# HUSH LITTLE BABY

J. A. BAKER

B
Boldwood

First published in Great Britain in 2024 by Boldwood Books Ltd.



Cover Design by Head Design

Cover Photography: iStock



A CIP catalogue record for this book is available from the British Library.

Paperback ISBN 978-1-83561-179-1

Large Print ISBN 978-1-83561-175-3

Hardback ISBN 978-1-83561-174-6

Ebook ISBN 978-1-83561-172-2

Kindle ISBN 978-1-83561-173-9

Audio CD ISBN 978-1-83561-180-7

MP3 CD ISBN 978-1-83561-177-7

Digital audio download ISBN 978-1-83561-171-5

Boldwood Books Ltd
23 Bowerdean Street
London SW6 3TN
www.boldwoodbooks.com

I shall pass through this world but once. Any good, therefore, that I can do or any kindness I can show to any human being, let me do it now. Let me not defer it or neglect it, for I shall not pass this way again.

— STEPHEN GRELLET

The greater the power, the more dangerous the abuse.

— EDMUND BURKE

*To our youngest additions. This is for you, little ones. Loved, always.*

# 1

# MELISSA

There was no escaping it – the noise that emanated from that house. It pulsed and echoed in my brain. Even from this distance, I could hear it: the strength of their voices. The anger in their inflection. It drowned out the sweet sound of the adjacent birdsong, obliterating the susurration of leaves as the breeze picked up, shaking the branches of a nearby tree. Then came the blare of a television followed by a high-pitched shriek that set my teeth on edge. I winced, the abrasive tone of the near scream rucking my flesh.

It wasn't the first time it had happened, that level of noise, that type of fracas, and it wouldn't be the last; that much I did know. I passed this way every day, had for months now, observed how inept and careless they were. How they went about their lives, ignoring their own child. Disregarding his needs and cries for help. Something had to be done to help that poor baby and I realised at that moment that I would have to be the one to do it. I had made attempts in the past to speak to them, made veiled pleas for them to change their behaviour, but my words had fallen on deaf ears. I'd tried. God knows, I had tried. In my defence, should anybody ever ask, at least I could say that I had attempted to do the right thing, to talk them round, make them see the error of their ways, but they simply wouldn't listen. Nobody listened. Mine was and still is, a lone voice, ignored and carried off into the four winds. Trying to intervene to help that youngster and make myself heard above the hubbub was like howling into a void. And so, at that moment, that tipping point that would stay with me forever, I made up my mind. I knew what I had to do. It was something dangerous. Something illegal, but it had to be done, no matter what.

I stayed crouched behind the shrubbery, every part of me concealed. It would have been easy, taking him at that moment, picking up my pace as I strode away from the house, glancing over my shoulder while curling my fingers tightly around the handle of his pram and walking off down the street as if nothing untoward was happening. I could have done it. But I didn't. It was a warm day, the last vestiges of a dying summer still with us; she had put the baby outside in the pram while she got herself ready. The street was empty, blinds partly covering the windows to block out the glare of the hot sun. Such a lackadaisical move, leaving him alone like that. And dangerous. Anybody could have taken him.

Including me.

But I didn't. I watched instead, my head full of plans. I waited and I watched and I waited some more. I could see her through the window, partly visible, distracted by her phone. Distracted by the television. Her mind focused on anything other than the baby she should have been caring for. He was in there too, my son. My only child. He had plummeted in my estimation. I thought he was better than that. It was clear to me at that point that he wasn't. He had been influenced by her presence, dragged into her slovenly, brutish ways.

At some point in their small, miserable lives, they would look back at that moment in time and wish they had had a stricter regime with their son, been quieter, given more thought to his welfare and allowed my grandson to live in a house that was less fraught. A quiet, loving home surrounded by people or a person who genuinely cared for him. But for now, everything was a mess. A haphazard approach to parenting that left much to be desired. No, it was worse than that. Their treatment of my grandchild reeked of neglect. And I wasn't prepared to stand for it. So I went home and I made my plans. I was meticulous. As meticulous as I could be given what I was about to do. It felt extreme, but I had no other option. They had done it to me, backing me into a dead-end.

And so, the following week, I did the same, crouching behind shrubbery, watching and waiting until the time was right. It didn't take long for the time to be right. I knew it wouldn't. Once again, the pram was placed outside their small garden while they did whatever it was they did inside that house. I had already worked out my technique, counted how many steps I needed to reach the pram, how long it would take for me to clasp at that handle and whip the baby away to safety. Timing was everything. My plan was set out with military-like precision. My mind was made up.

Ten quick steps. That was all it took to remove Gabriel from that toxic household. I leaned in and caught a glimpse of his sleeping face, his long, dark lashes fluttering against his pale, porcelain-like skin as he slumbered, unaware that his life was about to become infinitely better. I was in charge now. Things would improve. He would be happy. He would be loved. And that was all that would ever matter.

## 2

## MELISSA

Being alone has made me resourceful, forcing me to take on tasks that ordinarily, would have been done by my husband. Cleaning the guttering, drilling walls, carrying out minor repairs on my car – I'm proficient at them all. When a light appears on the dashboard or when the drains need unblocking, I'm not gripped by panic and I don't stand doe-eyed, looking helpless. I can deal with it. I am also highly adept at managing my finances. I'm not immensely wealthy but I do have savings. Which is just as well, given I now have another person in my life. A tiny mouth to feed. Somebody who needs clothing and looking after.

I glance at him, my little grandson, and can't suppress my smile or the soft thump of my heart that kicks in every time I study his features. I am in love with every part of him; his perfectly formed face, his full mouth and dewy skin giving me a lift, putting a spring in my step as I push him to safety. I reluctantly shift my gaze to my car that is parked up nearby then glance back at him for fear of missing a single second of not looking at him. My life with him in it will be a shinier happier version of my current lacklustre existence. This is the start of something special. We'll have a close relationship, Gabriel and I, each of us dependent on the other. I will care for him and he will fill the void in my life that has been there for too long.

I stop for a second and take a long, juddering breath. Listen to me, getting ahead of myself, eagerness and exhilaration muddying my thinking, my mind full of naïve notions of how this is going to be. It will be difficult; I'm not stupid. I do know that. We've a long journey ahead of us. I need to stay focused, not get pushed off course by quixotic concepts of what could be. Because people will soon be out searching for us. Missing babies make headlines. The world stops what it is doing to try and find them. Being vigilant is key. No getting carried away by foolish puerile daydreams. No thinking I can relax because I can't.

A bubble of air gathers in my chest, a fist of anxiety trapping it in place as I begin walking again, my sights set firmly on my car. A few more steps and I'll be there. Just a few more yards and I can shed the worry of getting caught. The idea of Gabriel being suddenly snatched away from me and handed back makes me weak-limbed with dread.

I feel the air behind me shift. My blood turns to sand, my skin puckering as I hear the voice.

'Well, isn't he a little beauty? What's his name?'

A thunderous clap explodes my ears, an army of angry insects buzzing and swirling around my brain, battering against my skull, trying to break free.

'Edmund. His name is Edmund.'

Edmund was the name of my father-in-law, the first name that springs into my thoughts. My own father's name isn't worth mentioning. I refuse to give him space in my head.

I make to move past him, this old chap who is impeding my progress, but he steps to one side and peers into the pram, his grey whiskers springing out from his face like a mass of silver antennae trying to break free from their anchored base.

'I had an Uncle Edmund once. Not as good looking as this little chap, though.' He smiles at me, revealing a row of perfectly white, ill-fitting dentures that clack together when he speaks. 'I take it by the blue clothes and blue pram that this is a little chap and not a little lady? Because you never really know these days, do you? With all this non-binary and gender-fluid stuff. So hard to tell and I didn't want to upset the apple cart, so I thought I'd better check.' His smile seems genuine, his voice soft, and his manner gentle and measured. I am sure he is a perfectly decent guy but he is stopping me from doing what I came here to do. His idle chatter is holding me back. Time is of the essence. I need to move, to get away from this place and I need to do it quickly. I have visions of pushing past him, my fingers splayed against his chest as I press hard and nudge him aside. I can almost hear the clatter of his old bones as he falls onto the concrete, his cries of pain and bemusement ringing out into the air when I stride past him, desperate to extricate myself from this situation. But as it turns out, I don't need to do anything because right on cue, Gabriel begins to stir, his snuffles becoming more noticeable, a distinct whine to his timbre as his stomach wakes up and cries out for sustenance.

'He needs feeding. Sorry,' is all I can manage as I bump the old guy aside with my hip and unlock my car, all the while ignoring his offers of help, and wishing he would leave me alone.

Placing a recently awoken, hungry baby in a car seat shouldn't daunt me but today's endeavour proves a little more difficult than I anticipated. Gabriel's snuffles turn into a cry, his shrieks soon reaching a pitch that could shatter glass. Sweat breaks out on my forehead and neck, running down my back, coating my arms and hands and making everything a hundred times more difficult. My fingers are hot and clumsy. I can feel the old man standing behind me, his presence as irritating as Gabriel's endless howling. Soon his parents will notice their child's absence. Panic will be set in, everything put in motion as the emergency services are notified. Within a matter of minutes, this area will be swarming with police. I need to hurry, to speed up my movements and get rid of this person who is loitering behind me like a lost child. I can almost feel the heat from his body as he edges closer, curious to see what I am doing, why such a seemingly simple task is taking so long.

'I'm fine. We're fine,' I shout over my shoulder, hoping it will be enough to send him on his way.

I keep my eyes fixed on the buckle of the car seat, pressing it down repeatedly with hot, slippery fingers, and breathing a sigh of relief when it finally clicks into place.

'All sorted,' I say brightly, my forced tone overcompensating for the awkward situation. I slam the door shut and step back onto the foot of the old onlooker. He is unperturbed, watching me closely. Monitoring everything I do and say. Perspiration runs down my neck, gathering around my collar, sitting on my top lip like a tiny oil slick. 'Now I really need to get on and get this little man fed.'

'And then home to his parents afterwards, eh?'

I recoil, his words twisting my guts and making me dizzy. I say nothing in return. A dry, cloying sensation fills my throat. Is he a neighbour? Did he see me taking Gabriel? He appears harmless but I can't trust anybody. He's an old man. A pensioner who probably sits at his window day after day, watching the world go by. All-seeing, all-knowing. I need to leave.

I shake my head and turn away, too flustered to reply.

'It's a good job these young 'uns have grandparents like you. Gives them a well-earned break, I should imagine.' His voice lowers, his despondency tangible as he continues. 'I lost my daughter. She was just a little girl. Eight years old she was. Meningitis. There wasn't anything they could do to save her. I would have loved to have seen her grow up and have little ones of her own but I guess it wasn't to be.' He stares in the car at Gabriel, the loss of his own child, his sadness and longing evident in his expression.

Guilt burns in my chest, a stinging, clawing creature that slams into my ribcage, knocking all the air out of my lungs. He's being kind – I know that. I'm not completely callous and unfeeling. God knows, I've had enough heartache of my own over the years. I know how it feels, that sense of loss: those continual feelings of wretchedness. He's a lonely, old man in need of company and means no harm, but I need to move quickly, to leave this place. And I need to do it right now.

I lift the pram into the boot and slide into the driver's seat, then turn on the engine, pressing my foot down hard on the accelerator. The vehicle picks up speed when I swing it around out of the parking space, and that's when I see him: the elderly gentleman. The one person who seems hellbent on stopping me. He is standing close to the edge of the pavement, waving at me to stop, his fingers clutching something, his eyes wide with desperation. I can't do this. I don't have time for any more conversations or recollections of his earlier life. As sad and heart-rending as they are, time is against me and I need to get moving, to get a head start before the police turn up and begin their search. I push my foot down even harder on the pedal, Gabriel's screams filling the car and beating in my ears. The rev counter spins, the car gaining in speed just as the old man steps out in front of me, his arms raised above his head. He is saying something, gesticulating wildly and waving at me to slow down and stop, but I can't and I don't. It's too late to brake and I am all out of time.

The thud of him hitting my bonnet is enough to stun Gabriel into a muffled, confused silence. It's only when I tear down the street, glancing behind in my rear-view mirror for the briefest of moments, that I spot the cuddly toy lying in the road next the old man's body. Gabriel's cuddly rabbit, its stuffing spread out over the road, its head and arms ripped from its torso by the wheels of my speeding vehicle.

I gasp, my heart a wild, thrashing thing in my throat, but I don't have time for guilt or fear to penetrate my tough veneer – the suit of armour I have created for myself in order to survive the harsh realities of life. I don't have time to think about whether the poor guy is alive or dead. I have done a terrible thing but at this juncture, my grandson – my beautiful, precious grandson – is the only thing that matters to me. I push my foot down even harder on the accelerator and head off towards the place that will become mine and Gabriel's new home.

# 3

## 1970

His anger filled the whole house: a profound, physical force that permeated walls, eating through solid brick, corroding everything in its path. Nancy flinched as he pushed past her, the baby pressed hard against her bosom, her bony frame and small breasts providing little protection for the child should her husband's anger escalate. She held her breath and said a short prayer, watching his hunched figure as he strode from room to room, back arched like a predator stalking its prey. He was looking for reasons to lash out, to justify his dark mood, his need for violence. She tried hard to not be that reason.

'Tell her to keep the noise down. It's like having a herd of fucking elephants up there.' He raised his eyes to the ceiling, lip curled in disdain at the barely audible noises of their daughter moving about in her bedroom above them.

*This too will pass.* The thought rattled through Nancy's brain as she willed her daughter to be quieter, for her to sit silently on her bed until her father's temper dissolved and all was well again. She counted the seconds. Seconds turning into minutes as she yearned for time to move on. For him to become normal once more. Whatever normal was. Nancy bit at the inside of her mouth. Normal was the wrong word. There was nothing normal about their lives or this house. Roger's moods oscillated between being mildly suspicious to being incandescent with rage. Happiness no longer featured in his range of emotions. It was as if it had leaked out of his pores and been replaced by paranoia and distrust that rapidly morphed into fury at the slightest provocation.

Nancy swallowed, held her baby even tighter, and crept out of the room. Her stockinged feet shuffled along the carpet. Her movements were as light as air, limbs liquid as she did her utmost to be as unobtrusive as possible. A ghost moving around her own home, gripped by fear. Paralysed by a growing panic that his smouldering temper would ignite without warning, scorching everyone in the immediate vicinity, including his own children.

The baby began to yowl. A frost prickled Nancy's skin; her blood, in sharp contrast, heated up, bubbling and boiling in her veins. More noise. A screaming baby would tip him over the edge. The blue touchpaper would soon be lit.

A thin arm still holding her child in place, she grappled with the door handle and escaped into the garden where the air was cool, the breeze a welcome sensation as it lapped against her bare limbs and face. How was it possible to be so hot and yet so cold at the same time, perspiration coating the back of her neck while she shivered uncontrollably?

At the bottom of the garden, birds gathered, pecking at the damp soil, foraging for food. How easy their lives were with their ability to fly away into the vast, blue sky, escaping their problems and moving from place to place whenever the mood took them. How free they were. She stood for a short while, watching them, rocking her fractious child until he eventually quietened down. She had thought of leaving this place before now but knew how difficult such a decision would be, packing her things and escaping her husband's clutches with a small child at her side and a baby at her breast. Where would she go? She could barely make it through the day without wanting to cry and gnash her teeth together, the grinding exhaustion constantly tugging at her, fear of her husband and caring for her children sapping her of all her strength. It wasn't the money. She had enough. She wasn't immensely wealthy but she had enough to get by. It would mean a step down in her living standards. Possibly moving to a flat somewhere in the centre of town. That thought didn't fill her with glee but neither did it scare her. So no, it wasn't about the money. She had more than most and had heard stories of women who were trapped by poverty, kept in their place by abusive husbands. That wasn't her story. It wasn't her story at all.

So what *was* her story, her reasons for staying? Why on earth was still here? That thought pierced her brain daily and she knew that soon, she was going to have to do something about it; to stop being the frightened, kowtowing wife and become something less brittle. A stronger person. A person who takes the initiative and isn't scared of leaving all this behind. Because *this* was no longer a home. It was a prison.

A roar from inside the house cut into her thoughts. The quietened baby nestled close to her chest, his soft snuffles pulling at her heartstrings as she ran back into the kitchen. Keeping her baby son and her young daughter safe, that should be her priority, not constantly giving in to the demands of a brutish man whose moods changed as often and as unpredictably as the wind.

The door closed behind her at the same time as Roger slammed his fist onto the counter top, sending plates spinning onto the floor. She wouldn't ask what the problem was. It would be a minor issue. It always was. Besides, no matter what it was that had riled him, it didn't warrant thumping inanimate objects or breaking crockery. Still, better he smashed his fist into something hard and immovable than her face. She stared at the worktop. He would be bruised, his fingers and flesh an inflamed, pulpy mess if there was any justice in this world. She turned away, staring out at the garden, shushing the child's soft moans and trying to hide the elation she felt at the thought of her husband's hand swelling to twice its normal size and causing him untold pain. Often she had dreamed of being the one who inflicted that pain on him in various ways. Putting poison in his food. Smothering him while he slept. Pushing him from a great height. But then, that would make her as bad as him. Was she really prepared to stoop to his depths? Once upon a time, her answer to that would have been a firm no, but just lately, her feelings had shifted, his actions and fluctuating moods pushing her closer and closer to the edge of a deep, dark abyss. An abyss filled with frenzied retaliation and savagery.

'I'm going to feed and bathe this little one. I'll not be long.' She kept her voice low. Gentle and non-threatening.

That was how she would get through this – by being invisible. By being half the woman she once was. There was a gaping hole in the very centre of her where her bravery and integrity used to be. She visualised herself stuffing cotton wool in that hole and allowing Roger to punch her repeatedly until he finally realised that she was beyond being hurt and damaged. He had already taken the most vital parts of her. There wasn't anything left for him to destroy. Except her children, that is. Dread darted beneath her skin, threading its way through her veins, pulsing and thrashing about inside her as a reminder of what sort of a man her husband was. What sort of a woman she had turned into for not leaving him. She wasn't poverty-stricken and she wasn't stupid. What she was, was frightened of being alone. Frightened of being in control of herself, because if she was going to be completely truthful and brutally honest, she no longer knew who she had become. She was, and had been for some time now, a stranger in her own life. The invisible woman. That's who she was. A dull, featureless individual who no longer had any control over her own life. Things had to change. *She* had to change.

She found her daughter playing quietly in her room, her head dipped the way it always was when trouble was looming. Such a clever, astute child, keeping herself salted away from all the nonsense that Roger stirred up because he was a man who couldn't control his own emotions.

'You don't know how it feels, Nancy,' he had once said as she placed a cold compress on her swollen cheekbone after enduring one of his beatings. 'Count yourself lucky you don't have the black dog pawing at your head, desperate to be let in. It's almost impossible to control it. These dark moods are dreadful.'

'You admit you're out of control then?' she had replied, the last remnants of bravery that she had within her, spilling out of her mouth unchecked as she held the cold pack in place.

He had ripped the compress out of her hand, and thrown it against the wall. And she had sat, waiting for the white-hot flash of agony as he drove his fist into her face again. Except that didn't happen. Instead, he stood, limbs quivering, eyes lowered. Nancy had counted the seconds, waiting for the hit, waiting for the relentless waves of pain, until eventually, he spun around and stalked out of the room, slamming the door behind him, shaking the very foundations of the house. She had won that one, but times like that were scarce and becoming more and more scarce by the day. It was as if the monster inside him had reached a pitch, tearing itself apart, and now there was no way of putting it all back together.

'You okay, honey?'

The little girl looked up, her blue eyes and smiling face melting Nancy's pounding heart.

'Yes, Mummy. Are *you* okay? I heard shouting downstairs.'

'I'm going to feed your brother, then I'm going to put him in the bath. You want to help me?'

'Yes, Mummy. I'll help. Shall I tidy my toys away first?'

Tears burned at the back of Nancy's eyes, the love she had for her children such a powerful emotion that she felt sure it was the only thing that kept her body upright. Without them, she would fade away into nothing, her skin falling from her skeletal frame, leaving behind a pile of desiccated old bones.

Nancy nodded and managed a tight smile before heading into her bedroom and perching on the edge of the bed where the baby latched onto her breast and drank thirstily. It was the softness of his skin that she adored, the small, narrow indent at the nape of his neck where his fine, downy hair rested in a tiny V shape. She would protect him. She would protect both of her children. She would do whatever it took to make sure her babies stayed safe in this place, this frighteningly unstable and hostile environment they called home.

# 4

## MELISSA

After driving away, I find a wooded area a few miles out of town and pull into a layby to feed Gabriel. I had already made up a few bottles of milk in preparation for the long drive, placing them in a cooler bag before putting them on the back seat of my car. He falls asleep after the first feed and I take advantage of his silence, laying him out on my knee and changing his nappy then strapping him back in his car seat. I forget about my own needs and put in over a hundred miles until he wakes again, a small yowl building in his chest as hunger begins to kick in once more.

The plan to take Gabriel was complex and way trickier than I expected. Even getting access to my own money proved enormously difficult. I had to stick to the daily cash withdrawal allowance from the ATMs and then get the rest over the counter at the bank. By that time, I had already changed my appearance, cutting my hair and wearing glasses instead of my usual contact lenses in readiness for taking him. I also applied a thick layer of make-up, something I rarely wear, and withdrew the remainder of my savings under the scrutiny of the assistant who fired endless questions at me that I duly ignored. I bought a pay-as-you-go phone and ditched my old one in the River Tees, throwing it off the Infinity Bridge at midnight, watching as it sank without a trace, then headed home and slept soundly, knowing my plan was taking shape.

Finding a rental cottage proved to be even more complicated. I spotted one in the classified ads in a national newspaper and rang the number, asking if I could pay the first six months in cash rather than using a credit card or paying by direct debit, and was immediately refused. The second one was further afield and took me up on my offer straightaway, the owner clearly attracted by the idea of easy money that they could hide away and not declare to the taxman. It took a full day to drive up there, hand over the required amount and pick up the keys, and then drive back home to the north east. By the time I got in shortly after midnight, exhaustion had dug deep into my bones.

I spent the next week visiting local market towns, places I could easily get lost in and not be recognised, and bought baby clothes and food for myself, baby formula and bottles, and everything I would need to keep the two of us alive. It's odd how all the things we accrue over the years that we consider necessary suddenly fall away and are deemed trivial when life takes a sudden and unexpected turn. We need very little to keep us safe and warm and fed. Everything else is just detritus.

I glance in the rear-view mirror, moderately pleased with the change to my appearance, and then step out of the car and clamber into the back seat with my beautiful grandchild, lifting him out of his seat and holding him close to my chest. The heft and scent of him makes me giddy, a feeling of euphoria at getting this far blooming in my abdomen and soaring through my veins. We can do this, Gabriel and I. We are on the path to our new lives and it feels so damn good. Better than I have felt in a long, long time. No longer am I gripped by a sense of hopelessness, his predicament in that dreadful house eating away at me like acid. I haven't just freed Gabriel; I have also freed myself, now released from the paralysing loneliness that over the past few years has crippled me. He isn't just my grandson. He's my best friend. My only true friend. I think of the people who have let me down over the years, both family and friends alike who ran for cover when things got difficult for me, never to reappear. That doesn't matter now because I have my grandchild here with me. He is worth a hundred of each and every one of them. He is all I will ever need.

I open his bag and remove the bottle of milk. It's not cold but I give him it anyway. It's not going to kill him. Babies are tougher than we realise. I doubt his mother was meticulous with her feeding regime. Another reason why he is better off with me. Not everything is going to fall into place but we'll work it out as we go along.

He guzzles it greedily, his eyes meeting mine, and that's when I know that I have done the right thing. The trust is there: the way he holds my gaze, how he places his little hands around my finger and grips tightly. It's as if we're the only two people in the world. This little person is all I will ever need. We have already established a bond that cannot be broken. It's like being immersed in a warm bath on a cold winter's day, the feeling I now have as I hold him close to me. I don't ever want it to end. Visions of his father as a baby fill my head. He was a beautiful child. I wonder what happened along the way, why he chose to ignore me and cut me out of his life and then I remember her, his wife. The way she came along and ruined everything. It was her. It's always been her.

The bottle is soon empty and I wonder if I should increase his feeds. He's a growing boy and in no time at all, he will be sitting up and playing, interacting with the world around him. Before I have a chance to think about it any further, he lets out a wail, the suddenness of his piercing shriek taking all the air out of my lungs. Hunger. It must be hunger. He needs more milk. In a matter of seconds, he is crying so hard that his face turns red, his body becoming feverish and clammy.

I try to stay calm. We're alone here on this road, surrounded by towering trees and foliage. Only one crumbling farmhouse in the distance. Nobody can hear him. If I lose my head over this small and relatively simple problem, then we are done for. Babies cry. All the time. I need to get used to it. And yet still, panic grips me. That noise, his screams. I need to stop the noise.

My hands grope around inside the bag, landing on something cool and solid. I lift out the next bottle of milk and place it near Gabriel's mouth but he turns away, refusing to latch on. My heart speeds up. I try again, and once more, he swings his head away, arching his back and wriggling about in my arms. Desperate for him to calm down, I plunge my hand into the bag and rummage again, my fingers landing on one of the dummies I bought for him. I put into his mouth but it falls out onto the floor and his wails continue unabated.

*Stop screaming! Just stop it.*

Perspiration coats my flesh, the heat from both of our bodies making it difficult for me to concentrate. I stand the bottle up next to where I'm sitting and curse when it falls sideways, milky drips pooling on the fabric. My attempts to soothe Gabriel are unsuccessful, his wails and screams growing to a nerve-shattering crescendo. I reach to one side to grab the bottle and wipe up the stains but Gabriel's wriggling body knocks me off balance and I end up a dropping it again on the floor at my feet. I can feel the wetness of the baby milk as it leaks onto my bare legs. Using one hand to hold Gabriel, I reach down to retrieve the bottle but it slips out of my grasp and rolls under the seat.

'Christ almighty!'

My growing rage does nothing to quieten him, his body now rigid as he prepares to let out another howl of anguish. As a last resort to soothe him, I lay him over my shoulder and hold him in place with my other hand, rubbing at his back in a circular motion simply because I don't know what else to do. Sweat runs down my face. I can taste the salt as it cascades over my mouth and gathers in the cleft of my chin. This is hard. It is all so fucking hard.

The belch that emerges out of Gabriel's mouth stops me, my anger dissolving, realisation dawning. How could I have forgotten such a thing? Babies need winding after they've been fed. His shrieks die away, his body suddenly limp on my shoulder. The closeness and softness of him, the fact that I allowed him to continue being in pain without knowing what to do, brings tears to my eyes. I shake away thoughts that I may be out of my depth here, and well out of practice. I won't entertain such ideas. We're here now. There's no going back. No room for negativity or regrets.

I lift him off my shoulder, one hand cradling his head, his heaviness a sign that he has fallen asleep, and lay him in my arms, my face close to his. I whisper reassurances in his ear, telling him how much I love him and that we will always be together, no matter what, and then spend the next few seconds listening to his breathing, the steadiness and regularity of it reassuring me that everything is going to be okay. Only when I'm certain that he is completely settled do I strap him back in his car seat, ensuring the angle is perfect so his head doesn't loll forwards as I drive. It's going to be a steep learning curve, caring for him, I know that now, but him having to endure a trapped ball of wind is infinitely preferable to being in a noisy, chaotic environment where his cries are ignored by his parents day after day. I've done the right thing taking him. This is just the beginning of our journey.

I retrieve the bottle of milk from under the seat and wipe away the stains, then strap myself in and set off. Gabriel sleeps for most of the journey. We stop once more for another feed and a nappy change and arrive at Rannoch Moor in Scotland shortly before 8 p.m. Darkness is setting in, the sun dipping below the horizon, its circular outline a shimmering, orange orb that is a sight to behold. We're completely alone here. Just me and Gabriel in a small cottage in the middle of nowhere. It's perfect. We will be perfect. This is an adventure: the beginning of the rest of our lives.

# 5

## 1970

The whisky bottle was empty. Dread and apprehension rattled in her skull before worming their way downwards and slithering behind her ribcage, making it difficult for her to breathe. She dropped the glass bottle into the bin and tiptoed past the living room where he sat, head lolling, hands placed firmly on his lap. It was what could come later that made her fearful, the volatility of it. He would either sleep it off and wake refreshed, or the alcohol would exacerbate his already declining mood, the festering darkness that lived within him, pooling and augmenting before exploding out into the open. Every word that came out of her mouth would be misinterpreted, twisted and bent out of shape until she could no longer remember what it was she had said that had caused him to fly into a rage. She always tried to be as unobtrusive as possible when his mood was on the turn, finding ways of keeping herself busy. Finding ways to keep out of his line of fire. And he always found ways of locating her, pulling her away from whatever it was she was doing and dragging her into his world, asking pointless questions, waiting to pick apart her answers until she no longer knew which way was up.

The little one was bathed and fed, his eyes heavy with sleep. She settled him down in his crib and placed a kiss on his forehead. He was adored beyond measure. She wanted him to know that. She had enough love inside her to make up for his father's lack of care. She was sure that deep down, when his mood was right, when the wind was blowing in the right direction, when everything in the universe came together at once for his delectation, then the boy's father did hold some affection for him, but all those things were too fragile to predict. The love that a parent feels for a child should be absolute and unconditional, not dependent upon flimsy, changeable circumstances. Nancy wanted to be part of a happy loving family, but was finding it increasingly difficult to hold it all together, to keep up the façade of normality that was expected of her. One day, she would snap, and just lately it felt as if that day was creeping ever closer.

'Can I give little George a kiss, please, Mummy?'

Once again, tears sprung to her eyes, the gentle pleading and yet at the same time, affectionate tone of her daughter's voice leaving her weak with helplessness. She had always been a demonstrative child, climbing on Nancy's knee and throwing her arms around her neck, squeezing and squeezing until they both giggled and fell back, breathless. That was one positive aspect to cling onto: that Roger's overbearing temper and dark moods hadn't stripped their daughter of her positive outlook. It could happen. Nancy had heard of youngsters who were damaged by such things. Damaged and traumatised by what they had witnessed in their own homes. But it hadn't manifested itself just yet. Her daughter remained gentle and upbeat, despite frequently being caught in the middle of the storm that tore through their house on a regular basis.

'Of course you can, my lovely one. Here you go.' She lifted her daughter up and watched as the young girl leaned down and placed the softest of kisses on her brother's cheek.

'Night, night, baby George. See you in the morning.'

Nancy smiled at the girl's words, more tears threatening to fall. Sadness was her overriding emotion of late. Even the most joyous of moments left her feeling desperate and flattened. The juxtaposition of near happiness tinged with a sense of being trapped seemed to exacerbate her turmoil. She didn't necessarily want to leave her home; it was, after all, half hers. She simply wanted her husband to be happy and throw off the mantle of misery that was permanently perched on his shoulders. That wasn't too much to ask, was it? She sighed, knowing it was. And finding forgiveness for the violence he meted out to her was another thing entirely. It weighed heavily on her mind. Could she do that? Could she stay and forgive a man who treated her as something less than human? Not that it mattered. It was no more than a pipe dream, that one day he would wake, a transformed person. A better man. Forgiveness was possible. A person suddenly changing their innate characteristics and becoming somebody different was not. It wasn't *impossible*. Just highly unlikely. Roger's black moods were growing more ferocious. More frequent. He wasn't about to change. Not for her. Not for anyone. It was just who he was. And she abhorred him for it.

'Come on, lovely one. Let's get you sorted now as well. Get your pyjamas on and jump into bed and I'll read you a story.'

They left the baby's bedroom, closing the door with a muffled click, and made their way to the girl's room.

'Does Daddy hate us?'

Nancy's blood turned to ice. Her body suddenly felt heavy, her limbs wieldy and leaden. She stopped and took a long, rattling breath, turning to her daughter and painting on her brightest of smiles before speaking.

'Of course he doesn't. He loves us all very much.'

She wanted to scoop up her daughter and her precious baby and run, and to keep on running as fast as she could until this house, this life she had chosen for them all, was far, far behind them.

But she didn't. She went through the usual bedtime routine of tucking in her daughter and reading to her in hushed tones her favourite story, the fear of disturbing Roger a constant factor. Fear of losing the moment and breaking their brief spell of happiness and contentment always in the forefront of her mind.

'Will Daddy ever hurt baby George?'

*Oh dear God!*

And there it was again. Nancy had dimmed the light and kissed her daughter goodnight when those words hit her, slamming into her with all the force of a speeding truck. Her fingers fluttered to her chest, her other hand clinging onto the doorframe for balance. She couldn't breathe. Every pocket of air had been sucked out of the room.

'No, of course not, darling.' She wanted to add that it was a silly question, except for the fact that it wasn't.

It was a perfectly acceptable question. Her daughter was astute and had seen and heard things that no child should ever see or hear. But it wasn't just that. She couldn't dismiss it as a silly or pointless question because what if it were true? What if, one of these fine days, Roger, in one of his many rages, took it out on their defenceless children? He was more than capable, wasn't he? He had it in him to lash out and do unspeakable things to those around him. She had seen it first-hand. Experienced it. Had the battle scars to prove it.

*No.*

She batted the idea away. It was ridiculous to even consider such a notion. An outlandish thought. Roger was many things, most of them deeply unpleasant, but he wasn't an abuser of children. He saved that sort of treatment for Nancy.

The children were perfectly safe in their home with her. They were safe with their father. Weren't they?

# 6

## MELISSA

The smell was the first thing I noticed when I pushed open the door. I had left Gabriel sleeping in his seat while I dragged our belongings out of the car and unlocked the front door of the cottage, a small frisson of excitement building in my gut, only to be quashed when I flicked on the light and looked around. It was inescapable, the pungent smell of damp that greeted me along with a wave of disappointment when I glanced at the décor. The place had quite clearly been unoccupied for some time, its fixtures and fittings reminiscent of my own upbringing in the sixties. It was neither quaint nor retro. It was dull and dated. Telling myself it wasn't important, I unloaded our things and lifted Gabriel out of the car, and now here I stand, wondering what the hell I'm doing here and where to start in order to make the place comfortable and habitable. In a bid to keep my movements and plans hidden, I have ended up paying for a cottage that is nothing short of a disgrace.

My eyes sweep over everything in the room and find it all wanting. The original flagstone flooring is small compensation for the rest of the cottage. The armchair by the open brick fireplace is practically threadbare, the two-seater sofa the same. Cushions have been strategically placed to cover the biggest holes and each arm has a lace doily slung over it. I shudder to think what lies beneath. In the corner stands an old standard lamp that is leaning badly to one side and hanging at the windows are curtains with a pattern so vivid and haphazard, it's enough to make anybody dizzy and nauseous. A thick layer of dust sits along the mantlepiece and across the table top. The only comforting, albeit lonely-sounding item in the room, is the old, wooden clock that ticks along rhythmically, echoing around us, reminding me of how isolated we are. Cut off from the rest of civilisation. Just me and Gabriel alone in this place. I picture my home comforts, my central heating and comfortable, clean furniture, then shrug away that thought and focus on making things right. This is the path I chose. Everything before me is what I should have expected. We're in a small cottage in an isolated part of Scotland. What did I imagine would await me – a five-star hotel with room service? I think of the cash I paid in advance and silently chastise myself for being so naïve. It took a chunk out of my money. I have plenty left but expected more in return for my investment, not this hovel before me.

There isn't time to unpack any of our cases or make a start on tidying and cleaning as Gabriel soon begins to yowl on my shoulder, his legs kicking hard against my chest. He's such a compact little thing, it's little wonder he guzzles back those bottles of milk as regularly as he does. It won't be long until he will be ready for solid food. I reach into the bag and take out the last bottle of formula, then sit on the sofa and watch as he gulps down the creamy liquid while I gag at the musty smell of the room. As he feeds, I think about my tidy-up mission. There's a lot to do in here. Too much. The owner is an elderly man who lives on the outskirts of Edinburgh. It's likely he hasn't visited this place in decades and leases it out to bring in some much-needed income. When I met him to pay the rent and pick up the keys, he looked in poor health, his skin pale to the point of being translucent, his silver hair, thin and wispy. Stooping badly, he took the cash, counted it slowly and handed me the keys. I never made it past his doorstep but his own house looked in dire need of repair: the front garden overgrown and full of weeds, the inside walls as far as I could see, dirty and grimy, with patches of mould creeping across the ceiling. His own home was squalid. I should have known what awaited me in this place. I should have known.

Gabriel finishes his milk, his lips smacking together when I sit him up and rub at his back. A stream of tiny burps escape from his half-open mouth and I thank God it will mean no more shrieks or crying from him.

His eyes follow my movements, his expression one of contentment. Smugness engulfs me. His parents have no idea where he is. They deserve to feel anxious and desperate. Concerned for his welfare. They sat day after day, glued to their phones while he was placed outside in his pram where anybody could have taken him. Where somebody *did* take him. He is better off here with me. I am the one person who loves and needs him. The one person who will take care of him. The only person who is capable of keeping him from harm.

I pick him up and walk towards the hallway that leads to the bedrooms, then turn on the light in what will be Gabriel's room. I sigh and bite at the inside of my mouth. It's not perfect but it's an improvement on the outdated, grubby living room. With white walls, a double bed, and an old, oak wardrobe, it will suffice. There's room for a cot for Gabriel even though I haven't brought one. I stand for a few seconds mulling over our sleeping arrangements. I could take the mattress off the bed and push it up against the wall then have a think about how to protect the other open sides to stop him rolling off and onto the floor. There will be a simple solution. Nothing is impossible. Going out to buy a cot isn't an option. I swore to myself when I was planning this, that visiting the shops is something I will only do in emergencies and I intend to stick to that rule. It will work out. Everything will come together in the end. This is just the beginning. There are bound to be hurdles along the way. The question is, will they be greater than the rewards? I don't think so. My gut tells me that everything is going to be just fine.

There isn't time to think about sustenance for myself. Gabriel clings to me and cries every time I attempt to put him down. I enter the bathroom, prepared for the worst. It isn't great but neither is it awful. Although old-fashioned, it's mould free and the smell of damp isn't as strong in this room.

A quick glance at my watch tells me it's almost time to put Gabriel to bed. Relief courses through me. I'm tired. It's been a long day and my back is aching from hauling him around.

With my free arm, I lean down and turn on the hot tap. A river of brown sludge pours out, the pipes rattling in protest as they empty themselves of years of sediment. I wait, determined to remain positive and am relieved when the groans and clatters disappear after only a few seconds, and the water runs clear. I watch, quietly pleased at the strength and heat of it as the tub fills up. Steam billows around me, the warmth a welcome sensation after a long drive and an exhausting day.

I test the temperature to make sure it's acceptable for a baby's delicate skin, then turn off both taps and walk back into the hallway where our suitcases stand. I should have unpacked first. My thinking is all out of kilter. Sweat prickles my hairline when I bend down to search for a towel. I grunt, fraught and hot as I try to open the case with only one hand. Gabriel, as if picking up on my own dilemma, begins to cry, his spine suddenly rigid, his feet pummelling against my abdomen with such force that I'm unable to catch my breath properly.

'Please stop it, little man. I just need a couple of seconds, that's all.'

I lay him down on the tiled floor, aware of how hard and cold it is, and quickly unzip the case, dragging out items of clothing and throwing them behind me. His cries quickly escalate, adding more pressure to the situation and compressing my inability to find something as simple as a towel.

*Just stop it!*

Blinded by sweat and desperation, I pull out a white bathrobe, other items tumbling and scattering over the floor. A toilet bag that is precariously perched atop a pile of clothes falls out and lands on top of Gabriel, covering his face. His cries turn into a shrill howl. My head pounds. I sweep the bag aside, too frightened to look at him in case there are any marks or God forbid, cuts and bruises, and scoop him up, holding him close to my chest where my heart hammers away like a huge metronome beneath my ribcage. This should all have been easy and effortless and I've made a terrible mess of it. I need to do better. It's all so much more difficult than I imagined.

My breathing is a succession of faltering gasps as I stand up and pace the floor, doing what I can to soothe and calm him. God, this is hard. This is so fucking *hard*.

'It's okay, it's okay. Grandma is here. Everything is going to be fine.'

I'm not sure everything is going to be fine, but I'll do my damnedest to try and get us to a point where we can function without too much trauma and upset. All I want is for my grandson to be comfortable and happy. Surely I'm capable of such a simple task. I did it before many years ago with his father, so I can undoubtedly do it again, can't I? Age and a long hiatus may have dulled my skills but I'm determined to master this thing. Looking after a baby should come naturally and yet it feels so terribly difficult, everything a monumental effort.

I lift him off my shoulder and stare down at his face, an image of his father springing into my mind unbidden. I blink, try to wash away those memories, those visions. It's too painful. I wonder how it has come to this. My grandson is a sharp reminder of how quickly things can change. How we can lose everything we hold dear, our lives and everything we thought would last forever slipping between our fingers like grains of sand.

His cries slow, becoming quieter. I snuggle him closer and take a good look at his face, inspecting it for marks and scratches. Nothing there, thank God. Everything is skewed, my gait unsteady as I pick up the fluffy robe and head into the bathroom. The floor feels spongy under my feet, the walls leaning awkwardly. I stop and take a few deep breaths. I'm about to bathe a baby. I've got to stop these moments of panic and self-doubt and get a grip. Where has my confidence gone? The self-assurance and resilience I felt sure would help get me through this undertaking? I need to get them back.

Trying to control my breathing, I kneel next to the bath and take off Gabriel's clothes, peeling away each layer with as much care and precision as I can, scrutinising his face, still checking for bruises or any signs of damage or distress. Suddenly, our eyes lock, and in that brief moment, I swear I see a flicker of recognition. It buoys me up, that look of acknowledgement and trust. He needs me and has faith that I'll take care of him.

'Come on then, little man. Let's get you washed and ready for bed, shall we?'

He is cradled in my arms, his warm, soft skin against mine, the most beautiful thing I have ever felt. His azure eyes are like deep pools so inviting, I want to dive right in and never leave. My pulse slows down, the thudding in my chest slowly returns to normal. I smile. He is mine now. Gabriel, my grandson is all mine. He is safe and happy here with me. Nobody will ever find us.

# 7

## 1970

*If only they knew.* That was the prevailing thought in Nancy's head as she smiled and nodded, sipping soup from her silver spoon and wishing she were elsewhere. Didn't matter where. As long as it was anywhere but here, sitting at this table, with these people who thought they knew everything about her and her husband. They didn't know about her ongoing fears and her damaged body and they didn't know about Roger and his twisted mind and propensity for violence. They thought of him as a trusted colleague and a good friend. A hardworking doctor: easy-going, kind, thoughtful. A man who would always be engaging and charming in public. Strange, thought Nancy as she sat quietly, observing the dynamics of the dinner party, how his rages and bouts of depression that turned him into a monster behind closed doors didn't rear their head in public. Funny that. Maybe that black dog that he claimed pawed at him, desperate to be let in, could be controlled and kept at bay after all.

'Isn't that right, darling?'

She raised her eyes at the sound of his voice, static filling her head, a line of white noise roaring in her ears as she listened to him speaking.

'I was just telling Margaret about how little George is already sleeping through the night. Such a marvellous little chap he is.'

The murmurs of appreciation and adoration at his statement made her want to howl and scream with despair while tearing out her hair in large clumps. How blind these people were. Blind and idiotic, their faces alight with joy, ears pricking up as Roger regaled them with tales of his family, glossing over his inexcusable ways, allowing them to think of him as a doting father and affectionate, caring husband. On instinct, her fingers traced a line over her cheekbone, her most recent scars and bruises concealed by make-up, the cuts and marks on her body slowly healing. One of these days, he would take it too far, do something unthinkable. Something irreversible and unforgivable. But for now, she would have to sit and smile and nod in all the right places. Let these people, these damn useless group of individuals who thought of themselves and Roger as intelligent and affable, think that all was well in her world.

'Yes, he's a little bundle of joy.' She tried to keep her tone light, to keep her face a mask of happiness and not let the bitterness she felt in the darkest corners of her soul creep in. 'We are very lucky and love him very much.'

It would be noted if her husband detected just the slightest hint of sarcasm or malice in her voice. Noted and spoken about at length after everyone had left. Picked apart until the carcass of her reply lay in ruins. And then the arguments and beatings would last long into the night while their daughter either slept soundly upstairs, blissfully unaware, or (as was usually the case) lay curled up under her covers, her small hands clasped over her ears in a bid to block it all out.

So it was better for everyone if she continued with the play-acting, plastering on a façade of contentment while her own features bled and melted away beneath, exposing bare bone and a mass of bloody, twisted sinew. That's who she was now – a bag of bloodied bones and very little else.

Roger's smile, the tilt of his head, the way his eyes narrowed as he assessed her answer for signs of mockery or cynicism before deciding he was happy with her response, made her quiver, dread snaking in the pit of her stomach. A nest of coiled vipers waiting to strike. She waited, watching him, holding in her breath until the barely imperceptible nod of his head told her he was happy with her response. She breathed deeply, air slipping out of her mouth in a slow, sour stream. She wondered if he knew or cared about what was going on inside her head or the fear she felt in his presence and the hatred she had for him boiling in her veins. Or if he gave any thought to her at all.

*I'm here. I'm a person just like you!*

It was a huge effort to not scream those words at him. To make him realise how much pain he caused her and to tell him how deeply unhappy she was at the way their lives had turned out.

It wasn't always this way. When they were first married, he was a witty, pleasant man, but the pleasant, easy times were becoming scarcer. His fists, his raging temper – that fearful, raging temper of his – made sure of it. If she could take her children and run, if she could just muster up the courage to do it, then what would happen? It was hard to visualise the next step, her imagination stunted by the hidings he gave her, her confidence squashed and pulverised to nothing by his harsh words and constant derision as he meted out yet more blows to her already broken and bruised body.

The rest of the night passed quickly. She had learned by now how to conduct herself in the presence of his colleagues, people who passed themselves off as close friends. She spoke politely, served the carefully prepared dinner, meekly accepting compliments on her culinary skills, stressing that she couldn't do it without the help of her husband, spewing out the required words for fear of reprisals later at her lack of gratitude for the fact he helped lay the table.

'He's a wonder, Nancy. Can you hire him out?' Deirdre Parsons waved her empty wine glass about in the air, her lipstick bleeding into the thickly applied make-up on her face. Nancy tried to avert her gaze away from the thin, scarlet veins that jutted out from beneath her bottom lip and the pale smudges of pink dotted on her teeth.

Nancy had seen the way Deirdre looked at Roger, laughing gutturally at his carefully rehearsed anecdotes, the ones Nancy had heard hundreds of times before. The ones that made her skin crawl. He repulsed her with his slick, perfectly delivered patter, and putrid lies.

'Oh, would you like a refill, Deirdre?' Nancy stood and collected a new bottle of Merlot from the sideboard. She couldn't find the right words to reply to Deirdre's trite, childish question. Sometimes, silence said more than words ever could.

The woman must be as stupid as she was drunk if she wasn't able to see what was right in front of her face. Nancy's husband was a violent egotistical monster who had the ability to charm those around him whilst masking the festering evil that lay beneath. He was clever, Nancy would give him that, but she couldn't think bad of Deirdre as she herself was just as stupid for carrying on with this sick charade. He had them all dancing to his tune and she was tired of it.

A sudden wave of exhaustion hit her hard. It was late and she'd had a long day, cleaning the house, preparing food, cooking over a hot stove and all while looking after two children, one of whom continually suckled from her aching breasts. He didn't see it or refused to – how difficult life was for her, having to entertain his friends when the demands of a young baby sapped her of all her strength.

'Only half a glass?' Deirdre turned to her own husband, who was engaged in conversation with the woman next to him, his eyes glazing over as he glanced down at the woman's cleavage, his cheeks reddened by the food and wine. 'Are we making this a late one, Samuel? Or are we heading home soon?'

Without removing his gaze from the woman's chest, he too picked up his glass and waved it under Nancy's nose. Her hands trembled when she filled it up, the crimson liquid reminding her of blood. Roger's blood. She pictured him lying on the floor at her feet, his twitching body in its death throes as she plunged a knife deep into his chest again and again and again until there was nothing left of him but a grotesque mass of savagely distorted flesh.

Nancy blinked then turned and topped up Deirdre's glass again, her own voice echoing in her ears as she complimented Deirdre on her sartorial style and elegance, the stark reality that her husband was still alive and well and observing her every move like a knife being plunged into her own heart.

'That shade really suits you, Deirdre. The design of the dress and the red swirls are so wonderfully vibrant.'

*It matches your eyes.*

The words rang in Nancy's head, sticking in her throat and remaining there. She would endure a sound beating later if they slipped out. She may endure a sound beating anyway just for breathing. The clock ticked away behind her like a death knell, each passing second a reminder of how exhausted she was and how these people would only leave when every morsel of food had been eaten and every last drop of expensive wine, consumed.

'Thank you, darling. It was from Petra's in town. Terribly expensive, but worth it, I think.'

Nancy observed how Deirdre's head turned left and right as she surveyed the other people seated around the table, her mouth slightly agape as she waited for their approval. Most were busy talking or eating, but a few gave her an appreciative nod of the head, murmuring how beautiful she looked and how an expensive outlay can be a worthwhile investment.

'Appearances are so important, don't you think?' said Jeanette Whitcome, a woman of whom Nancy had always been a little wary.

More murmuring and nods of agreement from those who were listening. Nancy could swear she caught Jeanette eyeing up her outfit before turning her attention to a lady sitting opposite whose name Nancy couldn't remember. Glancing down at her own clothing and shoes, items bought many years ago when she had time to go shopping for clothes for herself, Nancy felt her insides shrink into a tight ball. These days, looking after the children and making sure the house was clean and tidy took up all of her time. Roger rarely looked at her any more so it didn't seem to matter. She rarely looked at herself. Her cuts and bruises didn't shame him. He simply didn't see them. He didn't see her. She was a nobody to him. A nuisance in his midst.

She hoped Roger hadn't seen Jeanette's look of what she felt sure was disdain, at her attire. He would take it as an insult, imagining slights where there weren't any. Roger wasn't the kind of man who would want his wife to be viewed with derision or pity. Appearances meant a lot to him too. Not enough to keep his fists away from his wife's face or to make an effort and care for his children while his wife went shopping for a new dress, but enough to keep his standing in social circles as high as it could be by throwing lavish, expensive parties and making sure everyone was waited on hand and foot by an exhausted wife whose face felt as if it might explode every time she plastered on a fake smile or uttered another pedestrian phrase glittered with compliments to keep everyone happy.

Nancy took a stuttering breath and sat down. It was all getting to be too much. This whole fucking stupid act of appearing normal was more than she could bear. She had reached a tipping point and dreaded to think what would happen if she acted out her real, hidden desires. Desires of killing her husband, grabbing her children and leaving this mess of a life far behind. Blood pounded in her ears as she tried to regulate her breathing. Around her, the talk continued, threads of different conversations spreading across the table and pounding in her brain. She turned to the person next to her and smiled, aware always of Roger's watchful gaze. His need for her engagement with others to prove how perfect his life was, was all pervading, a clanging bell in her head as she joined in with the talk, nodding and chipping in when all she wanted to do was curl up on the floor and go to sleep. Her reserves of energy were bottomless when it came to protecting herself and avoiding confrontation. Somehow, she would find enough strength to make it through the rest of the evening without any glitches.

It was another hour before the first couple made to leave, and another hour until the last couple called for a taxi and bid their goodbyes. Fatigue was eating its way into the marrow of Nancy's bones. Almost 1 a.m. The children would be up in just five or six hours. Keeping her smile and amiable persona burning for the last quarter of the evening had been difficult, but somehow, she had managed it. She lost that social grace at her peril. Roger was often too tired for conversation or engaging in small talk after the children had gone to bed, but he was never too tired for violence. He dug deep when it came to that aspect of his life, his antennae finely tuned in to her actions. If she lapsed in her duties as a convivial hostess and became cold or distant to their guests, she would pay for it later.

'We must do this again, Nancy. You and Roger are the most wonderful hosts and really know how to throw a memorable dinner party.' Jeanette leaned in and gave Nancy an uncharacteristic hug, her perfume a deep, musky scent that hung in the air after they parted.

It was the alcohol talking. She and her husband were bleary-eyed, her earlier reserved demeanour smudged away by the copious amounts of wine they had drunk. Nancy could feel Roger's presence behind her, the heat from his body prickling the back of her neck. She didn't dare turn to look at him, focusing instead on being her best self, telling Jeanette that they were welcome anytime and that it had been a pleasure to have them.

'It's no trouble at all. It's been a marvellous evening. Thank you for being here and please do come again.' The words came easily, Nancy spewing out rehearsed lines, her smile wide despite feeling so tired she could cry.

There wasn't time to move away or formulate a fitting reply when Jeanette spoke again – a reply that would help extricate Nancy from the unfolding situation and make Roger aware that she didn't approve of what had just taken place. It was as she listened to Jeanette's words that she realised what an astute woman she was, and perhaps her earlier glance hadn't been at Nancy's lack of fashionable clothing, but at her broken body and fractured mind. A recognition of Nancy's plight. Empathy and compassion. An ally.

'Take care of yourself, my darling,' Jeanette said softly. She leaned towards Nancy and gripped her hand, her voice lowered but still powerful enough to be heard. 'And call me if you ever need any help.' Jeanette glanced over Nancy's shoulder, her eyes narrowing at Roger, her lips forming a thin, disapproving line that told them that she knew. 'Help with anything. Anything at all.'

The thought of closing the door and turning to face Roger after they had left filled Nancy with dread but it needn't have mattered because he did it for her, slamming it shut once their taxi had trundled off out of view. He loomed over her, eyes full of fire, splinters of ice in his voice.

'Call me if you need any help? What the fuck is that supposed to mean, eh?'

There wasn't time to respond. The slap came immediately after, followed by a kick to the ribs once Nancy had fallen to the ground. She felt another swift, hard blow to her stomach and let out a protracted moan. Then nothing.

# 8

## MELISSA

Bath time with Gabriel wasn't as easy as I expected or hoped it would be. I had forgotten how slippery and wriggly small babies can be, their tiny limbs and smooth skin difficult to hold onto. The small mark on his head has gone now, thank God. I lean farther in to check and gently run my finger over the place where he banged it. It was the tiniest of movements. One minute, he was lying in my arms as I leant over the rim of the bath to wash his hair and the next, he was on his side in the water. I don't even remember how it happened, how he managed to remove himself out of my arms. There wasn't and sill isn't any lasting damage, aside that is, from my frazzled nerves.

Nobody said this was going to be easy. Looking after babies is enormously difficult. They require round-the-clock care. I'd like to think that the thought of it isn't fazing me. But it is. After bathing him, I suddenly feel overwhelmed. The things I once did without thinking, things that came instinctively with my own child, now feel like a chore. I'm already exhausted and the thought of Gabriel waking during the night for another feed makes my skin ripple with trepidation. Bathing him has got to be the most difficult part. Surely after this, things are going to get better? Once I've mastered how to hold him properly and got him into a secure bedtime routine, everything else will feel much easier. I unclench my jaw and think about our sleeping arrangements. Another thing to fret over. Another mistake I have made.

*The bed.*

Anxiety bites at me. I've forgotten to sort out the mattress. Gabriel doesn't have anywhere to sleep. I give the briefest of thoughts to his pram and immediately dismiss the idea. It's too small. Perfectly acceptable for a brief daytime nap but too narrow and confined for overnight. A small amount of anger at my own ineptitude builds in my gut. I swallow it down and try to control my breathing, then place Gabriel on the sofa and surround him with cushions, much to his consternation. I set about dragging the mattress off the bedframe and shuffling it along the floor. The quilt is too big for him, the thought of him getting smothered during the night just something else to worry about. I throw it aside and grab one of the coverlets I brought with me, then line up a pile of folded blankets and pillows around the perimeter to stop him from toppling off onto the floor. It's not what I had planned and neither can it be permanent. I can see that now. I sigh, staring down at our less than adequate sleeping arrangements. We can't spend every night like this. Despite my resistance to going out and being seen in public, I am going to have to go to the nearest town and buy a proper cot. The least I can do is give Gabriel somewhere to sleep at night. I'm hoping the news of his disappearance from north east England hasn't spread to Scotland just yet. I've got my disguise if it has. I think back to earlier, the sensation of the plastic against my skin as I wrapped my fingers around the handle of the pram and took him away, then the dull thud of the elderly man as he hit my car.

*Oh God, what have I done?*

Reality hits me like a raging bull. The long drive to get here, Gabriel's crying, they stunted my thoughts and reactions making me focus on the present, but now it's all back and I feel sick at what I have done. The police will be there by now, swarming the entire area. The thought of it makes me dizzy, my blood an uncomfortable fusion of fire and ice. It felt like the right thing to do at the time but distance and exhaustion have made me question my motives. Too late now. I'm here and there is no going back, no turning back the clock. Wherever I decide to go in town, however uncomfortable it makes me feel, at least I will always be able to head back here to our safe little hideaway. Our sanctuary. It may be rundown and dated but nobody knows where we are and that is the main thing. It's the only reason we are here – anonymity.

Despite trying to block them out, images of the old man hitting my car continue to puncture my thoughts. My brain is flooded with the notion that I have broken the law over and over and over. That I am now a wanted person and have badly hurt an unsuspecting passer-by. Unsavoury visions infiltrate every part of me. Visions of me as a criminal, my face filling every TV channel, my name being read out on every radio station. I push them all away, all those dark notions and images. He will have been perfectly okay. He didn't look badly injured. It was a minor occurrence. He will have stood up after I drove off, dusted himself down and carried on with his day. That guy was old school. Hard as nails. I tell myself this to keep the guilt and the obvious truth at bay. The truth that he might be dead. The truth that I am possibly a murderer. It was a hit and run. He was a pensioner, a vulnerable individual. A lump forms in my gullet; a gavel bangs against my skull. I take a shuddering breath to calm myself. I need to stop this. I've got to push against the tide of negativity that is threatening to drag me under. I have a baby to care for and don't have the time or energy to worry about an incident that I couldn't avoid. He stepped out in front of me. I didn't have time to stop.

*It wasn't my fault.*

I repeat that phrase over and over in my head as I prepare Gabriel's feed, scooping out powdered formula and spilling as much on the kitchen counter as I put in the bottle. By the time I finish, the countertops are a sea of pale-cream powder and I have cemented the idea in my head that the old man is currently sitting in his house, drinking a can of beer and pondering over what took place. It will be a tale he can tell his pals at the pub – how the middle-aged woman almost ran him down after strapping in her grandchild and racing off at top speed. He will wonder how it all happened and will laugh and shake his head before opening another beer, settling into his favourite armchair and watching his usual TV programme. I tell myself this because thinking such thoughts is easier than considering the alternative.

'Come on, little man. Let's get you fed and off to bed for the night.'

I lay him in the crook of my arm and watch transfixed while he drains every drop in less than a minute. He begins to yowl as I pull the teat from his puckered mouth and once again I wonder if I should be increasing the amount.

His cries are raw, catching me in my solar plexus. Making me wonder what I've got myself into. The mess I have created for us both. I head into the kitchen to make another bottle with Gabriel laid in my arms. It's horribly difficult making up the formula with only one hand while Gabriel screams and arches his back. This small area doesn't lend itself to a tired woman trying to placate a howling baby while making up a bottle. The kitchen is dark and dated, my bags still littering every surface. Sweat gathers around my hairline, running down my face and neck in thin rivulets while he continues to cry. Holding him still becomes more and more challenging, his solid little body resisting my grip. I stop and take a breath, hoisting him higher onto my chest and holding him tighter while I add water to the bottle and screw on the lid. Anger and frustration mingle and merge somewhere deep inside me. My scalp prickles, lines of perspiration continuing to trickle down my neck.

'All right! For God's sake, just shut up, will you? Just bloody well shut the fuck up!'

Gabriel's screams grow louder, my coarse demands doing nothing to quieten or comfort him. If anything, I've made it worse. The flesh on my arms and neck is lava hot, sweat running down my back. I need to add extra water in the mixture to thin it out but his cries feel like nails being dragged down a blackboard and I can't seem to concentrate. I just want to do something to stop the noise. My legs heavy, my body weighted from sheer exhaustion, I head back into the living room and slump down onto the sofa, too exasperated and too damn angry to notice the thump of his head against my arm. I place the teat in his mouth, watching intently as he begins to suck, willing him to drink it all down and sleep. Please God, just let him sleep so I can have five minutes of undisturbed peace. Five minutes while I can unpack properly and make myself a cup of coffee and a snack.

His face turns a disturbing shade of pink after a couple of seconds. Unperturbed and determined to settle him, I push the teat further in, not knowing what else to do. He gags, then turns away from the bottle and lets out an unearthly growl. A fountain of thick, creamy milk spurts out of his mouth in a foamy trajectory and lands on the floor at my feet in small, vomit-like lumps.

He's choking. My grandson is choking.

'Oh dear God!'

I sit him up, one trembling hand cupped under his chin, my

other hand patting and stroking his back until the gagging and retching gradually eases. He takes a long, croaky breath. Tears roll down his face, the colour slowly returning to his cheeks as he wheezes and gasps.

'I'm sorry, Gabriel. I am so, so sorry.'

My own breathing is ragged, tears blurring my vision. Lumps of semi-solid milk are splattered over my clothes. I stare at the stains, guilt and terror at what could have been, rippling through me. Guilt and terror at my ranting and cursing. He's a baby. He could have choked and died. What was I thinking? What the hell was I thinking? I check his chest again, the rise and fall of it the most reassuring thing I have ever seen. He's alive. He's breathing. Everything is going to be okay.

My legs are weak when I stand and place him over my shoulder. His small body is pressed close to my chest as I head back into the kitchen and add more water to the bottle, shaking it until the consistency thins. It was a stupid thing to do. I was stupid. I need to be better, to up my game, be a better carer. A loving grandma, not a screaming harridan.

We sit on the sofa in the living room and he begins to feed again, his eyes locked onto mine as if what has just taken place never happened. My heart is still thrashing around my chest, my body damp with perspiration. With only a few ounces left, his eyes begin to droop, his lips slackening off the teat. I gently remove the bottle and dab at a dribble of milk that runs out of the corner of his mouth, using a cloth to mop up the excess. He lets out a truncated sigh and is asleep in seconds.

I am overcome with relief, immediately laying my head back and letting out a ragged breath. I am beyond exhausted, my limbs like lead, my nerves frayed at the edges. Is this how I imagined it would be? Did I know that escaping the country to a remote location in the Scottish Highlands with a small baby in tow would be so gruelling? Probably not. Would I do it again? I wish I could say absolutely. In a heartbeat. I wish I could say that I have no regrets. But I do. I have so many doubts and fears.

I look around the room while Gabriel sleeps. Outside, darkness is setting in. This has been a difficult day; there is no denying that fact. There have been hiccups since arriving – many of them – and we are completely alone here. Nobody to step in and give advice when I come unstuck. Living in a busy, bustling town hasn't prepared me for this – this sense of loneliness, especially when things have gone wrong. I've made mistakes today, plenty of them, but I still refuse to believe that Gabriel would be better off with his parents. I did the right thing taking him. All I need is a little more time to build up a routine. Then everything will improve. It has to. After today, I refuse to believe that things will get any worse.

He lets out the tiniest of purring sounds, his mouth curling at the corners into something resembling a smile. I place him on the sofa and stand up, walking over to the window. Dust motes swirl when I pull back the curtains and glance out, expecting to see the rugged landscape. I am met instead, with a veil of blackness. A stone sinks to the bottom of my stomach, jagged and heavy. It will take time to adjust, that's all it is. These feelings of trepidation and loneliness that I'm currently experiencing are transient things. I've had a major change in my life. It wouldn't be right to arrive feeling the same way I did when I left. I was gripped by euphoria when I took Gabriel, adrenaline pulsing through my system. That feeling has now subsided, only to be replaced by a growing sense of solitude and, if I'm being perfectly honest, acute anxiety. *This is normal.* I repeat that phrase over and over in my head. The elation I felt when I took him was never going to last. The all-pervading darkness outside, his crying, my feelings of fear and loneliness, they are all perfectly normal.

I close the curtains and pick up Gabriel again, the sensation of holding him in my arms, a fierce reminder of why I'm here. I stand for a few seconds, wondering what that reason actually is. Is it to save Gabriel or is it to save myself? The past rushes at me, a cold wall of water hitting me full force. My day-to-day existence wasn't perfect before I came here. I've been lying to myself, pretending everything was ticking along nicely when it wasn't. Coming here with Gabriel was something I knew I could do to try and improve my life, and his. That's all I've ever wanted to do – to be the best mother and grandmother to my family. It hasn't always gone as planned but I can atone for that by being here with my grandson and making sure he is safe and happy, not left in the incapable hands of his parents.

I carry him into the bedroom and place him on the mattress, laying out the small blanket over his slumbering body. The obvious thing to do is unpack and tidy the cottage while he sleeps but I am so tired, I feel as if a concoction of powerful sedatives has been injected into my veins. Besides, Gabriel may wake in a few hours for another feed. Dread is a tight vice clamped around my skull. I have no idea how long he sleeps for or whether he goes through the night without waking. I pray he sleeps through but given that he is only four months old, the chances are he will wake a couple of times to be fed. Irritation and disappointment at my levels of incompetence gnaw at me. I shake my head solemnly. I should know his routine. And I don't. My own failings as a grandmother are highlighted by my lack of knowledge regarding his care. Was I this inadequate with my own child? Is that why things have turned out the way they have – because I was lacking as a mother?

My head is fit to burst. Even my clothes feel tight and cumbersome when I get undressed. I unfasten my blouse and step out of my trousers, throwing them on the floor next to the mattress, then I climb in beside Gabriel, his soft snores lifting my mood and warming my heart. I need to dispel this negative attitude, rid myself of these moments of self-doubt. It's going to be all right; I will make it all right. I have no other option. We're here now and there's no going back.

# 9

## 1970

Everywhere hurt. Every move, every breath and twitch were agony. After getting up and taking as many painkillers as possible without overdosing, she set about tidying up and clearing the table, washing pots as quietly as she could so as not to disturb anybody. Her ribs weren't broken. She was experienced enough to know the difference between a break and a bruise, not a skill she wished to possess but possess it she did.

Roger had actually helped her up after she hit the floor.

'Nancy, why do you insist on making derogatory remarks, trying to humiliate me in front of my friends?'

She had wanted to reply, to tell him that she hadn't uttered a single word, but knew it was pointless. His mind was made up and defending herself was futile. Jeanette Whitcome had seen through his ruse, was able to detect what sort of a man Roger really was, and he didn't like it. His vulgar, crass ways had been put under the spotlight and he had lashed out, his propensity for violence once again rising to the fore.

'I'm really exhausted,' he said, giving her a wan smile as he headed for the stairs. 'You can leave the dishes until the morning if you would prefer. I can help you after breakfast. It's completely up to you of course, but I know what you're like. You'll no doubt want to do them straightaway. It's no wonder you feel so tired all the time, Nancy.' And with that, he was gone, his shadow trailing behind him like a grey, malevolent spectre.

She had glanced in the mirror. No blood this time but there would be bruises. It took her an hour to tidy everything away. Climbing into bed and lying next to him repulsed her. By the time she slid between the sheets, he was snoring loudly, every breath he took making her skin crinkle with disgust. Sleeping in the spare room wasn't an option. The last time she attempted such a move, she had awoken to his face leering over her, his eyes dark with fury. He had dragged her up and led her back to their bedroom, pushing her down onto the mattress.

'We're husband and wife. This is where you belong, here next to me. Not in a separate room on your own.'

Sleep had come easily, the painkillers numbing her aching limbs and now it was morning and she could hear George beginning to stir. Another day to get through. Breakfasts to be made, children to be washed and dressed. Roger was still asleep, his mouth slightly open, eyes shut tight. She had visions of jamming her fingers into his eyeballs and stuffing a sock in his mouth then watching him choke to death while she held her hand over his nose. Many times, she had wanted to push him down the stairs or add something poisonous to his food. Killing him would probably have been easier than leaving him. And then he would surprise her by doing something kind and thoughtful such as flowers or an evening at the theatre, telling her how beautiful she looked and how deeply sorry he was for his behaviour. He knew when he had taken things too far and she had thoughts of doing something drastic. Not that she ever would. She was a coward. That rankled her as much as his abhorrent behaviour – the fact she did nothing to stop him. Helplessness and fear were terrible emotions to bear. They were weighty and corrosive, toxins that swilled around her system, slowly eating away at the very centre of her being. But after last night, after hearing Jeanette's words, seeing the recognition of Nancy's plight in her expression, perhaps escape from this dreadful marriage was closer than she realised. She wasn't alone in her misery. There was another person out there who understood what she was going through; somebody who had the intelligence to see straight through Roger's façade and spot the detestable, destructive man beneath.

Her legs were heavy as she swung them out of bed and stood up, a definite sluggishness to her movements. A glance in the bathroom mirror made her wince. No bruises but the reflection of a woman who was old before her time stared back at her. Dark circles hung below bloodshot eyes and grey hairs had begun to spring from her head like thick, silver wires. She had to get out of this house and this marriage. She needed to do something before Roger took every little piece of her and she became a walking shell of a woman. That is, if she wasn't already. She certainly felt hollow, despairing and so very sad and low, her mood trailing in the gutter. She couldn't go on like this. Something had to change before her mind became as broken as her body.

She quickly washed and dressed in yesterday's clothes and was in George's bedroom ready to scoop him up before he cried and woke Roger. The longer her husband slept, the better it was for everyone. Ten minutes to make a cup of tea and feed her baby, that was all she wanted. Ten peaceful, undisturbed minutes without his heavy presence watching over her, monitoring everything she said or did, looking and hoping for flaws in her behaviour so he could resume his barbaric ways, his acid tongue and heavy fists tearing at her soul and cutting deep into her flesh.

All was quiet in the kitchen. She slumped into one of the

chairs and held George to her breast, stroking his soft, downy hair while he fed from her. It was a Saturday; she would let her daughter sleep. Why drag the child out of her soft, warm bed when it was cold and windy outside?

Nancy looked around, wondering what it was that first attracted her to this house. The size played a part. And the state-of-the-art fittings. Coming as she did from a working-class family, meeting Roger felt like a step-up in the world. He wasn't immensely wealthy but over the years, he had worked his way up, gaining promotion after promotion and as he did so, their finances grew; enough for her to begin saving money without him knowing or missing it. She had the means to leave. What she didn't have was the guts. Until now, that is. Jeanette's words had set a spark inside her, igniting a flame of hope that things could change. Allowing her to think that escape was possible. Would she miss this house if she left? Possibly. Would she miss the memories it held? Absolutely not. Those, she would gladly banish from her mind at the first opportunity.

A creak from above cut into her musings. He was up. Her time alone to gather her thoughts had been brief. She swapped George over onto the other breast and stood up, making her way towards the living room. She didn't want to be in the kitchen while Roger busied himself with making his breakfast. She couldn't face his inane chatter, the way he hummed away to himself while poaching eggs and making toast, talking about the weather and any number of unimportant topics like they didn't have a care in the world. She had neither the energy nor the enthusiasm to join in with his sick little charade. She was past being the dutiful wife and painting on a happy face. Her resilience was waning, her ability to continue with this pretence and this way of life all but coming to an end. She had no next step planned, nothing in her mind that she could pin her hopes on, but she did know that she had to do something.

Thoughts of calling Jeanette lingered in her mind. Did she have the guts to do it? Perhaps. Or maybe not, but at least it was there, that offer of help. It burned bright in her mind, like a beacon of hope. Something she could hold onto in the darkest of moments.

'Coffee?'

Nancy lifted her head to see him lean his head in through the doorway, hair combed, eyes fresh and sparkling as if last night didn't happen. As if he didn't knock her to the ground and drive his large feet into her ribs. This marriage was a sham. It was over. If only her husband could see it for himself. He was an expert at teasing out purported hidden meanings in her words but oblivious to the obvious. Blind to the damage he caused day after day after day, his callous words and wicked ways a huge wrecking ball in their lives, knocking down the walls of their marriage, the aftermath of his destruction marring her ability to think clearly, to work her way out of the dark corner where she had lain for so many years, fearing for her life. But not any longer. Her escape route was starting to take shape in her mind. Jeanette had thrown her a lifeline, made her realise that she wasn't alone. Nancy may have taken a beating for it, but in her thoughts and heart, she thanked that lady a thousand times over.

'Thank you but I'm okay for now.' She smiled, hoping it reached her eyes. Hoping he didn't detect her current mood. Her hatred of him. How she wanted to leave him, to escape this place with her children and go somewhere far from here. A place where he would never find her.

Because he would. He would make it his sole aim to seek her out and bring her back. His ego wouldn't allow her to stay hidden for long, if at all.

Even up until a few weeks back, she thought she could tolerate it, hoping things would improve, but her daughter's recently uttered words about him hurting the children alerted her to how stupid it was to stay here. Hearing her child's questions was like having cold water poured over her, waking Nancy up to how senseless and blind she had been, continuing to live here, exposing her children to his violence and wildly oscillating moods.

*Call me if you ever need any help.*

Jeanette's offer of assistance continually filled her head. Did she have the nerve to pick up the telephone and tell a woman she barely knew what was happening to her in her own home? Was she brave enough to make that call and ask for help? Jeanette's husband was a close colleague of Roger. They worked side by side in the hospital. She thought of the hell that would break loose once Roger found out about the call – which he would – and dismissed the idea. He and Andrew, Jeanette's husband, would often lunch together. Words would be said, secrets spilled. Andrew would be on Roger's side, his loyalty to his friend uppermost in his mind as he sat in the staff canteen telling his long-time pal and confidante about his wife's conversations with Jeanette, unaware of the punishments that would be doled out to Nancy afterwards.

So no. It was out of the question. But what Jeanette had done was strengthened Nancy's resolve, given her something to aim for. Made her realise she wasn't invisible or isolated, and that was more important than anything else. She had never really been alone in all of this; it had just taken Jeanette's words to make her see it.

Nancy took a shaky breath as George continued feeding, making sure to appear composed under Roger's watchful gaze. There was somebody else she could turn to.

*Nancy, if you stay, you'll rue the day.*

The last time she'd spoken to her sister, they'd parted on bad terms. Hayley, her only sibling, tired of Nancy's inability to take her children from the house and flee, had hung up, her exasperation at Nancy's inability to extricate herself from Roger's malignant clutches a solid barrier between them.

*Come and stay with me. Simply grab a few things and leave.*

That was just under two years ago. Since that time, their conversations had been perfunctory, speaking on the phone for only a few minutes each time, with Hayley asking after the children and sending a small gift for George a few weeks after he was born, her vexation at Nancy's continuing weakness evident in her tone.

She could go there. She could take the children and get the train to London. Hayley would meet her at the station and help her. And then all of this would be a thing of the past.

Excitement glimmered in her mind. It was possible. For so long now, her brain had been fogged up with fear; logic lost amidst her terror and a need to simply make it through each day. But now, armed with the words of allies and the realisation that she was braver than she ever knew, escape seemed within her grasp. The pinprick of light in her mind ballooned, allowing in warmth and a raft of possibilities. Hayley had moved home since she and Roger last visited. Nancy wasn't even sure if he had the new address, but she would find it.

Strands of long-forgotten memories looped around her mind, slotting into place. She had scribbled Hayley's new street number and road in the old address book. Nancy used the book rarely, her contact with the outside world limited, but she definitely had a memory of writing it down.

George unlatched from her nipple, a dribble of milk running down the side of his face. She leaned down and kissed the top of his head. Imbued with a sudden surge of enthusiasm, her mind now clear of the thick, swirling mist that had crippled her for as long as she could remember, she stood up. She had to get that address book and slip it into her handbag. Tearing out the page would be a huge clue to her whereabouts. Taking the whole book would prove less problematic, keeping Roger guessing. He may not even notice it was missing. The rift between her and her sister would make Roger less likely to suspect Hayley of harbouring her. Come Monday, when Roger was back at work, she could put her plans into motion. For now, she would have to continue with the pretence of being a happily married woman. A loving and compliant wife. She could do that. She had managed it for the past twelve years. Another two days wouldn't make that much difference.

The deadweight of her aching body lightened, hope putting a spring in her step, giving her something to aim for. She placed George over her shoulder and shuffled upstairs where she removed his sleepsuit and nappy, putting a fresh one on him and dressing him in a powder-blue outfit.

'There we go. What a beautiful boy you are. Let's go and see your sister, shall we?'

She held him close to her chest and as quietly as she could, they went into Melissa's room and sat on the chair in the corner, watching the child slowly wake up, her limbs languid as she stretched and yawned, her eyes fluttering against the fingers of morning light that crept into the room from behind the blinds.

Nancy's voice was as light as air when she spoke, her tone gentle and full of optimism, and perhaps even tinged with the slightest trace of confidence. 'Morning, sleepyhead. What a wonderful week we're going to have. Such a wonderful week ahead for the three of us.'

# 10

## MELISSA

My eyes are glued together, fatigue weighing them down. It takes a couple of seconds for me to orient myself to my surroundings. Gabriel has begun to snuffle, his pitch building up to what I now recognise as a cry of hunger. I glance at my watch, squinting to see the hands on my old analogue wristwatch. 3 a.m. The witching hour.

Memories flood into my tired, befuddled brain. Dark, distant memories. Unwelcome ones. I think of my mother and how she tried to care for George and me while her world fell apart. So often, I think of how she should have tried harder, done more to make our lives that bit more bearable. Yet she didn't. Her courage failed her. When she did finally do something after years of suffering, it all felt too late. Everything was too damn late, the damage irreparable. This is my chance to right those wrongs, to make sure my grandson flourishes and doesn't spend his formative years cowering under the bedsheets, terrified of the endless shouting and the screams of terror. I survived it and I'm here now, acting as a loving grandmother to my grandson, but even in this quiet, sedate environment, it's harder than I imagined. I'm tired, unused to Gabriel's routine. We travelled a long way to get to this place and now that we're here, everything feels out of kilter, my energy levels waning, my ability to tend to his every need sorely lacking.

I rub at my eyes, my vision blurred and grainy, then reach out to touch Gabriel, to feel the softness of his body and to convince myself that this situation is real, that unlike my mother, I have at least found the nerve to leave everything far behind us. I may not be perfect but I've got my baby and he's safe here with me. My little boy. I have done what my mother wasn't able to do all those years ago. I have found the courage to remove a baby from danger, and for now, that is enough.

I slip out of bed and tiptoe to the kitchen, making up a bottle, increasing the volume by two ounces, then make up another, and pop it in the ancient, noisy box in the corner that passes itself off as a fridge, before heading back to the bedroom just as Gabriel's cries become more insistent.

He latches onto the teat and sucks, the noise of his hungry gulping filling the silence of the room. He's almost the same age as George was when everything spiralled out of control. When it all went horribly wrong. I shake my head and fight back tears. Everything was already on a downward spiral. Things simply sped up and took a turn none of us could have ever predicted. A lump is trapped in my throat, tears burning the back of my eyelids. I swallow and let out a trembling sigh.

Enough. I need to focus on the present. Raking over the past will not solve my immediate issues. Gabriel needs me to be the best I can be. I rub at my eyes with my free hand and suppress a yawn, hoping this feed will be enough to send him back to sleep. He finishes in record time and opens his eyes, looking around as if suddenly aware of his new environment. And then he smiles, and at that point, I know that everything is going to be perfect.

'Awake, are we now eh, little man?' I take another look at my watch. It's just after 3.40 a.m. and he is fully alert, his eyes roaming around the room. A dull headache sets in at the base of my skull, the urge to lie back and sleep for a decade such an overwhelming sensation that it feels as if it is a permanent fixture, something that will never leave me. This is the hardest part, the bit I didn't consider or give any thought to – the exhaustion. It's overwhelming. Fighting it off feels like pushing a boulder uphill.

I swallow down the tears that threaten to fall and lie next to Gabriel, staring at him, still amazed at how perfect he is. Even in the dim light of the room, his face is clear to me; his blemish-free skin and sculpted features enough to restore some energy into my tired, old body.

We stay like that for a while, his small sighs lulling me into a near slumber. Eventually, his eyelids droop and I watch as he effortlessly slips into sleep, his mouth shaped into a small O. I lie for a few seconds, mulling over my past, present and future until my own eyes become gritty and I can no longer stay awake.

* * *

My eyes snap open. Sweat is coursing down my back and chest. I was dreaming. No, not a dream. A nightmare. A horrible, vivid nightmare about Stuart. A pain shoots across my head. I rub at my face, pressing the heel of my hands into my eye sockets to clear the film that sits across my eyeballs, distorting my vision.

I blink repeatedly and look around the room. It's starting to get light outside. I check my watch. 6.30 a.m. Soon it will take longer and longer for the sun to rise, the darkness encroaching in small, indiscernible measures. Soon the murky evenings will last longer than the hours of daylight. I swallow and suppress a shudder, trying to blot out the thoughts of another long winter.

Stuart's face fills my head. The Stuart I once loved and married. The same Stuart who awoke one morning and told me that he no longer wanted to remain as my husband. I was completely blind-sided by it, his words cutting me to the quick. Robin, our son, had already left home at that point and Stuart had explained, without an ounce of compassion, that being left alone with me was more than he could bear. I was sucking all the joy out of his days, ruining our marriage with my endless bouts of depression. He left that morning, claiming my erratic ways were too much for him. He had tried, he said, to make it work but I had given him no choice with my changeable moods and behaviour.

'I've tried to work with you on your issues, Melissa, but it seems that you don't want to know. If you ask me, you enjoy wallowing in your own misery. We could have worked through this together, but you have shut me out, leaving me with no choice.'

Watching him load up his belongings in the car and drive away was the lowest point of my adult life. My childhood is another matter. The two are not mutually exclusive and each brings their own share of heartache and unhappiness. We sold the house in record time, our recent renovations helping to bump up the asking price and bring in plenty of interested parties. I needed somewhere to live that was warm and dry. My apartment was, and still is, a shell. A place where I existed. Until now, that is.

I glance at Gabriel then think back to the nightmare. The one where I was standing over Stuart, bashing his head in with a hammer. It's a recurring theme in my dreams: me meting out violence to my ex-husband in various bloody and horrific ways. We were meant to stay together for the rest of our lives, not move off in different directions as strangers. And then shame washes over me at feeling satisfaction for dreaming about such ghastly scenarios.

Perhaps deep down, I am as bad as my father, violence embedded deep inside of me. I shake my head and wrap my arms around myself. No. I'm not him and never will be. I'm a caring mother and doting grandmother and would never hurt another living soul.

*Except for that hit and run incident. You left an old man for dead.*

I suppress a sob and fight back tears, closing my eyes against the tide of dark thoughts that continually drag me back to the past. A past I would sooner forget. It was around that time that my relationship with my son, Robin, also began to falter. That era of my life is hazy and misshapen, blurred around the edges. Many events are difficult to piece together and some days are clearer than others, but the hurt of knowing that my family is fractured is something that cuts me to the quick.

Stuart said that perhaps I should seek professional help. What I needed was *his* help. But it was all too much for him. He couldn't do it and so he left, telling everyone that I was the problem, refusing to admit that his lack of compassion and patience were the undoing of us.

I shake off the memory of the nightmare and slip out of bed, trying not to disturb Gabriel. If I can get showered and dressed before he wakes, it will make everything so much easier.

The pipes and nozzle give a sudden cough and a splutter before kicking into life, steam billowing out from behind the nylon curtain, which is thankfully, clean. It's strange how, when put under pressure in an alien environment, we become grateful for the smallest of mercies. I quickly wash and shampoo my hair, trying it up in a bun after getting dry and slipping into loose-fitting slacks and a thin sweater.

Gabriel is rousing as I pass the bedroom. I hurry and make up three bottles, putting two in the old fridge for later. I've forgotten how feeding a baby takes up so much time, the preparation of making up the formula an endless and mundane task, detracting from what should be a joyous experience. I find the whole process to be prosaic and tiresome and not the happy adventure I had hoped for.

My stomach kicks into life at the thought of breakfast. After feeding Gabriel, I'll make some coffee and toast. Caring for him is draining, both mentally and physically. I need to remember to eat. I cannot spend every minute of every day tending to only his needs. I think I will scream if I don't find time to sip at a cup of tea or eat a sandwich. I love him dearly but this round-the-clock caring is taking it out of me. I clench my fists and stand for a few seconds, trying to pull myself together. It isn't his fault. He's a baby. I have to do this. This is what I wanted, what I felt compelled to do, and there is no turning back. We're both here now and I've somehow got to find the energy and the motivation to keep going.

Gabriel is lying on his back, eyes wide open when I head back into the bedroom. I tiptoe closer, not wanting to disturb or alarm him. For one terrible heart-stopping second, I fear that something is wrong as I stand close by watching him, waiting for that familiar rise and fall of his chest to assure me he's breathing properly. Nothing. No movement or crying. My skin grows cold. Then I see him breathe and I relax, my own chest a series of small convulsions fuelled by relief.

'Come on, little man, let's get you fed, shall we?'

I wonder how long it will take for me to stop panicking, for my new life and all that goes with it to fall into place. I wanted everything to be seamless, the transition from Gabriel being with his parents to him spending all day every day with me, an effortless shift. And it isn't. The path has been littered with problems and self-doubt. I pick him up, the warmth of his body against mine allaying my doubts. It's still early days and he is healthy and loved. What more does any child need?

My mind wanders as he feeds. The urge to check the news is overwhelming but with no Wi-Fi or television, it's an urge I am forced to ignore. I wonder what sort of chaos I have left behind and whether Stuart has seen any of it or been questioned about my actions. I visualise his stricken expression, the way he has of blinking rapidly when he is put under pressure. The twitch in his jaw. The pallor of his skin. I hope he is thinking of me, wondering where I am. What my plans are for the future. I've got full control of our grandson now and he has nothing. For once, the balance of power is tipped in my favour. I've waited a long time for this, to steer my own ship, not have others push me around, telling me what's good for me. I know what's best for me. The days of being the underdog are over.

Perhaps throwing my phone into the river and cutting myself off from the rest of civilisation wasn't such a good idea after all. Even a snippet of a headline would give me a clue as to what is being said about me and what I've done. And then there is the story of the old man. He will be uninjured. Had he been killed, the police would surely have found a way of tracing me. The fact they haven't is testament to that and proves I've done nothing wrong. Gabriel is clearly safe here with me and the old man is alive and well.

Still, being able to lay my hands on a newspaper would assuage my lingering doubts, putting to rest my worries and frustrations. The nearest village is a forty-minute drive away, the main town even further. The realisation that my plan isn't as meticulous as I thought, weighs heavily on me. Being isolated has its pitfalls. I bite at the inside of my mouth until the sting and metallic taste of blood forces me to stop. Enough worrying and angst. It's tiresome, dragging around these negative emotions.

They are weighty and destructive and I don't need them. Caring for Gabriel is tiring enough.

I finish feeding him, then dress him and prop him up against a stack of pillows while I flit around the room, hanging up clothes and doing what I can to unpack our things and spruce up the place. He allows me five or so minutes before he begins to fidget and make noises that I know will soon turn into a piercing cry that will shred my nerves.

I scoop him up and swirl him around in the air, trying to emulate the feelings of euphoria I felt yesterday when I took him and made the journey here, but feel nothing. Gabriel's mouth puckers, his face creasing as he prepares to let out a scream. I sigh, readying myself for it, my stomach twisting with dread and apprehension. Then I visualise the police swarming Stockton-on-Tees and the surrounding areas, and manage a smile. A warmth spreads across my flesh, my face burning with excitement and triumph. They have no idea. The route here to this cottage had few cameras. Once I left the main roads, my journey will have disappeared from their radar. It's just me and Gabriel now. We've made it. We have actually made it. We're in a tiny, rundown, old place in the middle of nowhere. No neighbours. Nobody around for miles. And I'm not sure if that's something to celebrate or whether I have made the biggest mistake of my life.

## 11

## MELISSA

'You'll not find anything like that round here.' I stare at the heavily whiskered face of the sales assistant and suppress an eyeroll as he continues speaking. 'Nearest place for that sorta thing is possibly Pitlochry or even further afield at Aberfeldy which is only an hour away. Mind you,' he says, squinting and staring out of the window, 'you'd have tae set off pretty soon before the storm hits.'

I refuse to get drawn into a conversation about the weather. Strong winds and a bit of rain are small potatoes after yesterday.

'Thanks for your help,' I say as brightly as I can, the wig making my head itch and the heavy make-up feeling like a dead-weight on my skin.

I turn to leave, eager to be back outside, away from the staring eyes of other shoppers. The longer I spend in the company of anybody other than Gabriel, the greater my chances are of being recognised. That is, if news of his disappearance has reached this far north.

'You'll be staying locally for a holiday then, I take it? You should have requested a proper cot for the bairn before you drove all this way.'

'It's fine,' I murmur over my shoulder as I pull open the door and wheel Gabriel over the threshold and out into the sharp breeze. A quick glance at the headlines of the stack of newspapers tells me that news travels slowly up here. No mention of a kidnapped child. Nothing about a hit and run. I'm safe. For now.

I feel the intensity of his stare as I exit the shop. I look back into the face of a middle-aged, bearded man who is perusing the shelves, his eyes shifting to me as I leave. He monitors me closely through the open doorway while I adjust my bag on my shoulder and lower the hood on the buggy to protect Gabriel against the growing wind. Nobody knows me here. No need to worry. I'm being paranoid. Still, perspiration makes me clammy, the heavy make-up smearing on my skin.

I stare up at the sky. Clouds the colour of gunmetal press down on us. I'll take my chances with this purported storm and drive to Aberfeldy to buy a cot.

My reflection in the shop window takes me by surprise. I hardly recognise myself. Even if the news was being circulated in this area, the wig and make-up narrow the chances of people recognising me.

Gabriel smiles and gurgles as we reach the car.

'Come on then. Let's be brave and take a drive into town.' I unfold the buggy, strap him into his car seat and start the engine, relieved to be away from the shop and the inquisitive eyes of that man. I back out on an empty road. Gabriel snuffles for a short while then sleeps while I savour the silence.

We arrive without incident, Gabriel waking as I lift him out of the car and into the buggy. It becomes apparent as I wheel him around, that as picturesque as this town is, it isn't the place for purchasing baby equipment. I berate myself and my stupidity for being so remiss and neglecting to buy the correct equipment before leaving England. I lie to myself, repeating in my head that his well-being is what counts, that he is loved and cared for and that that is enough, but deep down, I know it's not true. My errors are a hindrance. I promised plenty and have delivered little. It's not good enough. *I'm* not good enough. Maybe Stuart was right. Maybe my low moods get in the way of everything. Spoil everything. Maybe I'm not up to the job of looking after my own grandson.

My fingers are hot as I clasp them around the handle and push, my knuckles a waxy, white ridge. Heat gathers under my collar. I take a shaky breath and close my eyes. This needs to stop. This constant stream of self-deprecation and doubt has to stop. It's pernicious and counter-productive.

'Food,' I say as I push the buggy. Gabriel watches me with bright, inquisitive eyes. 'We'll buy some food while we're here.' He responds with a small yowl and I feel my flesh pucker. *No more crying. Please, no more crying.* I can't stand any more of his screams. The rumble of the wheels soothes him. He lies back and gurgles, his eyes still wide with alarm as I wheel him through the streets, over undulating surfaces, up and down kerbs, and through the crowds of shoppers that line the streets. My feet twist beneath me. The wheels of the buggy rumble and warp, tipping to one side. I'm going too quickly. I need to slow down, to get a grip and stop panicking.

'We're here,' I say, suddenly breathless with anticipation as I stop and stare at the doorway of a supermarket, its bright lights and piped music an inviting scene amidst the chaos of the high street and the crowds that bustle and slalom their way past me.

The aisles are busy with shoppers. I keep my eyes lowered. I can't afford to become too confident or complacent. Need to keep my guard up, remain vigilant and be an invisible entity in their presence.

I fill up the handbasket and make my way to the checkout.

'What a bonny wee one.'

My heart speeds up. I place my items on the conveyer belt, my gaze averted from the voice beside me. I keep my shoulders hunched, my back arched and angled away from the voice.

'Got such a cute little smile, hasn't she?'

This woman hasn't picked up on my silence and body language. She doesn't have the good sense to leave us alone. I can't escape her questions so go along with the pretence. If Gabriel and I are to remain anonymous, taking on new identities may prove to be useful.

'She certainly has. Such a good girl for her great-aunt.' The lies slip easily off my tongue.

'That's lovely to hear. How old is she?'

My skin frosts over. Too many questions.

'Three months,' I say. 'Big for her age.'

I manage a tight smile. It feels like a grimace. The dated old cottage in Rannoch Moor seeps into my thoughts, the appeal of its remoteness and even its dated décor pulling at me. I need to leave this place. We should be there, not here in this brightly lit, overcrowded supermarket with its incessant noise and curious customers.

A wad of notes spill out of my purse as I unzip it. The money flutters away from me, spreading over the grimy, tiled floor. My face burns. I stand frozen, my limbs solid blocks of wood. I want to escape, to grab Gabriel and just run and keep on running until all this is far behind me.

'Here, let me help you, hen.' She bends down to pick up the cash, her slim fingers gathering up ten-pound notes and passing them back to me with a smile.

'Thank you.' My voice is croaky, my gratitude hidden behind a veil of fear. Despite my disguise, I feel vulnerable and exposed. I'm coming undone, my nerves sizzling beneath my flesh as she watches me, her eyes roving over my clothes and tight expression. A twitch takes hold beneath my eye. I bat it away with hot trembling fingers, thoughts of smeared make-up running down my face increasing my state of panic.

She hands over the remainder of the money and cocks her head to one side. There is no disingenuity there, just helpfulness and kindness. Yet unease still cripples me, rendering me inert and useless. I avert my eyes away from her face, her probing gaze and smile stirring up the feelings of disquiet that are making it hard for me to breathe properly. It's as if she can see through to my thoughts, to the deceitful person loitering behind the crude attempts I have made to hide my real identity.

I grab at my bags of shopping and start to push Gabriel away from the checkout, my eagerness to be out of the place overriding everything, including my dexterity. A tin of beans falls out of the bag and rolls across the floor. I kick it away. It's just a tin of beans. Getting out of this place is all I can focus on.

'Excuse me.' Another voice of reason. Another good Samaritan. Christ almighty, will these people not leave me alone? 'You seem to have dropped something.'

Before I can tell him that it doesn't matter, a young man dressed in a navy tracksuit chases the tin towards the exit, catching it before it rolls out of the door.

'Here you go.'

I snatch it out of his hand and grunt, my chest and throat in a spasm. I tried to keep a low profile but once again have made mistake after mistake, drawing attention to myself and Gabriel. Will I never learn? Our presence in this area will be noted and remembered. I hope I'm right and that my wig and make-up render me unrecognisable and completely different to the e-fit that will be currently emblazoned across the internet and all the news channels on the television back in England. My erratic behaviour, however, is another matter, my actions in the last few minutes marking me out as unhinged.

'Thank you. Sorry, need to get this one home and get him fed.'

*Him.*

I realise my error too late. The lady who helped pick up my money is watching me, her eyes tapered, bemusement etched into her features. My legs are leaden as I rush out of the shop, my mind honed in on reaching my car, getting Gabriel safely strapped in his seat and leaving this town, going back to a place where nobody knows me. Our safe place. I should never have come here. Disguise or no disguise, it was a stupid, reckless move.

I'm breathing heavily; my chest is tight. By the time I put Gabriel and the bags of shopping into the car and strap myself in, I am gasping, every breath a huge effort. I lean back and close my eyes for a short while. I just need a few seconds to regroup and start thinking clearly.

The knock close to my face reverberates through my bones, forcing me to sit up straight. She is standing next to my window, the woman who helped pick up my money. Her body is bent over, her face inches away from the glass as she peers in, her eyes occasionally flicking to Gabriel, who is cooing happily in his car seat, before resting back on me.

Do I drive away? Make myself even more conspicuous by my strange behaviour? I have many things to fear; my crimes are serious. Taking a child without consent, even a child who is related, is a possible prison sentence. Then I think about the old man and whether he is alive or not. I swallow and drum my fingers against the steering wheel. Do I do the thing that any normal, innocent, decent person would do and open the window to see what she wants? I smile at her and glance at my watch, tapping it with my forefinger, hoping she sees it as a sign that time is against me. Hoping she leaves me alone. She remains standing, her brows knitted together in confusion. I pray her puzzled expression is confusion and not anger. I don't need any enemies. People who will turn against me and contact the authorities. Common sense is telling me to open the window and be gracious and courteous. My nerves, however, are screaming at me to get the hell out of this place, to drive as quickly as I can and leave her standing there. I take a long, shuddering breath, clasp my fingers around the steering wheel and think long and hard before making my move.

# 12

## 1970

He was in his study, his head lowered as if pondering over something hugely important. She had learned through bitter experience that such a pose didn't necessarily mean he was deaf and blind to her movements. There had been occasions when it was a ruse, a thing he did to catch her out. A way of provoking an argument.

*Where are you going?*

*Why are you tiptoeing past my study?*

*Who the hell do you think you're talking to?*

The last retort had been fired at her after she had dared to insist that she hadn't been tiptoeing at all, merely walking past as discreetly and unobtrusively as she could to allow him some peace and quiet. Sometimes, there weren't any right answers. Only words that antagonised and riled him, giving him the opportunity to warrant having yet another flare-up of anger. She felt sure he enjoyed it: the power trip, the massaging of his ego. Letting her know that he was master of the house and that he made the rules. Rules that changed as often as the wind and were impossible to follow.

The address book was in the drawer of the telephone table in the hallway which was close to his study. She would take it later in the day when he was occupied elsewhere: pottering in the garden perhaps, or drinking his mid-morning cup of coffee in the lounge which he often did on a weekend. The lack of noise in the house was her enemy. They rarely listened to music and infrequently switched on the radio or the television in the middle of the day. The sound of a drawer being opened would echo around each room. Roger cast a heavy presence in their home. Removing one small item was an enormously difficult manoeuvre. So many stringent limitations on what she was able to do, and she had glibly accepted it over the years because her current life and its many restrictions had crept up on her bit by bit until it became the norm and she knew no other way. But all that was about to change. Looking over her shoulder would soon no longer be her default stance. In a short while from now, she would be free of this place. Free of him and his overbearing ways and horrific temper.

Already, she was planning it, enjoying the buzz it gave her. On the pretext of going on her usual visit to the bakery for fresh bread, Nancy would call her sister from the phone box two streets away. Her heart was a rapid thud, the thought of speaking to somebody who could help her, making her giddy with excitement. She would do well to keep her feelings of exhilaration under wraps. His eagle eye would spot the difference in her demeanour. That was his forte – being able to read her mind. Even her thoughts were no longer her own, but not for much longer. Soon she would begin to rebuild her life. She would remember who she used to be before she met Roger, and more importantly, who she could become. That part gave her pause for thought. A better, stronger mother. A powerful role model for her children.

It wasn't easy, trying to suppress the excitement that bubbled in her abdomen – it swirled and exploded like popping candy – but she had to keep it locked away because the ramifications of Roger discovering her plans didn't bear thinking about. It would be an end to everything. Possibly an end to her.

She gathered the children, telling them they were going out for bread for Daddy. She felt the burn of Melissa's stare as the child assessed her words.

'Is he coming with us?'

The look of peril in her daughter's eyes shrivelled her insides. This was why she was making this move: to protect her children. To shift them from the darkness of his shadow, his elongated, all-pervading shadow that loomed over them day after day.

'No, darling. This is going to be a surprise for Daddy. We're going to get some extra special treats.'

She would explain about the telephone call when they got to the phone booth. Melissa was a bright little girl; she would know how to keep a secret. Besides, Roger had little time for his daughter. Any attention he showed the children, which was scarce, was given to George. It became apparent how deep her husband's misogyny ran after their son was born. George was the boy he wanted Melissa to be. When he did decide to be father-like and playful, it was George who received his attention.

Nancy slipped out of the door, calling behind her that she was going to the bakery and would be back in fifteen minutes. Roger's low, non-committal grunt was a sign that he was busy, possibly immersed in something work related. This was her time. These fifteen minutes could mean everything. They could change her future and the future of her children.

With George safely tucked up in his pram and Melissa's small hand holding onto the chrome handle, they set off, the warm breeze lapping around them, caressing her face. Helping her feel alive once more.

She knew the number, had it stored in her head, reciting it out loud as she dialled. She could even ask Hayley for her new address, cast it to memory and not have to go through the arduous process of locating that damn stupid book. Her breath bubbled up, becoming suspended in her chest while she waited to speak to the one person who could save her. Her leg was jammed in the semi open door of the small booth, one hand clasping the handle of the pram. Melissa stood next to her, one half of her small body inside the confined space, the other half exposed to the elements as she cooed over her baby brother.

Nancy counted the rings, her heart hammering out a solid beat behind her breastbone. Then a click as somebody picked up at the other end.

'Hello?' She spoke first, her breathless greeting cutting over her sister's attempts to reply. 'Hayley, is that you?'

'Nancy? Is everything okay?'

Tears pricked her eyes at the sound of her younger sibling's voice. She swallowed, the lump in her throat painful, like shards of broken glass. So many unshed tears. A river of emotions pushing at her defences, trying to burst through as she listened to Hayley's words. The innocence of her tone. The security it promised. But she told herself there would be no crying today. She would save the tears for later. They would be happy tears once she made it to London, Once they were all safely tucked away in her sister's new home.

'Yes, it's me. I'll need to be quick. So sorry to gabble but I need your help, Hayley. I desperately need your help. I've got the children with me.' She dropped her voice to a whisper, sneaking a glance at Melissa, who was happily chatting away to George. Her words came out in a rush, her breathing fast and erratic, a sour taste swilling around her mouth. 'Can we come to yours? I need your new address. I'm doing it, Hayley. At long last, I've found the courage and I'm finally going to leave him.'

## 13

## MELISSA

The car growls when I press my foot down hard on the accelerator, the wheels crunching on the tarmac as I move away from the woman standing next to my car. Guilt and mortification dilate in my pores, pooling over my flesh. I press the back of my left hand against my forehead to alleviate the ache that is setting in there. This is ridiculous. I'm drawing attention to myself with my inconsistent and juvenile behaviour. I hit the brake, the wheels screeching in resistance, before reversing back to where she is standing, her brow knitted together as she observes my absurd behaviour.

A pulse beats in my neck. I lower the window with no idea of what I'm about to be faced with. I have no answers at the ready for the barrage of questions and accusations that she will probably fire my way. All I have is my gut feeling that I did the right thing taking Gabriel. A stranger won't see it that way. She will see me as a wanted person. A criminal.

'Sorry,' I say breathlessly. 'I didn't see you. Is everything okay?' Once again, lies slip easily off my tongue. I'm becoming quite the master at it. They drip from my mouth like warm oil. My own voice echoes in my head, each word sounding alien and ill-fitting. Everything is not okay. Things will only be right once Gabriel and I are back at the cottage in Rannoch Moor, away from this lady. Away from the rest of the world.

'I was going to ask you the same thing, actually.' Her face softens and she smiles at me, tipping her head to one side, her stance gentle and non-threatening. She looks at me like a parent trying to comfort a distressed child. 'I noticed you seemed to be struggling to manage back there in the shop and wanted to make sure you were all right. Looking after little ones is really difficult. We all need as much help as we can get.'

I'm unsure how to react. She seems genuine, her features soft and rounded, her voice calm and pleasant. No abrasive words. No shouting. No apparent judgement. And yet, I don't know her. Just like me, she could be lying.

'I'm fine, thank you. Had a bit of a bad day.'

She holds out a business card and places it in front of my face. A loud hissing sound fills my ears, a line of static echoing my head. Who is this lady and what does she want from me? I glance in the rear-view mirror, my thick make-up now seeming garish and clown-like, and then look down at the card.

'My name is Lorna. I run a baby group in the Town Hall every Tuesday and Thursday if you're interested. It's an informal get together where people can meet and chat. Quite a few folk who go there are glad of the break. There are lots of other adults around who can help look after the little ones while parents and grandparents and even great-aunts like yourself, enjoy a well-earned cup of tea. Sometimes just chatting with like-minded people can alleviate the stress.' She smiles, her head still leaning to one side, her expression pleasant and welcoming.

Did I detect a note of scepticism when she said the words *great-aunt*? I think about her offer and don't know whether to feel flattered or insulted. What I actually feel is relieved. She hasn't recognised me. She isn't about to call the police.

'Thank you,' is all I can manage to say, my throat thick with emotion. 'I'll certainly bear it in mind.' My fingers are still trembling when I put the card in my coat pocket. Later, when I'm away from the town and these people, I'll dispose of it, tear it into a thousand pieces and throw it in the bin. Gabriel and I are fine as we are. We don't need anybody else. As nice as this lady is, we are better off on our own.

'Please do. We're always on the lookout for new members. The more the merrier.'

I close my window and give her a weak smile and a perfunctory wave before driving away.

Despite trying to forget what just happened, despite telling myself that I don't need her or her business card or any of her offers of assistance, her words loom large in my mind. It simply isn't possible. Why on earth would I give any thought to mingling with strangers and run the risk of being recognised and reported to the police? And yet there it sits, her invitation, taunting me with its presence. It's a lonely old business caring for babies. I'll admit that I've found it daunting and difficult at times. I sigh and fight back tears. Now I'm the one being disingenuous. It's been more than difficult. The whole thing has been one long struggle. I hoped to make up for the past by painting a shiny new future for myself and my grandchild, but it's proving harder than I ever imagined it would be. Thoughts of my baby brother, my father, my mother, drift in and out of my mind. Thoughts of that time in my life: that day. If I could just go back, change things, make it all better. Make a better job of it...

I rub at my face, make-up smearing over my sleeve, then head out onto the main road before she has a chance to stop me again. Before I weaken and ask her for her help.

Gabriel sits quietly in his seat as I drive, my gaze fixed firmly on the road ahead. Once we get back to the cottage, everything will seem clearer. We can continue sleeping on the mattress on the floor. He's safe enough there, and besides, having thought about it, I like the idea of having him by my side every night. It will allow us both a level of much-needed comfort. God knows we could do with it right now. The world feels like a lonely old place. Frightening and precarious. Full of inconstancy and peril. Neither Gabriel nor I need baby groups, and we don't need other people. We have each other and that is enough. I repeat it over and over in my head until it feels real. Until I convince myself that it's actually true.

The cottage is chilly when we arrive back. I turn on the wall heaters. Later, when Gabriel is in bed, I'll think about stoking up a fire. The store out the back has a decent supply of logs, enough to keep us going for at least a few weeks. It's one thing the owner of this cottage has got right. Everything else is questionable.

Gabriel lies on his playmat while I tidy the living room, dusting and polishing surfaces and vacuuming rugs. It doesn't take too long for things to look brighter and cleaner. More like a home than a neglected, old cottage. Sweat blooms on my chest and back. I stand and tie back loose strands of hair that have fallen free, pulling them away from my face. The wig that caused my head to itch lies discarded on the sofa and the many layers of make-up I applied before going out feel like a heavy mask. I take a tissue and wipe it off, smears of orange, red and black streaking over the paper. I continue wiping until my skin feels clear again then catch sight of my reflection in the mirror that hangs over the fireplace. A tired, old woman stares back at me. Lines litter my face; my hair is thinning and the skin on my neck is almost translucent. Once again, misgivings creep in and I begin to doubt my own abilities. How can somebody my age care for a baby? I don't have the energy I once had. My reflexes aren't what they used to be and I am tired. So very, very tired. I slump down into a chair just as Gabriel begins to yowl for attention. I know that I wasn't the best mother in the world. I tried, God knows I tried but something went awry along the way, so how can I possibly hope to garner enough physical and mental strength to care for my baby grandson?

I rub at my eyes and stand up. I have to stop it. I can't allow any more negativity to bleed into my thoughts. I pick up Gabriel, collect a bottle from the fridge and sit in one of the old armchairs, watching as he guzzles the milk like a baby who has been starved. I think that he is probably ready for being weaned onto solid food. I dread the thought of it. It's just something else I have to do. Something I didn't prepare for or even think about even though this whole scenario is what I wanted. I created this. I shouldn't complain or gripe when all of this is my doing. I swallow down the lump in my throat and bat away any feelings of fatigue that nag at me.

'Can't have you going hungry, can we?' I say quietly, forcing myself to sound happy. Forcing myself to be a caring grandparent when exhaustion and frustration are threatening to engulf me.

I place a dry kiss on the top of his head and carry him into the kitchen, balancing him on my hip whilst studying the instructions on the side of the packet of baby rice. I need to mix it with some of his milk and then try him with a couple of spoonfuls.

The whole process of unscrewing lids and opening packets and mixing with fluid whilst balancing a baby on my hip is an arduous task and takes longer than it should. By the time I manage to complete it, Gabriel has begun to whine and I am hot and bothered again, my hair plastered to my head, rivulets of sweat running down the side of my face.

'Come on, let's try you with some of this, shall we?' My voice is hoarse, lacking in any softness or compassion or any of the qualities required when speaking to a baby.

I perch him in the corner of the sofa, realising that I haven't brought a plastic spoon in with me. I make a dash back into the kitchen to collect it and come back in seconds later to find Gabriel slumped forwards, his body laid flat on the seat, his head hanging over the edge of the sofa. I shriek, the noise in my throat a guttural howl. I scoop him up with clammy hands and cradle him close to my chest. Seconds. That was all it took. I dread to think what could have occurred had I taken any longer. This is just the beginning. They are the sort of things that will happen once he becomes properly mobile. I need to make sure every room in this cottage is safe and secure, move all stray objects out of his reach and keep a closer eye on him. I made a terrible mistake. It could have proved fatal. Just one more inch and he would have slid off completely, his head hitting the hard floor. I think back to that other time, the mayhem and the worry, the terrible, blood-curdling screams, and shut it all out of my mind.

'This was never going to be easy, was it, eh, Gabriel? Nobody ever said it was going to be faultless.' My voice is dry and croaky. My hands are trembling. I'm trying to inject some softness and levity into my tone but a length of barbed wire sits at the base of my throat, my voice a dry rasp.

Once again, I prop him up and place cushions around his body to keep him upright, then scoop up a small amount of baby rice on the spoon and put it in his mouth. His lips smack together, the gluey substance coating his gums and tongue. His face is a mask of passivity.

'You want some more?'

I ladle up a bigger amount and repeat the process. His face reddens. His eyes begin to water. He inhales sharply. Then a cough followed by an explosion of creamy porridge-like substance fires my way as he expels it from his mouth.

'Oh God, please don't choke! Not again.'

I pat his back and wipe at his mouth, clearing the sticky food from his face, telling myself I can do this even though I don't think I can. He takes a deep, rattling breath, his tiny chest heaving with the effort of simply trying to get enough air into his lungs. Why is this so bloody difficult? I may not have the energy levels I once had but I'm not completely decrepit, and I'm definitely not an idiot. But it's been thirty years since I've looked after a baby. Nevertheless, I don't recall it being this tough last time around. Lorna's face slips into my mind unbidden. I shake my head as if to knock it away. I don't need Lorna or her baby group. I don't need anybody. We're doing just fine on our own. I keep saying it even though I know it's not true. I'm willing to bet there are hundreds if not thousands of new mothers up and down the country who are having the same sort of struggles. My difficulties are nothing new. In a few months, I will look back at this time and wonder why I found it all so taxing.

The thought of the future, my uncertain future, weighs heavily on me. There was a time when I could have predicted what lay in store but now, everything feels flimsy and changeable. Visions of the police descending on the cottage blacken my thoughts, turning everything to ash. I wish I could banish all these negative emotions but tiredness and fear are allowing them in. They roam around my brain, sneaking up on me, reminding me of how inept and ridiculous I am. How stupid and thoughtless, taking Gabriel without thinking things through properly.

*Stop it!*

I continue rubbing Gabriel's back in small, circular motions until he rights himself and can breathe properly. Tears are running down my face and a huge, rock-shaped lump is wedged in my throat. I wipe at my cheeks and nose with the back of my hand and silently berate myself. Enough of this self-pity and uncertainty. It has to stop. Nobody else is going to step in and help me. I need to get a grip and pull myself together. Be the decent grandmother and carer he needs me to be.

'Okay, a smaller amount this time, eh? No more scaring me like that, young man.'

I manage a smile, my chin quivering as I speak, and place a thumbnail-sized portion of the rice onto the spoon. He opens his mouth and a small amount of elation unfurls in my chest as he takes it and swallows it down without any problems. I give him one more spoonful and then lay it down on the bowl. He's had enough for now. *I've* had enough.

'Perhaps a little more later before bed to fill up your tum, eh?'

His eyes twinkle like small diamonds, his mouth curls up into a smile. He's replete and happy. I am wrung out and exhausted.

The afternoon passes without event. I resist the urge to curl up on the bed and sleep soundly. Gabriel spends the next hour kicking about on his playmat while I busy myself with more cleaning chores. Each task is interspersed with hugs and the occasional walk around the cottage to help familiarise both him and me with each of the rooms.

It's only as the sun begins to sink that the feelings of helplessness and solitude begin to creep in once more, a lead weight pressing down on me. More unwanted thoughts plague me: what if I fall ill unexpectedly? Who will care for Gabriel then? Everything feels so precarious, any positive emotions I had falling away like confetti. Small pieces of my mind scattered around me. Outside, any remaining light fades from a pale ochre to a wash of grey that soon switches to a blanket of deep, impenetrable darkness. Alone once more.

A clap of thunder knocks all thoughts of unforeseen events

and catastrophes out of my head. The sky outside is lit up by a streak of lightning so vivid, it feels surreal and dreamlike. Holding Gabriel tightly to my chest, I stand next to the window and watch as the predicted storm finally moves in.

'Here it is, the bad weather we were warned about. A good few hours later than expected. At least we're warm and dry in here.' I almost add, *and safe* but swallow down those words. Slipping in the bath, choking on food, falling off the sofa. Just a few of the perils from the past twenty-four hours.

The sky is illuminated, a vast pattern of stars visible between the ominous-looking clouds, their complex constellation a sight to behold. Another apocalyptic rumble of thunder has me backing away from the glass. I draw the curtains and carry Gabriel through to the bedroom, closing the door behind us as if to protect us from the elements. Perhaps growing older and being the wrong side of middle-aged, rather than infusing me with confidence, has stripped away all my self-assurance. Experience is a two-way street. Whilst learning from it, it also teaches us the dangers and hazards of life. Having a vulnerable individual in the house has made me acutely aware of how easily an environment can change from one of safety to one of extreme danger. Storms don't frighten me; it's the aftermath caused by their ferocity that scares me. Weather-related issues set my nerves on edge but the storms whipped up by the behaviour of others are harder to handle. The fallout of those destructive paths lasts forever, damaging the present and shaping the future of those involved. We can all kid ourselves that overcoming such things is possible but deep down, it isn't that simple. Each damaging event digs a deeper groove into us, embedding ruts into our psyche that cannot be smoothed out.

'Come on, little chap. Let's get you bathed and ready for bed, shall we?'

Gabriel kicks about in the old, enamel tub while I wash his hair and gently clean his face and body. Drying him off, feeding him and settling him in bed helps restore some of my confidence in my ability to do this thing. I am all he has so I had better dig deep into my reserves of energy and be the best I can be in order to make him feel loved and happy. There isn't anybody waiting in the wings, no hired help. Nobody to step in and give assistance if required.

He is asleep in seconds, his eyes heavy, his small mouth pursed in contentment. Today has been full of ups and downs but it has ended on a high. The storm is passing.

# 14

## MELISSA

I wake with a start. Something is wrong. I listen out, trying to pick up on any unfamiliar sounds that will give me a clue as to why I have such a strong feeling of unease. My eyes slowly adjust to the darkness as I lie there, my body stiff with anticipation. Is the thunder still rumbling on in the distance? I doubt it. I pick up my watch from the side of the bed and squint at the face; it's too dark to see anything. My phone is still tucked away in my bag, turned off and for use only in emergencies. I suddenly realise I am truly alone and miss the connection to the outside world that technology provides.

My ears become accustomed to the noise: a low, grating sound, like a feline purr.

*Gabriel.*

I sit up and scramble around the bed, touching and pawing for him. I can feel the heat coming from his small body before my groping fingers finally land upon his saturated sleepsuit.

'Oh God!'

He's burning up. I back off the mattress and flick on a small lamp. Gabriel is lying there, his clothes damp, his face a frightening shade of crimson. Sweat has matted his hair and his breathing is noisy and laboured. I listen, horrified, as his chest rattles and gurgles like an old boiler with every single breath he takes.

Panic coils around my throat, swirling upwards and tapping at my temple. We're alone here, in the middle of nowhere and Gabriel is ill. My grandson, the child that I snatched from his home, is very sick. Somewhere deep down, I always knew something like this was going to happen, that bad luck would creep upon us to try and teach me a lesson. I have to do something – anything – to make him well again. Caring for a healthy baby is difficult enough; trying to look after an ill one without any medical assistance or intervention is well beyond my capabilities. I've got to do something to make him better or everything will come undone; all my efforts thus far, the ground we have covered to get here, will have been for nothing.

Medicine. I need some baby paracetamol to bring down his temperature. I know that I brought some with me. One thing I got right at least.

I place my hand over Gabriel's forehead, anxious at how hot he is. I need that medicine as quickly as possible. Except I can't remember where it is. In a bag somewhere in the kitchen would be my guess. I should have tidied it after cleaning the living room. Except I didn't. And now I'm faced with this.

I feel as if I'm being punished for some past sin, having to face this alone, every hour that passes bringing a new set of problems. I leave Gabriel in the bed and run to the kitchen. The strip light scorches my eyes, its white glare at least helping me to find the bag that contains the medicines I brought with us.

The rattle and crinkling of the plastic carrier bags crashes into my brain while I rummage and pull out boxes and tins and bottles, placing them on the kitchen counter with a clatter until eventually I locate it, wedged in at the bottom below a collection of heavy items. Of course it is. What did I expect – that any of this would be easy and effortless?

Grabbing the unopened box, I pull out the bottle and plastic syringe, narrowing my eyes to read the small print of the instructions on the back. He's allowed 2.5 ml. It doesn't seem like much for a baby whose temperature is raging but I know better than to administer more than is needed. That way lies real danger. Babies are tiny, fragile creatures. I'm alone here should anything go wrong. I can't afford to take any chances.

Back in the bedroom, an air of disquiet winds its way under my flesh. It's silent. All I can hear is the steady thump of my own heartbeat. Where is Gabriel's rattling breathing, the wheeze of his chest? His plaintive cries? I clamp my teeth together until my face aches and approach the bed with caution, preparing myself for the worst and praying for the best. Every move I make feels cumbersome, my own breathing difficult and onerous.

Gabriel's eyes are closed. He is soundless and still.

*No. Please God, no!*

I reach down and touch his forehead. He is still clammy. I stare hard, concentrating and praying until I can see the faint rise and fall of his chest. My legs buckle. I want to cry with relief. He's alive. My boy is alive. He is ill, however. The fever hasn't left him. He needs medicine. My fingers are wooden when I attempt to get the correct amount of the gloopy liquid from the bottle.

Holding the syringe tightly, I part Gabriel's lips and inject the medicine into his mouth, then pick him up and cuddle him into my chest. He lets out a low splutter, followed by a sigh. I pray that the medicine does its job in record time and brings his temperature down. I wouldn't know where to find a doctor or a hospital. All I have is my common sense and ingenuity, and both of those seem to be in short supply of late, my recent mistakes a reminder of how rusty my baby-minding skills have become.

Gabriel begins to weep. Fluid. He needs fluid. I fill a clean, sterilised bottle with water and he gulps it back, then I take his milk out of the fridge and we sit together on the sofa as he slowly takes a third of it before falling asleep in my arms.

I sit for half an hour, dreaming of smoking a cigarette and drinking a glass or two of wine. But of course I don't do either of those things. What I actually do is continually check his temperature, watching as the fever gradually recedes and he feels and looks normal again. My relief is palpable. I cannot allow myself to think about what would have happened had he not responded to the medicine, how much his temperature would have continued to rise, damaging his little body and internal organs, possibly even killing him. I cannot allow myself to think about it because the thought of that transports me back to a place I don't want to visit. A time in my life when happiness was rudely snatched away from me, never to return. So instead, I continue to watch over my sleeping grandchild, making sure he is in a deep, undisturbed slumber. Only then do I carry him back to bed, laying him down as I would a fragile flower. I climb in the bed and lie down next to him, monitoring his breathing until in the end, I also fall asleep, the trauma of the evening taking its toll on me, bone-aching fatigue pulling me into a long and deep torpor.

* * *

It's light outside. I blink and yawn, those first few seconds of wakefulness lulling me into a false sense of security, making me forget about the important stuff. Making me forget about Gabriel. It hits me like a speeding train, the memory of last night. His illness. His irregular breathing. I sit bolt upright, looking at my grandson as he continues to sleep.

His face is ruddy again, his hair matted. I don't need to touch him to check his temperature; I can feel the heat pulsing from his little body. The bottle of medicine is by the side of the bed. Should I wake him, or administer it while he sleeps? I think about the choking episode from earlier and feel my own temperature rise, a surge of intense heat and a spike of cold clashing in my veins at the idea of him gagging again.

I reach down and fill up the syringe, then gently place my arms around Gabriel and lift him to my breast, his head tipped slightly forward. He doesn't stir. This is a bad thing; I know it is. He usually wakes if I pick him up. With him cradled in the crook of my elbow, his head lolling, I give him the medicine then tip his head back ever so slightly. He doesn't gag or regurgitate it. His small mouth works slightly, his lips opening and closing as he swallows it down.

Time passes slowly, each second a minute, each minute feeling like an hour. I wait, observing him closely, waiting for the medication to do its thing. His breathing is regular – that's one positive thing, but he still doesn't wake up. I tell myself that I'll give it another fifteen minutes and if he still doesn't rouse then I'll have to take action. I have no choice. The thought of driving to a hospital and facing a barrage of question from overbearing doctors and nurses fills me with dread, but not as much dread as if I were to do nothing and the unthinkable happened. Again. I shiver and rub at my eyes. I need to find a solution to this situation. I know that babies develop fevers, get viruses and high temperatures. I tell myself that it's just his immune system doing its thing, helping to build up a resistance to a whole host of germs that swirl about us every day. Gabriel's body is adjusting, that's all it is. Once the medicine kicks in, he will wake up and smile at me and everything will be back to normal. I say a small, silent prayer, cuddle him closer, and wait.

Through the curtains, I can see the day edging its way in, the half-light of the early morning slowly giving way to full sun. A clear sky after last night's storm. I wonder if it's cold and crisp out there. I could take Gabriel out for a walk; the ambient temperature may help to cool him. I just need him to wake up.

The sheer terror of each passing minute as he continues to sleep, shreds my nerves until at last, his eyes spring open as if shocked into wakefulness. He doesn't smile but neither does he appear restless or out of sorts. The medicine is clearly working and for that, I'm immensely grateful. A spark of optimism ignites in my veins, flames of hopefulness streaking through me.

'Good morning, lovely little chap. How are you feeling today?' My voice is croaky, fear and uncertainty making it hard for me to speak clearly.

He watches my face then lights up the dull room with a wide, toothless grin. A sob rises up my chest. He's on the mend. Thank God. He is gradually on the mend. No hospital visits. No doctors. All he needs is me. I should have trusted my own instincts all along. Proof if ever it was needed that we don't need anybody else in our lives. All we need is each other.

# 15

## 1970

'I'll drive up north to collect you. There's no way you can travel to London on the train with two little ones and then navigate your way on the underground.'

Nancy sighed, a faint crackling sound filling her ears. 'That's really kind of you, Hayley, but you can't. If he sees you here, he'll know that something is up and then that will be that.' She straightened her coat, pulling up the collar to keep off the chill, and peered around the half-open door of the telephone box, her voice a whisper. 'Good girl, Melissa. Keep playing with George. Mummy won't be long.'

'I can drive up in the early hours and you can be out of that godforsaken house before he even wakes. And not before time, if you ask me, Nancy. Not before bloody time.'

Nancy wanted to say that she hadn't asked her but held her tongue. This was never going to be easy. She needed her sister's help and couldn't afford to risk getting involved in any arguments or disagreements with her only sibling. Besides, she'd had a gutful of confrontation. Enough to fill a hundred lifetimes. Now was the time for amicable exchanges and pleasantries.

'Please, Hayley, you don't know him like I do. If you come to the house, he will hear you. I would also need to have our bags packed the evening before. If I get the train, I can grab our things after he leaves for work on Monday morning and be at the station well before lunchtime.'

She waits for her sister's reply, her suggestion hanging between them, before speaking again. 'And even if you drove up early morning, you wouldn't get here till lunchtime. He sometimes comes home for a sandwich if there isn't anything in the hospital canteen that takes his fancy. I can't take the chance of you two running into each other. I just can't. All hell would break loose.'

Hayley sighed, her voice edged with exasperation. 'Okay, but if you change your mind, I don't mind driving up to collect you and the little ones. I could set off in the early hours and be at yours just after he leaves for work. That way, he won't see me, will he?'

Images of Hayley turning up early or Roger leaving the house a little later and the pair of them meeting burned bright in her mind. It would be a catastrophe. The consequences of that encounter didn't bear thinking about.

'Thanks, but it's safer to do it my way.'

They spoke for a few minutes, Hayley asking after the children until she finally took a long, trembling breath, her bewilderment about her sister's timing evident in her tone. 'Nancy, it's great you're finally doing this, but why did it take you so long? I mean, the man is a fucking monster. I don't want to think about how many beatings you've had to endure over the years.'

She couldn't reply, didn't have the words to articulate how debilitating it had been living as she had, with the threat of violence constantly hanging over her. How it had reduced her to nothing, taking away what little confidence she had and leaving her a husk of her former self. Hayley wouldn't understand. Nancy didn't even truly comprehend it herself so how could she expect her sister to grasp her thinking?

'Sorry, I'm not blaming you,' Hayley said swiftly. 'I'm just confused, that's all.'

Nancy could see her sister now, sitting on the sofa, surrounded by her home comforts, the things she had worked hard to buy. The things that had come easily to her. It felt as if adult life had always been a struggle for Nancy whereas Hayley's achievements had all but fallen into her lap. She'd met the right man who treated her with love and respect and had been able to carve out a decent career for herself as a legal secretary with the support of a good man at home, whereas Roger had insisted that Nancy leave her job as a nurse as soon as she fell pregnant with Melissa. She should have seen it then – the signs that he was domineering and heavy-handed. She should have taken notice of those red flags but was blinded by his charm and intelligence. She had married a doctor. Their lives were going to be perfect.

'No, it's okay, I know that. Things have been – tricky, as you well know.'

'I totally understand. Can't have been easy for you with two children, one of them a baby.'

Tears burned at the back of Nancy's eyes. She swallowed and rubbed at her face with her sleeve. No tears. Once they started, she wouldn't be able to stop them and that simply wouldn't do. She had to be strong for the children. Strong for herself. Travelling down to London with two little ones wasn't going to be easy; she had to reserve what little energy she had for the journey.

'Anyway,' Hayley said, her voice taking on a gentle lilt that put Nancy in mind of a soft, summer breeze, 'ring me when you get into Kings Cross and I'll come and meet you. Far simpler than me trying to give you directions over the phone and a lot easier than you going on the underground on your own with the children.'

They spoke for a few more seconds with Nancy promising to call Hayley as soon as she arrived in the city.

'It can be a bit daunting even for the most seasoned of travellers, so please don't try to get to my house without me accompanying you.'

They bid their goodbyes and hung up, Nancy feeling happier than she had in a long time, her body and mind as light as air. She felt as if she could take a leap and float up into the clouds.

'Who were you talking to, Mummy?'

Bending down on her haunches, Nancy took Melissa's face in her hands and gave her daughter a kiss. 'Can you keep a secret?'

The child's eyes sparkled with delight. 'A secret? Is it a nice secret? Like somebody buying me ice cream without me knowing about it? That sort of secret?'

Nancy nodded and gave Melissa a tight hug, the softness of her skin like being enveloped in a length of expensive silk.

'Something like that, my darling. I've just been chatting to Aunt Hayley about us visiting her next week. Would you like that?'

'That's so exciting!' Melissa's voice was a high-pitched squeal, her excitement a tangible thing that warmed Nancy's heart. It had been some time since her daughter had displayed genuine enthusiasm and joy, her emotions tempered by her father's unpredictable reactions should she ever dare to become too animated in his presence.

Nancy realised at that point that she hated her husband for sucking all the life out of her daughter; for forcing their child to tread on eggshells to avoid setting him off on one of his infamous rages. She was doing the right thing by leaving him. In a few months' time, she would look back on this period of her life and laugh at how weak she had become. How spineless and cowardly. She was none of those things and never had been. He had twisted her mind, made her think of herself as undeserving and worthless. That was what abusers did. They dripped poison into the minds of their victims, skewing their thinking, making them turn upon themselves. But not any longer. Soon enough, those days would be behind her. Every second that passed infused her with another layer of courage. By the time she and her children boarded that train, she would be wearing an invisible suit of armour: untouchable and invincible. As strong as forged steel.

'But remember, we mustn't tell anybody.' Nancy took a shaky breath, readying herself for the next part. 'Not even Daddy.'

Melissa's eyes flickered as she watched her mother closely. 'I won't tell him, Mummy. I promise.'

They walked to the bakery together, Nancy's mind full of ideas. She would take the money she had saved as well as her cheque book. Roger knew nothing of her separate account. Her savings were split between the bank and the wad of cash she had tucked away in her bedside cabinet. Roger thought he controlled every aspect of her life but rummaging through her underwear drawer wasn't his style at all. She still had something that belonged to her. Her secret stash. Like a member of a criminal underworld gang. That thought almost made her giddy.

'Will Daddy be happy if we buy him lots of bread?' Melissa was skipping. Nancy hadn't seen her daughter skip for the longest time.

'I think so. We'll buy his bread and when we get home, I'll make some juice and we can have a little tea party.'

'Like a celebration for our secret.' The child tapped the side of her nose and smiled.

'Exactly that. Now we'll not speak of it any more as secrets aren't supposed to be mentioned, are they?'

Another tiny squeal as Melissa slipped her hand into Nancy's, leaning in to hug her mother's slim legs. She let out a laugh and squeezed Nancy's fingers. 'What secret?'

Such sophisticated humour and mannerisms for a child of her age. Not so damaged by her environment after all. Nothing could go wrong. Nancy could feel it. She was almost there, their futures mapped out. Her attempts at carving out a new life for her and her children was almost within reach, the happiness they wanted and deserved so close, she could almost taste it.

'Come on, let's treat ourselves and buy half the bakery.' An unseen power pushed her on, the pram suddenly light beneath her fingers, Melissa's hand feeling so fragile, her touch was barely there at all. Nancy stopped and took a sobering breath. She had to remain grounded, not let Roger see her feelings of jubilation or all would be lost. He had a sixth sense for such things and would detect it as soon as she stepped foot inside the house.

'Would you like an iced bun, my lovely?' Melissa smiled and nodded her head, already doing her best to keep her own excitement under wraps.

'Yes please, Mummy. Should I eat it before we get home?'

And there it was – the affirmation she needed that getting out was the right thing to do. The fact her child was too frightened to relax and enjoy a special treat in front of her own father told her everything she needed to know – that their home was a prison and she was about to break free.

'You know, I think that might be a good idea. You can eat it on the way back.'

Another enigmatic smile from her child: a knowing smile. That's what it was. Their shared secret was their route to freedom and happiness, and they both held the key.

* * *

Melissa's fingers were sticky, her face caked in icing sugar. Nancy took out a handkerchief and spat on it, rubbing her daughter's hands and face vigorously. There must be no trace. No evidence of their daughter having had a sugary treat. No evidence of her acting like a normal child, enjoying the liberties and the innocence that many other children experienced and took for granted. It would aggravate him and an aggravated Roger was a dangerous one; he would begin to question every little thing, seeing Nancy's quiet behaviour as suspicious and furtive. He would make her nervous and agitated, her mask of happiness slipping away to reveal her true intentions beneath. She always was a terrible liar when confronted with his questions. He had done that to her – flattening her ability to manage her own thoughts and emotions and controlling everything she did.

'There we go. Let's make sure we're nice and quiet when we get home. I'll give Daddy his special bread and you can go and play in your room.' She nodded at her daughter who in return, gave a brief smile, shedding her earlier contentment and replacing it with her usual level-headedness. Already, she was a master at concealing her sentiments, and this, thought Nancy dolefully, is why they needed to leave.

Melissa could be trusted, Nancy knew that, and in return for keeping her confidence, Nancy would give her child a happier life. It was a healthy bargain. She deserved it. They both did, as did little George, who knew nothing of their current woes and worries but would at least have the chance to grow up in a household free of violence. A household brimming with love and opportunity. A household without Roger in it.

They walked back to the house together in near silence, each preparing themselves for what lay inside, readying themselves for his sour exchanges but hoping at the same time for smiles and laughter. Whatever was within those four walls, they would cope, knowing their time there was limited. Knowing their lives were about to get immeasurably better. Just two more days until she would be able to throw off the shackles of this poisonous house and hideous marriage, and then a more contented life would be hers for the taking.

## 16

## MELISSA

The day stretches out ahead of me. Within an hour of giving him his last dose of medicine, Gabriel's temperature spikes once more. Using what little knowledge I have of battling fevers in babies, I decide to take him out in the buggy, hoping the fresh breeze will cool him down. My euphoria at his sudden recovery has evaporated. We're back to square one. I take my new phone with me, unsure of whether I can even get a signal out here in the middle of nowhere. I still feel safer having it with me should Gabriel suddenly take a turn for the worse.

I put on his coat, place a blanket over him to keep off the chill, and we set off down the rutted path, his eyes closed against the glare of the full sun. I pull up the hood which provides some protection against the heat and light whilst allowing the cold wind to still reach his hot flesh and in turn, hopefully lower his temperature. It's a long shot and if this, along with another dose of medicine, don't work, then I don't want to think about what my next step is going to be. The idea of a hospital makes me shudder but leaving Gabriel to suffer is also unthinkable. He'd be in the right hands had I not taken him, a team of medical specialists able to diagnose him. I block out that thought. It's nonsense. Had I left him with his parents, he would be in the same position. They were both too busy with their own lives to pay any heed to an ill child.

Once again, Lorna's face pops into my mind. I bat it away but her name and offers of support refuse to leave, tapping away at my brain. She won't have any medical qualifications but what she may have is the number of a local doctor who won't pry into my details. Somebody who will understand my predicament and give me some medical advice. I can lie, tell them I'm here on holiday with my grandson. That's not so far from the truth anyway. And the doctor will give me a prescription for a course of antibiotics – because it's apparent to me now that Gabriel has an infection of some sort – and in a couple of days, after taking a few doses, everything in our little world will be back to normal. Or as close to normal as is possible, given the circumstances. A small, still voice tells me that it wouldn't happen, that they would need names and addresses, that their computer system would flag up any false identities. And then it would all be over.

Holes and dips litter the path but I continue, hoping the cold breeze does its job and cools Gabriel down. Once again, an acute sense of isolation gnaws at me. The roar of the wind is the only thing I can hear. It whirls around me, pockets of turbulence whipping at my face. This is what I wanted, isn't it? To be alone with my grandson. I expected a peaceful environment, somewhere where we could both lay low and become better acquainted. What I didn't expect were childhood illnesses that seem resistant to everyday medications. Perhaps, given my previous experiences, I should have expected it. Being a victim isn't my style, but if I rake back over my life and scrutinise it closely, everything up to this point has been difficult and warped, my existence a deformed, distorted version of how it should really have been. How I *wanted* it to be.

Gabriel lies still, his face now devoid of colour. I lean forward and touch his cheek. Still warm but no longer like molten lava. I was right. The cool weather is helping him. His eyes flicker with exhaustion. He is sleeping longer than is considered normal. It's this illness; it's taking its toll on him, like a wrecking ball battering his little body.

I keep my eyes fixed on him, studying every breath and movement. He yawns and I'm suddenly imbued with a surge of positivity. It doesn't last long. Out of nowhere comes an unearthly scream. My legs buckle. My heart speeds up and despite the cold wind, heat rises up my neck, prickling at my hairline. Once again, panic rushes through me, making me jittery and unsteady.

I unstrap him and lift him out, holding him close to me and cradling his head, hoping to calm him down. His sobs pulsate through both of our bodies. I don't know what to do next. I am all out of ideas and struggle to fight back my own tears, knowing they will only make things a hundred times worse. I need a clear head to deal with this escalating situation. His health is deteriorating. I think perhaps the time has come for me to get some help even though every fibre of my being is screaming at me to stay in the shadows and sort this thing out on my own. A louder, sharper voice in my head yells at me that Gabriel's well-being comes first, that I'm going to have to get him to hospital and run the risk of being recognised and caught, and that if I don't, he might die. Could I live with that?

With my free hand, I fish out my phone along with the card that Lorna gave me, relieved that for once, I did something right in not disposing of it. Gabriel lets out another howl of despair and I hold up the phone and spin around until I see two bars, then carefully punch in Lorna's number, and wait.

She picks up after just two rings, catching me unawares. I don't have any words prepared in my head and stand there in silence until Gabriel cries once more, dragging me out of my reverie.

'Hello? Can I help you?' Her voice is welcoming, a calming inflection in her tone that reassures me.

'You said to call you if I needed help. We spoke yesterday in the supermarket.'

'Of course! I remember. You're the great-aunt. Your little one is sounding a little out of sorts there. Is everything okay?'

'He's ill. *She*, I mean, *she* is ill.' A strong breeze blows my hair over my eyes. I shake my head to clear my vision. My heart is hammering. I gasp as I speak to her, my words full of fear and agitation. I'm coming close to losing it. I have to rein it all in, my terror at losing Gabriel and being found out. What happened to my ability to lie with impunity? 'I need to know where the nearest doctor is.'

There is a short silence, long enough for me to become apprehensive. Did she recognise me yesterday? Maybe she has already called the police and they're currently tracing all of her calls. Hysteria builds in my gut. I swallow and take a juddering breath.

'A doctor? What are her symptoms?'

'High temperature. Very high. It comes down after a dose of medicine but goes back up again within an hour or so. Just upset and out of sorts really. Where can I find a doctor? We're on holiday here and I need to see someone. As soon as possible.'

I'm wheezing now, Gabriel's squirming and crying and the growing wind making me tired and causing me to stumble. I lean into the handle of the buggy for balance, willing Lorna to help me without wanting to know any further details.

'Where are you staying? There's a doctor's surgery in Aberfeldy but if she's that poorly, you might be better off taking her straight to the hospital. If you let me know where you're at, then maybe I can come—'

I cut the call and turn off my phone. I can't take such a risk. Why couldn't she just give me directions and let me find my own way there? Experience has taught me that that's what people do – they let us down time and time again. The only person we can ever truly rely on is ourselves. I'm alone in this. I've always been alone.

Gabriel quietens down. I continue to rock him, his cries gradually petering away to nothing.

'We'll manage just fine on our own, won't we, little man? It's you and me against the world.'

Soothed and calm again after a few seconds, he snuffles when I place him back in the buggy. I lift out a bottle of milk from my bag and gently put it in his mouth. To my relief, he takes almost half of it before turning his head away and falling asleep again.

Weary, I sit on a hillock and look around. The terrain is barren as far as the eye can see, but also uniquely beautiful, with an undulating landscape, distant mountains and tracts of marshland that give the area a rugged feel. Not so bad in daylight. Night-times are a little more taxing.

I swig from an old bottle of water that I find at the bottom of the bag and take a bite from a cereal bar. Sustenance to get me through the day. I sit for a few more minutes, then stand and check on Gabriel, who is still fast asleep.

In the distance, a car passes, the low growl of its engine cutting through the silence. I turn my face to one side and keep my eyes fixed on Gabriel. I'm too far away for anybody to see me clearly but I'm not about to take any chances. With no heavy make-up or anything that will conceal my identity, keeping my eyes lowered and my face out of view is the wisest thing to do. I think of my phone call to Lorna and feel my stomach clench. It can't be her. It's too soon. The passing vehicle is just a coincidence. I'm being irrational. She has no idea of my location. This is just another moment of panic that is twisting my reasoning skills.

As soon as the car is out of sight, I grasp the handle of the buggy and set off walking again, continuing for another five minutes or so before turning back, the ruts and holes in the path making further progress impossible.

We are almost back at the cottage when I see a shape that sets my nerves alight – somebody is standing at the door. I bend down, concealed by a clump of shrubbery. I only hope Gabriel continues to sleep and doesn't wake with a yowl. My knees creak and my back shrieks with pain as I rest on my haunches. The cottage is isolated and I'm guessing by its dilapidated state, hasn't been occupied for years so who is this person and why are they here? It looks like a male figure but I can't be completely certain. Frustration and fear collide in my head. All I want is a quiet existence with my grandson and yet at every turn, it appears there is always somebody or something ready to ruin my plans. Perhaps Lorna *was* somehow able to somehow track my location. I sigh and berate myself at my own stupidity. Of course she wasn't. This is something unrelated. A bizarre coincidence. An ill-timed, unwelcome one.

I keep watching. Watching, watching, watching, a pocket of air trapped in my chest as I wait. And then something happens that makes me weak with horror and dread. The figure unlocks the front door of the cottage and steps inside. My insides turn to water. I have no idea what is going on but I do know that I need to get in there and demand that they turn around and go back to where they came from. Did I leave the key in the lock? No, I didn't. I dig into my pocket and curl my fingers around the small set of keys. Who is this person and what the hell are they doing here?

I stride towards the cottage, my jaw clenched tightly. As I get closer, I can see another vehicle parked next to mine down the side of the house. It's a black SUV. My stomach knots. I think of the police and wonder if they have managed to track me down. No. It's impossible. Absolutely impossible. They wouldn't use an unmarked vehicle for such an operation. And besides, why use keys to get inside? I've seen films and documentaries where they kick down doors in the middle of the night to catch people unawares, dragging them from their beds and arresting them.

The thudding in my chest is a heavy gallop by the time I reach the door and push Gabriel's buggy inside. I can hear somebody moving about but before I have chance to say or do anything, a figure appears and I am pressed up against the wall, a strong hand held firmly against my chest, a solid set of fingers clutched around my throat.

I try to scream but my windpipe is constricted. A powerful individual holds me in place. A male figure. I can feel the heft of him, am able to smell the foul stench of his breath as it wafts close to my face. He's wearing a hood, the top half of his face concealed from view. He has the strength of ten men as he holds me fast. I struggle to breathe properly. My legs kick out at him, and on instinct, I bring up my knee as hard as I can and catch him between his legs. He lets out a roar and stumbles back, giving me just enough time to duck out of his grip and make a dash towards Gabriel, who is still sleeping peacefully.

'Bitch! You fucking bitch!'

Before I can do anything else, he grabs at my hair, pulling it out of the clip that's holding it in place, and yanks me back towards him. I feel myself being overpowered but my limbs continue to thrash about, scratching and kicking at anything I can reach. His face connects with my hand. With splayed fingers, I dig my long nails into his skin and drag down as hard as I can, feeling a satisfying tug of flesh. His hood falls, revealing his features. Spots of blood pepper his left cheek and a long gouge runs the length of his face.

'What the fuck? Who the hell are you?' His voice is a deep bellow. Incredulity is etched into his features.

He lets go of my hair and brings his hand up to his face. His eyes are dark and wild with anger. He isn't done with me just yet. I spin around, searching for an object I can use as a weapon. If there is anything nearby, I need to get to it before he does. I have to protect Gabriel. Then this angry stranger does something that surprises me. He sits down and shakes his head, dabbing at his face with an old tissue that he fishes out of his pocket, and speaks. 'Who the fuck are you and why are you in this place?'

I'm panting, caught between wanting to hit him with something heavy and wanting to crumple to the floor and weep for an age. 'I'm renting it. Who the fuck are you and why are *you* here?'

More head shaking and dabbing at his damaged flesh. It's a long gash. I had no idea I could inflict such a wound and feel quietly pleased with myself. That was without even trying. If he attempts to do anything else, at least I know I'm capable of putting up a good fight.

'That can't be right. You must be in the wrong place, lady.'

'How so? I've paid my money and I have a key.' I dangle it for him to see, then slip it back into my pocket.

'So do I and I need this place more than you do, so you're gonna have to leave.'

I stare at Gabriel, then back at this man, who stands up and starts to walk towards me. He is grimy, sweat marks staining his sweater, stubble covering his greasy and bloodied skin. I need to think quickly, do something to show him that I'm not soft and about to give in to his demands. I was here first. I have a baby, a vulnerable individual. My needs are greater than his.

To my right is an old vase. It looks heavy. Enough to inflict more damage to his face. I pick it up and hold it aloft.

'And I have a small child to care for. A tiny baby. Now leave.'

He stops walking then shakes his head and lets out a raucous laugh. 'Don't be so fucking stupid.'

Anger darts through me. 'Stupid? I don't think so. Take a look in the mirror at your face. That cut is just for starters if you don't leave me alone.'

My fury soon turns to terror as he reaches into his pocket and pulls out a gun, his face clouding over, his smile now a lopsided grimace. 'Look, I didn't want to do this, but you're not leaving me with any choice.' He waves the barrel at Gabriel and nods at me, his eyes as black as coal. 'I need you out of here. Pack up whatever stuff you've got and get the fuck out of this place. Now.'

## 17

## 1970

It wasn't easy, hiding her plans from him, keeping her thoughts to herself and dampening down her enthusiasm, but she did her best to remain normal and level-headed; to be her usual, guarded, amiable self, always eager to please, but not too lively or energetic or he would suspect, thinking there was an ulterior motive to the change in her attitude and behaviour. Roger was a bright man academically, but knowing how to manage his own emotions and be part of a happy marriage were alien concepts to him. He knew nothing of real family life or how to behave in an appropriate manner towards his wife and children. Once, many years back, he had opened up to her about his own childhood (but only once because showing his soul counted as a weakness), telling Nancy how his father would beat him for the slightest misdemeanour, taking the belt to him if his homework wasn't completed on time, or how he would ridicule him if Roger gained anything less than top marks in class. For a clever, well-educated man, Nancy couldn't for the life of her understand how he couldn't see that he was repeating a history he utterly hated. One that had made him as a child feel wounded and worthless. It was as if that part of his brain had been stunted by the abuse, refusing to work as it should.

She handed him his coffee and fresh bread and shuffled out of the room, claiming that George needed feeding and changing. He let out a sound of agreement that was neither anger nor contentment. She hated this dance of theirs, the way he had of keeping her on edge. It was like being a snake charmer, never knowing if her next move would lead to an attack. All she could do was smile peaceably and back out of the room, hoping she had acted accordingly and not said or done anything that would set him thinking. A thinking Roger was a dangerous creature. A predator in waiting. He imagined slights where there weren't any, every single thing she said or did viewed through eyes of distrust.

Only two more days to go. Come Monday, she would dress Melissa in her school uniform, wave her husband off to work, then pack up their things and make the short journey to the train station where a new life awaited them. Nancy pushed down the fiery excitement that bubbled in her gut, and picked up George from his crib, nestling him close to her breast, where he fed contentedly.

* * *

Saturday bled into Sunday, the dawn gently breaking through the bedroom curtains as she lay completely still, listening to Roger's heavy breathing. They had spent the evening before reading, his mood remarkably steady and benign. That was the problem – she couldn't ever predict his reactions. To anything. What was acceptable one day was completely against the rules the next. And so she took each minute, each hour and each day as they came, treating them with the utmost caution, which proved to be a draining experience. That, along with feeding the baby, took every bit of energy she had, but even allowing for that, she still had enough in reserve to let a glimmer of happiness peek through and for that happiness to give her self-confidence a much-needed boost.

She climbed out of bed, sliding her feet into her slippers, and padded along the landing towards the bathroom where she washed, dressed in yesterday's clothes, and combed her hair. This had become her routine of late, floating silently through the house, unseen and unheard.

The children continued to sleep while she sipped coffee in the kitchen, her gaze drawn to the garden beyond. She would miss her outdoor space when she left this place, having spent many years keeping it weed-free and spending money on planters to spruce up a large, concrete patio area. It occurred to her as she stared outside how rarely the children played out there, how Melissa preferred the confines of her room, how having friends around for tea or a picnic on the back lawn was something that other children did. When she did move from this place and got her own house, she would make sure it had a garden: one that was big enough for Melissa and George to play in, for them to run and be happy and carefree – everything that was currently denied to them. She sighed and closed her eyes. It was tempting to sit there, drinking coffee, daydreaming about what could be, but she had a house to clean, dishes to wash, breakfasts to prepare. Life had to go on as usual. Until tomorrow, that is. Tomorrow couldn't come soon enough.

As quietly as she could, Nancy began the ritual of laying out the dishes for everyone, making sure Roger's plate was dead centre, his cutlery spotless. She was caught up in her usual regime, her mind honed in on other things, when he appeared and spoke, his voice sending ripples of foreboding down her spine.

'Why are you up so early?'

She spun around, well versed by now at painting on a neutral expression, making sure her voice was even and calm. 'Oh, good morning. I just woke up so decided to get cracking with preparing breakfast.'

'Something on your mind that woke you?'

She wrinkled her brow and smiled, her heart thrashing wildly in her chest. 'No, not at all. Just thought I'd be better off making use of my spare time in the kitchen getting everything ready before the children wake up.'

Her throat was as dry as sand, her palms clammy. God, this was proving to be so tricky, the constant evasions as he fired questions her way. The attempts at appearing normal when in truth, her insides were leaping about, her innards knotting and unknotting like slithering eels.

A protracted silence as he stood, watching her. Assessing her. Then, 'I often wonder what goes on in that head of yours, what thoughts wander freely in your brain while I'm out at work every day.'

A hammer bashed at her skull, the pain of it travelling behind her eyes and making her woozy. Another statement designed to trap her. Under the pretence of checking that the pots and crockery were acceptable to her exacting eye, she gripped the table and stared long and hard at the prepared dishes and cutlery to stop herself from losing her balance and falling to the floor. Then she took a breath and turned to face him. 'Most of the time, I'm focused on George and the house. I really enjoy cleaning our home and caring for our children.'

'Most of the time?' he said lightly, a smile playing at the corner of his lips. 'But not all of the time?'

An explosion of fear in her abdomen. A schoolboy error. Stupid semantics. She had fallen into his trap. He had set that jagged, serrated snare, pulled it wide apart, and she had walked right into it, its teeth snapping shut, keeping her in place.

'All of the time, darling. I sometimes put half an hour aside to read a book if George is sleeping, is what I meant.'

He didn't reply, his eyes narrowed, his pupils drilling into her until she felt the need to turn away, pretending to busy herself with locating coffee and teabags and filling the kettle. She felt the burn and intensity of his gaze. He was angling for an argument, longing for an obvious transgression to present itself, and if it didn't, then he would do his damnedest to find one. The atmosphere in the kitchen was heavy, his presence an overbearing force. Whatever she did or said would be twisted and misconstrued to suit the narrative that was currently raging in his head. It was better to remain silent and only speak when spoken to. To keep her answers brief and non-committal.

'How lovely, don't you think? That you have time to read while your husband is at work bringing in the money to pay for this place?'

She nodded and cleared her throat. 'Every day, I think how lucky I am. You're a wonderful husband. Generous and hard-working. An intelligent man.'

'But not kind or thoughtful, eh? Not sensitive or caring or compassionate?'

She swallowed hard and pushed a strand of hair out of her eyes with the back of her hand, trying to obscure the tremble in her fingers. This situation was escalating. She knew the signs, recognised them before they presented themselves in all their sickening glory. She needed to defuse the tension, do something unexpected to catch him off-guard.

'Here you go.' She handed him a cup of speciality coffee, the one that she knew he favoured. 'I also got this for you yesterday as I know how much you liked them last time I went to the bakery.'

The croissant was balanced on a small china plate, its top lightly dusted with icing sugar. On the side sat a small, silver dessert fork, precariously balanced across the rim.

Her heart thudded against her ribcage. She smiled and leaned forwards to place a kiss on his mouth. 'Always kind and thoughtful and everything I could ever want in a husband. I'll put some bacon on and scramble some eggs for you.'

A silent recital of a prayer remembered from childhood filled her head as she waited for his response. Had she overreached herself? Been too dramatic and syrupy? It certainly felt that way but panic had forced her into a dead-end. She only hoped she had done enough to stave off what usually came next.

His face remained impassive. Unreadable. Without saying another word, Roger took the plate and the cup of coffee from her and left the room, his quiet movements and lack of a reply sending an icy chill over her skin. She was going to have to be careful here, make sure every movement she made, every syllable that passed her lips was meticulously thought out and carefully constructed. No room for error. Just well-rehearsed routines and words that would stop his suspicions from being awakened.

One more day. That was all she had to get through. Only twenty-four hours until she could leave this disturbing atmosphere behind her.

Keeping her breathing in check, Nancy cracked two eggs over a bowl and opened a packet of bacon, the sliminess of the rashers making her gag. She suppressed the reflex and took two long, convulsive breaths before preparing her husband's breakfast for the penultimate time. That thought made her smile. No more of this sickening pretence. By the time Roger reached the hospital tomorrow morning, she would be almost packed. By the time he saw his final patient of the day, she would be on the train to London, her daughter safely ensconced in her seat while George nuzzled into the warmth of Nancy's chest. That thought made her smile. Soon it would be over and the rest of her life could begin. She poured the eggs into a pan, took a wooden spoon from the drawer, and began to stir. She and her children were almost free.

## 18

## MELISSA

At the edge of my vision, I see him falter, his eyes locked on Gabriel, who has now begun to wail.

'Sort it out. Make it stop. That squawking. Make it fucking well stop!'

His body is slightly bent, his feet moving about on the tiled floor, the heels of his shoes grinding up small specks of dust. The gun in his hand, however, remains steady.

'He's ill. I need to feed and change him then call a doctor.'

'No!' His voice rises in volume then returns to normal, almost a whisper. 'No doctor.'

I think quickly, deciding to tell him I'm leaving, taking all my things and getting out of here. The further away we are from that weapon, the safer I will feel.

'Right, well, I just need to take my belongings and we'll leave. You can have this cottage. You clearly need it more than I do.'

He glares at me, then shakes his head, his eyes darkening again. 'No. I've changed my mind. It's too late now. You've seen my face. You'll go to the police. Just shut the kid up and then sit over there on the floor.'

I snort at him. 'On the floor? I'm sixty years old, not sixteen. I definitely won't be sitting on the floor.' I'm surprised at the strength in my voice. My heart is being squeezed by an iron fist but I'm not about to kowtow to this man. I've met his type before, been beaten down by them. Watched the havoc they wreak with their ruthless, bullying behaviour. Memories of my own father nudge their way into my brain: how he behaved, ruining the lives of those around him. I won't give in to anybody who thinks they can tell me what to do. Not again. Those days are behind me. I am not my mother.

He watches me for a few seconds, then relents, waving the gun towards the old sofa.

'Right, on there then. Sit down over there. Do whatever it takes to stop that kid crying. The noise is setting my teeth on edge.'

I pick up Gabriel, lifting him out of his buggy, and place him over my shoulder. 'A baby's cry is designed to set your nerves jangling. It's a way of making sure their needs are met. I have to go and get his bottle from the kitchen, so if you don't mind?'

He thinks for about it for a second or two, then nods, following a few steps behind me, the gun aimed at my spine. I want to tell him to stop being so ridiculous, that I'm not about to come back in brandishing a knife when I've got a baby in my arms, but opt for silence and dark, vengeful thoughts instead. A gun is a powerful tool and controls all aspects of thought and movement when one is pointed at your back.

'I need to make him a bottle. I don't have any prepared.'

He doesn't reply but lets out a low grumble which I assume is his way of expressing agreement.

It doesn't get any easier, this whole process. If anything, it becomes more and more gruelling, holding Gabriel still as he yells and writhes about, while making up the bottle one-handed.

Powder spills on the kitchen counter. Gabriel's screams grow louder. Sweat coats my back and neck. And all the while, a weapon is being held to my back.

'Make it shut up! Make that kid fucking well stop!'

I spin around, a sudden rage taking over any fear I have of that gun. Fury at his lack of patience and comprehension of what I'm trying to do under the most difficult of circumstances fuels my anger and frustration. My emotions spill out, my voice a near shriek. 'What do you think I'm trying to do, for God's sake! He's ill. This baby is very ill. I'm trying to do this with one free hand and all the while, I've got a man behind me pointing a gun at my back! Now why don't you bloody well back off and let me get on with it, eh?'

I expect reciprocal rage, maybe even him pulling that trigger and my life slowly ebbing away as I slump to the floor. What I don't expect is for him to soften and nod, running his fingers through his hair wearily, as if the weight of the world is perched on his shoulders.

'Right, yeah. Sorry. I get it.' He takes a few steps back and lowers the gun enough for me to relax a little. I feel relief wash over me. 'It's just that noise. I don't know how you put up with it. It's fucking unbearable.'

I turn again and get on with making the bottle. 'Like I said, he's a baby. It's what they do. It's what you once did.'

Another grunt from him. Then, 'Whatever. Not that anybody would have taken any notice of me when I was a baby.'

And there we have it. A man damaged by his upbringing. I almost laugh out loud. He's not the only one. If this was a competition, I feel sure I would win. Memories of that day once again bloom in my mind. I ignore them, push them away. It's all in the past. Here and now is what matters. Getting Gabriel to a safe place, away from this maniac. That's what matters.

I screw on the lid of the bottle and shake it, Gabriel nestled in the crook of my arm. I watch the man's expression, keeping a close eye on the angle of the gun, my gaze lowered under the pretence of monitoring my grandson. The barrel of it is there, at the edge of my vision. It's hanging loosely by his side, but his finger is still wrapped around the trigger.

'Sounds like you and I have more in common than you realise. I also had a disturbing childhood. Doesn't excuse you for waving that gun around, though. Everyone has something in their past.'

He doesn't respond, following me at a safe distance when I walk back into the living room and sit down. I can feel the heat from Gabriel. My stomach knots itself. He needs to see a doctor.

'I'm Melissa. What's your name?'

I steel myself, prepared for shouting and contempt for my question. He remains quiet, watching me closely, his expression dark and defiant. Guarded.

'I saw it advertised, travelled to Edinburgh and paid cash for this place,' I say quietly. 'How about you? I reckon the old man who owns this old cottage has made a killing out of us and is sitting at home right now, counting his money and smiling.'

'Call me Jason. And yeah, same here. Saw the place advertised and gave him the money up front.'

I nod and glance down at Gabriel. 'Slimy old bastard. He stitched us up good and proper, didn't he?'

He sighs and nods his head. Slowly, I turn to look at him. No sharp movements. Nothing that will startle or upset him. His dark hair is tousled and greasy looking, his stubble at least two days old.

'This is my grandson. We're having a break here. What's your story?' I nod my head at his gun and raise my eyebrows. 'Hunting season in the Highlands?'

He doesn't reply, turning instead to look out of the window, a shadow briefly flitting across his face.

After taking half of the bottle, Gabriel lets out another scream, his head turning from side to side, his little body squirming and twisting about. I place him over my shoulder and glance at the man whose name clearly isn't Jason.

'I need to stand up with him and walk about. It might help to stop him crying.'

I don't wait for him to give me permission and do it anyway. He's not going to shoot us. Gabriel's crying may be annoying him but I cannot see this man taking a gun to a baby and pulling the trigger. Whatever his reaction, I need to do something to calm my grandson. I can see that these fits of screaming are making this guy edgy and nervous.

'Let's just say I needed to get away and stay somewhere remote,' he says gruffly. 'We'll leave it at that, shall we?'

I nod and give him a half smile before returning my attention back to Gabriel, who lets out another scream and kicks his legs about.

'This poor baby really does need to see a doctor.'

Like somebody with a split personality, Jason changes, his temper flaring, his face reddening and nostrils widening as he unleashes his bile on me.

'I said no fucking doctors, all right? You'll stay here and make him better. Give him some medicine or something, but there's no way you're heading out of here so you can call the police!' His voice fills the room, bouncing off every surface and turning my skin to ice. 'You've seen my face, heard my voice. I may as well hand myself in right now. No fucking way are you leaving here, okay?'

I thought I had forged a connection with this man but I was patently wide of the mark. He is edgy and unpredictable. A volatile individual with a gun. If I thought things were difficult before, his untimely appearance has multiplied my problems a hundredfold.

My legs feel weak and rubbery as I pace the floor holding Gabriel close to me to try and soothe him. His sobs and screams grow louder. My energy wanes. I am hot and tired and all out of ideas. My throat feels sore. I hold back a flood of tears. This is all my fault. I should never have come here in the first place. I wanted isolation but didn't bank on anything this remote and definitely didn't bank on a psychopath turning up with a gun. I've put Gabriel in danger. My life may not count for much but he is a child, a baby for God's sake, and I've put him in the line of fire. We're pitted against an unstable man with a deadly weapon. It doesn't get much worse than this. I dream of leaving here, driving back to my hometown, to my little apartment, locking us both in, closing all the blinds and curtains and ignoring the rest of the world.

'I'm going to change him and give him some more medicine. Just so you know.' My voice is remarkably steady, belying my inner terror and fury.

More incoherent mumbling from him.

'His things are in the bedroom. I need to go in there to get them.' It's hard to keep my emotions in check, to contain them and not tell him exactly what I think of his bullying tactics and disgusting behaviour. A baby. He held a gun to a tiny baby. If I could snatch that weapon out of his hands, put it to his temple and pull the trigger, I would gladly do it.

'I'll come with you.'

He stands and follows me into the bedroom, his gaze roaming over the mattress on the floor and the piles of clothes everywhere.

Gabriel's crying doesn't stop when I lay him down on the

unmade bed. If anything, it heightens, his body stiffening, his small fists clenching together. I scramble around for a clean nappy, a dry vest, and some fresh clothes. My fingers are stiff and unyielding when I attempt to take off his outfit. He is damp, each layer of clothing sticking to his small, hot body. I can feel Jason's presence behind me, his impatience and growing fury a tangible entity in the room. I manage to remove Gabriel's undergarments and put a clean nappy on him, and am just in the process of putting him in a different set of clothes when his colour changes from pale pink to a deep shade of crimson. His head tips back and his torse becomes as rigid as stone. I watch, horrified, as my grandson's eyes roll back in his head and foam gathers at each corner of his tiny little mouth. I begin to cry, my sobs mingling and merging with Gabriel's screams. I pick him up and spin around to glare at the gun-wielding man behind me.

'I need a fucking doctor and I need one now! If you don't let me call one, this child is going to die and it will be your fault. You might be able to cope with having a dead baby on your conscience but I certainly can't. Now put that stupid bloody gun away and call an ambulance because if you don't, I swear to God, I will rip that weapon out of your hands and blow your fucking brains out!'

# 19

## 1970

They ate their breakfast in near silence, George suckling at Nancy's breast as she sipped her coffee. Melissa picked at her food, taking just two bites of her toast before asking to be excused.

'Of course, darling.'

The words were barely out of her mouth before Roger spoke, his voice conveying just the right amount of simmering fury to make Melissa think again, lowering herself back into her seat without making a sound.

'Sit back down and finish eating.'

Nancy felt a tremor take hold in her hand. She flexed her fist to quell it, the vibrating sensation threatening to travel up her arm and take over the whole top half of her body.

'Looks like a bright day outside. We may even get to spend some time out in the garden if it lasts.' She spoke lightly, hoping Roger hadn't detected the slight warble in her tone, the way she swallowed nervously always a dead giveaway to her real emotions, the ones she was continually forced to squash down, out of sight.

He carried on eating, giving no response. Melissa nibbled at her toast, glancing briefly at Nancy before lowering her eyes and focusing on her plate. She knew the drill. Such a good girl. Always compliant and able to sense the growing levels of animosity in the house, and act accordingly.

Nancy waited until Roger had finished eating, then stood and took his plate, George cradled in her other arm.

'More coffee, darling?'

A shake of his head. Her heart sped up. Something was awry. She wouldn't ask. She would continue as if everything was normal in their fractured little world. She would ignore the cracks and splinters, doing what she could to heal them, to stop the gaps from widening and blowing everything apart.

'I'm going to put George in his crib, and then I'll come back down and clear the pots and wash the dishes.'

Melissa finished her toast and looked to her father for permission to leave the table. He nodded and she quietly slipped from her chair, pushing it under the table with small fingers. Before he could protest about Melissa's lack of manners or the fact she hadn't cleared away her breakfast pots, Nancy picked up her daughter's empty plate and carried it to the sink, placing it in the bowl as soundlessly as she could. One rogue clatter, one sharp scrape could be the tipping point that drove him into one of his rages.

Only when their daughter was upstairs in her room did Roger finally break his self-imposed silence, his words like having sharpened pieces of ice driven into her skin.

'So, what's the secret you're keeping from me, then? Because I do know that you have one.'

Her throat closed. She blinked and forced a smile, praying he didn't spot her nervous disposition, her thumping heart or the tic under her eye. She blinked and ran her fingers through her hair.

He always had the ability to reduce her to a gibbering wreck. It was a game he liked to play; a power game that made him feel superior. She wouldn't allow it this time. Not when she was so close to escaping his clutches. Not when she was so very close to leaving this house and his violence behind. Freedom beckoned and she would not let herself be swayed by his words or threats.

'I'm not sure what you mean, Roger?' She crinkled her brow and feigned confusion, shaking her head while rocking George, who had begun to cry. 'I don't know anything about a secret?'

Seconds passed, each one driving terror into her heart. She felt the weight of her husband's gaze; the intensity of it causing her face to heat up. Her skin crawled with dread as she watched him, his dark eyes locked onto hers.

'Go and sort George out, then once you've done that, this kitchen needs cleaning.'

He stood, then turned and walked away. Nancy felt herself shrink, hot, bitter breath expelling itself from her lungs in one swift motion. She waited a second or two to right herself, praying for her chest to stop convulsing, then took her son upstairs and placed him in his crib where he lay quietly, his earlier cries now simmering down. That's who they were, she and her children – the quiet people. The frightened ones.

Nancy padded downstairs into the kitchen, ready to continue with her act of innocence, but was caught by the slap before she took the final step down. He was standing at the bottom, waiting. Her legs buckled. She gripped onto the newel post and on instinct, brought her hand up to her cheek where he had struck her.

'That's for lying.' Roger's gravelly voice reverberated in her ears. 'Honestly, Nancy, I wish you would stop with this act, making me resort to doing things I don't want to do.'

Her head vibrated; her flesh stung. She fought back the tears.

All her energy had to be reserved for getting out of this house. For getting away from her husband.

Words crept around her brain, things she could say but didn't dare. They were at that point now: the point when anything and everything she said would be misconstrued and twisted. Saying nothing was her only weapon, the only way she had of protecting herself. Physically, she was no match for him. All she had was her thinking skills, her logic and intelligence, and they were screaming at her to remain silent.

She shook her head and tried to stand up straight. The next hit was aimed at her torso, his fist connecting with her ribcage as she folded over, her body bent double from the pressure of the blow. It hurt like hell but she had endured worse. He knew exactly where to strike, how hard to deliver the punches so his message got across but nothing was broken. It wouldn't do for her to be admitted to hospital and for his colleagues to discover his wife's injuries and start questioning his honour and integrity. That wouldn't do at all.

Nancy gasped, her hand clutched to her abdomen, her head lowered to her knees.

'Now start acting like a proper wife and clean that kitchen. I'll have more coffee once you're finished.'

She watched his feet move off into the living room then gradually pulled herself vertical, her hand gripping the banister rail. Her stomach throbbed and her skin stung but she refused to give in. It didn't matter if she cried or apologised or acted stoically; Roger's response would always be the same – to tell her to stop acting as if the world was coming to an end and to drop the amateur dramatics charade. Then he would ask for his footstool and pick up a book, his mind already focused on something else.

She shuffled into the kitchen. Clearing the breakfast table would give her some thinking time. He couldn't know about her plan. She thought of Melissa and how Roger could possibly have manipulated the child, tricked her into telling him. Later, when he was resting in the chair or sitting in his study with the door closed, she would speak with her daughter, tell her that even if she had accidentally told him, it wasn't a problem and that she wasn't in trouble. Nancy simply needed to know how much of the plan he knew. She needed to be one step ahead of him.

A serrated blade swept up and down her spine; her back was to the door while she washed pots and wiped down surfaces. He could steal in at any point and catch her unexpectedly, the attack taking her legs from under her. No time to prepare and brace herself. Nancy briefly shut her eyes and let out a shaky breath. The sooner she finished, the better. It was safer that way. Safer if she was able to sneak upstairs and whisper to Melissa, ask her if Daddy had spoken to her at all about Mummy's telephone call.

Nancy rubbed at her ribs where the blow landed, applying pressure to alleviate the pain, then wiped her hands on the tea towel, stopping to make sure everything was as perfect as it could be. No half measures when Roger was on the prowl. He had a keen eye for detail and an even keener one for mistakes. The countertops gleamed. The pots were in the cupboard, all lined up in perfect symmetry. The place was spotless. Just to be sure, Nancy tugged at the blinds to ensure they were clean and straight. If there was anything amiss, then he would need a magnifying glass to find it.

The stairs creaked as she climbed them, her legs jelly-like, pain weakening her, hindering her ability to walk properly. She needed to speak to her daughter. Asking Melissa to accompany her for a morning walk with George in his pram would be too obvious. Roger would see through such a trick. A walk yesterday and another one today would be too noticeable. Too contrived. She would check to see if he was ensconced in his study and then whisper her questions into Melissa's ear. She stopped and rubbed at her eyes. This level of subterfuge was exhausting. Her flesh was sore, her ribs bruised and aching. The skin on her face was on fire, flames searing across her cheekbone. She wondered how long her body could hold out before something ruptured. Perhaps her mind would go first, the damage from his fists swelling and ballooning inside her, the remaining strands of each blow reaching deep into her brain and blotting every remaining ounce of lucidity that she had.

'One more day.' She mouthed those words to herself as she climbed the stairs. 'Just one more day.'

George was wide awake, his eyes following the shadows above him. Outside, leaves rustled, the old oak tree next to the window swaying gently in the breeze, its branches creaking, its large shape casting an eerie glow on the white ceiling. Nancy picked up George and kissed the top of his head, holding him close to her, enjoying the softness of his skin against hers. 'Such a good boy, lying here quietly. Such a beautiful, beautiful boy.'

A creak behind her set her nerve endings ablaze. She held her baby even tighter to her chest, the need to protect him so strong, it stole the breath out of her lungs. Despite being in pain, she clung onto her little boy with such ferocity, it made her arms ache.

'Is everything okay, Mummy?'

The sound of Melissa's voice forced an involuntary tear out of her eye. She mustn't cry. If Roger were to come in the room right now, the sight of her weeping would aggravate him. He hated weakness, which was rich coming from a man so weak and insecure, he felt the need to hit his wife on a regular basis in order to elevate his own status as an overbearing and powerful man. Master of his own house.

Nancy wiped at her wet face and spun around to look at her

daughter, her wonderful, darling little girl. 'Of course it is, sweetheart. Come here and give Mummy a hug.'

They held one another tightly, little George nestled in the crook of Nancy's arm, both too engrossed in one another's company to notice Roger standing in the doorway, hands balled into fists, his lip curled up in disdain.

## 20

## MELISSA

He waves the gun at me again, his fingers curled tightly around the handle. 'Told you already – no doctors!'

I glare at him, my hatred for this man growing exponentially with every passing second. Gabriel's torso is stiff and hot to the touch. 'This child may well die if you don't let me call somebody to help him!'

Walking backwards, the gun still pointed at us, he goes into the kitchen and comes back with a wet cloth. 'Here, put this on him. Cool him down then give him some medicine.'

I grab at the damp square of fabric, white-hot fury pulsing through me, and place it on Gabriel's forehead. 'He's having a convulsion.' I try to keep my voice even and calm, hoping it will make him see reason. If he cannot comprehend how ill Gabriel is, or worse still, doesn't care, then I truly am dealing with a psychopath and despite my attempts to reason with this man, perhaps both Gabriel and I are done for.

'Where's the medicine?'

'There's some in the kitchen, next to the sink.' I am barely able to keep the fury out of my voice. Who the hell does this guy think he is?

He comes back into the room carrying the bottle. I roll my eyes and bite at my lip in frustration. 'I need the syringe. It's in the box. Get me the bloody syringe and hurry up.'

I'm past being polite now. This man has descended into our lives and taken over my living space. Gabriel is all that matters to me. This man is a nobody. An irritant in our midst. He returns a few seconds later with the plastic syringe in the palm of his hand. The gun is hanging limply by his side. He sees me looking at it and raises it once more. I notice a tremble in his fingers. He sees me staring at that too and grimaces.

'Give him the medicine then! I can't think straight with all that fucking noise.' His voice is a bark but I detect fear in there. Not as brave or as fierce as I initially thought. Lacking in concern and unused to having little ones around for certain, but is he really a cold-blooded killer? A little longer in his company and I might come close to working him out, to learn enough about his character and be able to spot the chinks in his armour.

Gabriel's body is so stiff, I can barely hold the bottle to administer the medicine. His cry has turned into a high-pitched whistling sound that terrifies me.

'You're going to have to do it.' I push it towards him and nod. 'Just press the syringe into the neck of the bottle and tip it upside down. And hurry!'

He stops for a second then places the gun on the floor behind him. His eyes are filled with mistrust when he turns around to look at me. I watch his actions, willing him to move faster as he fills it up in slow motion and passes it over to me. I lay Gabriel in the crook of my left arm and try to pass the syringe between his lips. His mouth is firmly closed and as I attempt to part it, the whistling noise turns to a deep moaning that prickles my flesh.

Sheer terror pulses through me. I pull his mouth further apart and inject as much of the liquid as I can between his gums, then sit him up, his chin resting between my thumb and forefinger, my other hand rubbing his back to make sure he doesn't choke.

An age passes before he lets out a breath. His chest rattles with the effort. He wheezes and coughs, the screech of his inhalations painful to hear. But he's breathing. I let out a loud staccato sigh. Gabriel's cries and moans gradually lower to a whimper and the redness of his skins abates, his usual colour returning. He is still warm but no longer feverish and stiff, his torso becoming limp and pliable again. I silently give whichever deity heard my hushed prayer a huge thank you.

Then I turn to Jason and hold the damp cloth out to him. 'I need more water on this. As cold as you can.'

Without waiting, he takes it and goes into the kitchen. The gun is still laid on the floor. I eye it, wondering what sort of reaction it would provoke if I picked it up and held it to his head when he came marching back in.

I'm still imagining his expression if I were to press the barrel into the soft flesh of his temple when he appears and passes me the wet scrunched up square of fabric. I've missed my opportunity. Not that I could have done it while holding and nursing my grandson, but the fact that he is becoming lackadaisical and leaving it lying around for me to take gives me a tiny scrap of hope. I have no knowledge of firearms of any kind and have never even held a gun before, but the feelings of self-preservation I have for myself and Gabriel are strong. Common sense would guide me. I am sure of it. Besides, this man isn't the monster he wants me to think he is. A monster would have killed us both by now. A monster wouldn't help me with medicine and cold flannels. I look at his face and what I see is a scared man. Possibly a man on the run from somebody or something. We are more alike than he will ever know. He is, however, unpredictable and filled with fear and rage. I still need to be careful. One downward turn of his mood. One flash of anger stoked by raw fear and anything could happen. I know how that works. I've seen it in action first-hand. I'm practically an expert at handling men who lose their tempers. Men who act first and think later.

I remove the cloth from Gabriel's forehead and put him over my shoulder, keeping him there for the next ten or so minutes, waiting until the fever begins to recede. 'I need to get him dressed. He's cooling down now.'

A nod and an indecipherable murmur.

I quickly get Gabriel changed and place him against my chest. His body grows heavy and he is asleep in a matter of seconds. Weariness bites at me. My bones and limbs are aching. The earlier walk, the shock of being confronted with this man, and then my grandchild's illness – they have collectively drained me of every bit of energy I had.

My knees click and groan when I bend over to lay Gabriel down on the mattress. The urge to lie next to him is strong, and even though I don't believe this Jason person is as dangerous as he would have me believe, I'm not altogether comfortable with sleeping while he watches over me. I'll battle the tiredness. The idea of that gun being close to us is enough to fight off any level of exhaustion.

'See. We didn't need a doctor after all. He's shut up now.' His gravelly voice cuts into my thoughts, the sound of it irritating me to the point of wanting to stand up and slap him hard across the face.

I stop looking at Gabriel and stare at him, struggling to keep the annoyance out of my voice. 'So, you never did tell me what your story is. Care to elaborate? Since you're not prepared to let me leave and we're stuck here together, I think the least you can do is introduce yourself.' I spit out the words, my tone feisty and sibilant.

He juts out his bottom lip and shakes his head. 'No story. And anyway, what about you? Why you out here on your own with a baby? Not exactly family friendly this place, is it?'

My turn to shake my head. 'I've already told you – I'm having a little holiday. You're clearly not. How many people get so riled, they feel the need to pull a gun on a tiny baby?'

A weighty silence sits between us. He turns away from me. I sit patiently, refusing to fill the seemingly endless void with inane chatter. Out here in a small cottage in the wilds of Scotland, time is something I have plenty of.

Then after what feels like an age, he replies. 'You don't need to know anything about me. I carry the gun for protection. I didn't know who you were and you entered this place when I thought it was going to be empty. You shook me up and I needed to defend myself.'

I purse my mouth to suppress the wave of laughter I feel rising up my throat. 'Defend yourself from a middle-aged woman and a baby?' I let out a caustic snort of derision. 'I don't know anything about you or your background but I do know that you're a proficient liar.'

'And you're not?' He sneers at me before lowering his gaze to the floor. 'You really expect me to believe you've come here for a break?' He lifts his head and looks around at the peeling wallpaper, the ancient furniture, and the many dated accessories. Even the threadbare rugs warrant a disdainful glance. 'Not exactly Disneyland, is it?'

I try to keep my expression neutral. Flames lick at my face, heating up my flesh. He doesn't know anything about me or why I'm here. At least I hope he doesn't. He hasn't shown any signs of recognition and he hasn't asked any questions about Gabriel. I'm guessing he already has enough happening in his own life and hasn't had the time nor the inclination to pick up on any news articles concerning a missing baby. We each have our own reasons for being in this place, and it seems we also both have something to hide. Not so different after all.

Another elongated silence. Then I speak, hoping I can reason with him. Hoping he will see sense in what I am about to say.

'Look, it seems ridiculous us both being here. If you let me and my grandson go, I can absolutely swear, nobody will get to hear about you. It's not as if I have anything to tell. I don't know you or anything about you. Once I leave this place, as far as I'm concerned, you don't exist.'

His reply is crisp and concise, each syllable enunciated with all the clarity of a whip cracking against stone.

'You both stay. I trust nobody and I definitely don't trust you.'

I am barely able to keep the exasperation out of my voice. Trying to reason with this man is like continually banging my head against a brick wall.

'And then what? Are we all going to stay here until we rot away? Our bodies diseased and emaciated because you refused to see the logic in my request?'

There is no getting through to him, this coarse-mannered and agitated stranger with his wildly oscillating moods and a stubborn streak so tough, it's almost impossible to break through it. But he isn't superhuman. He is just an ordinary man. At some point, he will need to sleep and when he does, I will make my move. I will gather up our belongings and leave this place far behind, driving as fast as I can while trying to forget he ever existed. I have enough money to rent somewhere else. Nothing is insurmountable. I've come this far; a little bit extra on my journey isn't going to hurt. Suddenly returning home seems appealing. It's a damn sight better than being cooped up in here with him and that gun.

He doesn't reply. I decide to elaborate, make him see that me revealing his whereabouts would also implicate me in an incident that could see me arrested. I think of the elderly man I left lying in the road when I made my escape and feel an upsurge of alarm swell in my gut. I swallow and focus on the here and now, on Gabriel's welfare and why I did what I did. What I am about to say doesn't come easily. I'm taking a huge risk, but this isn't an everyday situation and I need to do something drastic to get us out of this ridiculous deadlock.

'Would it change your mind if you knew that I've also got a story that I'd rather not tell? A story that could see me get into big trouble with the police if I was stupid enough to speak to anybody about meeting you and the fact the pair of us were stuck together in this old cottage?'

A pulse taps at my neck while I wait for his reply. I wanted this cottage. I wanted this life. I took Gabriel to keep him safe, but he is ill, and events have taken a sinister turn. It's time for me to leave while I can. Before this man's mind breaks completely and he kills both of us.

# 21

## 1970

She felt her daughter's manner and mood change, the air in the room fluctuating, the tension that was present stretching itself tighter and tighter over her bruised flesh until every inch of her skin sizzled and burned. He was behind her. She could sense him. Smell him even, the pungent, metallic tang of his anger emanating from his flesh like toxic waste.

'Quite the little party you've got going on here. Is anybody invited or are some of us being deliberately excluded for reasons unknown?'

Nancy could hardly breathe, each intake of air a gargantuan effort, her chest convulsing with every inhalation. She felt Melissa stiffen, fear beating through her small, terrified body.

'We're just enjoying a little cuddle. I thought Melissa would like to give her baby brother a hug. She is such a wonderful older sister, always so gentle with him, aren't you, darling?'

The little girl nodded, her eyes dark with apprehension. She attempted a smile and reached up to stroke George's face, her finger tracing a line over his cheek. Such delicacy under duress, thought Nancy. A braver person than Nancy was, and definitely a braver soul than her father could ever hope to be. He was the biggest coward she had ever met, using his fists on vulnerable people.

'Be careful, for God's sake!' Roger's voice filled the room and Melissa snatched her hand away, her skin mottled with fear. 'He's only a baby. You don't want to be dragging your filthy fingers all over him. Stop pawing at his skin.' He grimaced and shoved his hands in his pockets, his eyes roving over his daughter's pristine clothes. 'Go and get washed. And make sure you scrub under those nails. I'll be checking them when you get back.'

The pulse in Nancy's neck became a deep thud. She tried to catch her daughter's eye, to attempt to reassure her, let her know that this wasn't her fault, but Roger was watching every move she made, his dark pupils assessing everything. He wanted Nancy to do something, to make a move or say something that would justify his outrageous behaviour, but instead she stood, George a silent, unmoving bundle in her arms. It was, she thought, as if her young son knew. Even at such a tender age, he seemed to be able to pick up on the nuances of his father's erratic and impulsive mood swings, keeping as quiet as he could when trouble was looming.

Melissa quietly slipped out of the room, her body like a soft breeze as she made her exit. Nancy thought of her daughter, how distressed she would be, alone in the bathroom, attempting to scrub away invisible specks of dirt and grime. Scared her father would find some upon his inspection. Which he undoubtedly would. Roger was like a ravenous hunter now, a heat-seeking missile searching for its target, unable to stop until he wreaked as much havoc as possible. Nancy hated him for this. She hated him for the way he snuck around the house, trying to catch them out, twisting their words and actions and turning them into something malicious. She hated every inch of him and wondered if his patients knew the real Roger Fitzgerald. If they could ever begin to imagine how cruel and unforgiving he was towards his family. How callous and heartless he could be when the mood took him – which it did more and more frequently of late. The days of him wining and dining her to make up for his dreadful outbursts were becoming less and less frequent, his dark moods bunched together like heavy storm clouds, their bellies engorged, their contents filthy and contaminated.

In the next room, she could hear Melissa turning on the taps and filling the sink. She visualised her little daughter desperately scrubbing at her fingernails, terror befuddling her thinking and scotching her ability to carry out the task properly. Anger at the injustice of it grew in Nancy's chest, expanding and ballooning until she could stand it no longer. She elbowed her way past her husband, her baby son still clutched in her arms, and strode towards the bathroom before he could stop her. She would pay for her indiscretion later, but she would deal with that when it happened. For now, she had to focus on her daughter, the child who was terrified of her own father. Terrified of even existing for fear it may rile him.

The door closed behind her. She turned the lock and placed a comforting hand on the child's shoulder, then leaned down and whispered in her ear, the rush of water as it hit the porcelain drowning out her words.

'Did you mention anything to Daddy about the telephone call yesterday? I won't be cross if you did. I just need to know.'

Melissa shook her head, her eyes glassy with unshed tears as she whispered her reply. 'No, Mummy. I haven't spoken to Daddy all weekend. He ignores me anyway.'

Flames combusted in Nancy's chest. She would not allow this to go on any longer, this curtailing of their lives. This torturous bullying campaign. She refused to let her husband take every last piece of her and stamp all over her daughter's emotions, treating her worse than dirt. Enough was enough. They would leave tonight, just as her sister had suggested. She would wait until Roger was sleeping, then she would take her children and go, leaving everything she owned behind. Possessions weren't important. They could be replaced. What was important was the life of her daughter and her baby son. *Her* life. That meant something as well. She wasn't an object, something to be continually insulted and beaten. The time had come for her to rise up against him, for her biblical David moment when she would slay the giant and make a bid for freedom.

Near elation held her fast, helping to heal her bruised body and fortifying her weakened mind. Her skin was battered, her emotions as flimsy as tissue paper but they would strengthen once she was out of this house. Already, she could see Roger beginning to chip away at Melissa's brittle confidence, finding fault with everything the poor child said or did, and she couldn't stand by and watch it happen. She wouldn't. The time had come to break this vicious circle and not have her daughter subjected to the endless bouts of abuse she herself had endured.

'There you go, my love. Let's use a bit more soap.'

She leaned down and whispered in Melissa's ear, 'Tonight, I'm going to wake you and we're going to go and stay with Aunt Hayley. Our secret, yes? Just you, me and George.'

The girl nodded, her eyes momentarily losing their dullness as she stared up at her mother, those few words injecting a fragment of hope into her expression.

'Right, young lady,' Nancy said volubly, making sure to keep an exaggerated timbre out of her voice. He would detect any theatrical performances and punish her accordingly. 'Let's dry your hands and show Daddy.'

With her free hand, she vigorously dried Melissa's small

fingers, then placed the towel on the radiator. She rested a reassuring palm on the girl's back and hoisted George further up onto her shoulder before unlocking the door.

'Hold them out.'

He was standing directly outside the bathroom, his frame an imposing sight. Roger wasn't a huge man, average in almost every way, but the sight of him was jarring, causing Melissa to stumble.

'Stand up straight and let me see.' He pulled her upright and inspected each finger, examining each crease on his daughter's palm, glaring at her with loathing, his annoyance palpable when there weren't any faults to be found. Roger didn't like losing, and in this instance, he had lost. Finding a spotless child angered him as much as if Melissa had walked out caked in dirt.

'Lovely and clean for Daddy,' Nancy chimed, flashing him a wide smile.

The play-acting was horribly tiresome. It was right that they were leaving the house earlier than planned. Keeping up the mock pleasantries was more than she could bear. It was fogging up her thoughts and clouding her judgement, and she needed a clear head to make sure her escape was as well executed as it could be. No room for error. Not when she was dealing with a man like Roger who prided himself on being scrupulous in almost every aspect of his life. She observed his expression, the way his eyes glazed over as he attempted to delve inside her head, desperate to fathom what she was thinking. He didn't know what her plan was but he was bright enough to know that she did have one. Unlike him, she found lying to others a trying and onerous task. Roger did it with aplomb, wearing one face for the outside world and another for his wife and children. It didn't come naturally to her. The intricate webs of deceit he wove were deeply embedded in him whereas Nancy's only stretched to hiding behind a mask of happiness in the presence of others. She didn't have any friends, only acquaintances that were wives of Roger's colleagues, and she saw them rarely, making small talk at dinner parties and grinning inanely when required. Those women neither knew nor cared about her life. All they saw was a reserved and unerringly polite, middle-class woman. Aside from her sister and children, she was alone in the world. Except for Jeanette Whitcome, that is. Jeanette, who offered her a way out of this mess. And Nancy had ignored that offer. But it did inspire her to make changes in her life, giving her a brief glimpse of hope.

Roger continued staring at his daughter's hands, turning them back and forth before letting go of them with a disgruntled bark. 'In your room. And be quiet. None of that stomping around and disturbing everyone else in the house.'

Nancy seethed, her blood bubbling as she watched her daughter slink away, her shoulders hung low, eyes downcast.

'We need a chat, you and I. I'll be downstairs when you're ready,' he said, his voice full of grit and menace.

A thousand serrated knives tore at her insides. She should have left this house last night. She should have left months ago. Jeanette's words bloomed in her mind. It was stupid not getting in touch with her. At least she now had other plans to leave. She just prayed that she hadn't left it too late as she placed George in his crib and took each stair as slowly as she could with all dread and trepidation of a prisoner being led to the gallows.

## 22

## MELISSA

'Go on, then. Spill. I'm all ears.'

He is standing in the corner of the room, his figure casting a long shadow across the floor. I swallow and think hard. Do I really want to do this? To tell him what I've done and make myself a target? For all I know, there may be a reward out for Gabriel's safe return. This man looks like he could do with some cash, a rapid injection of money in his pocket to keep him going through this dark period of his life.

'I asked you first. Honesty needs to work both ways.'

He throws his head back and laughs. 'I'm not your fucking husband. You sound like a marriage guidance counsellor!'

My face heats up. What am I going to tell him – the truth? The reality of my situation is something that can be easily misconstrued and twisted. I'm on the right side of the situation ethically but definitely on the wrong side of the law.

'I took my grandson without asking. His parents don't know where he is, but that's because they were mistreating him. He's safer here with me.' I am almost panting, my chest heaving with the effort of speaking. 'Or at least he was until you turned up all guns blazing. Right, your turn,' I say, feeling triumphant about being so honest. Will this man do the same and reveal why he is here? Something tells me not, but I wait to hear what he has to say.

'Kidnap?' he says quizzically, his eyes widening. He couldn't look more horrified if I had admitted to killing somebody with my bare hands.

'That's a rather brutal way of putting it,' I say, my voice laced with annoyance. 'I'd say I've saved him from a life of misery. If you knew his parents and had seen what I've seen, you would understand.' I nod and stare at him. Now it's my turn to widen my eyes. 'So?'

'So, what?' he replies, his voice a near whisper.

'So, what is your story, Jason who isn't Jason. You know about me and what I've done. Why are you here?'

He dances from foot to foot as if stepping on hot coals. The gun is still dangling from his hand. I try to not look at it. I try to pretend it doesn't exist. Easier that way.

'I took some money. A lot of money. From an elderly man.'

'You threatened him with the gun?'

He lowers his eyes and I freeze.

'You shot him?' I can hardly breathe. 'Is he dead?' I can't keep the horror out of my voice.

When he doesn't reply or look at me, I know that I am standing opposite a murderer. A killer. If he is capable of shooting an elderly man, he will have no qualms about turning that gun on Gabriel and me.

'I wasn't the one who shot him.' He raises his head and meets my gaze. '*He* did it.'

'Who? Who did it?' My voice is a near shriek. The time for word games is over. I need to know exactly who I am dealing with. 'Who did it?'

'Sonny. My partner. He shot him. He wasn't meant to but the old guy tried to stop us leaving after we'd emptied his safe.'

Tears mar my vision. My lungs shrink. I try to focus on my breathing while my heart thuds and pounds beneath my sternum. 'Is he dead, this old man?' I think of the elderly gentleman who hit my car. The one I ran down.

*It was an accident!*

This situation is a nightmare. A hideous nightmare that has no end. Coming here was supposed to be a happy time, a positive experience that would benefit my grandson, and it has turned into something ghastly and warped. I would never in a million years have guessed that any of this could ever happen. And yet my own knowledge of how people behave and the cruelties and atrocities of which they are capable should have prepared me. I know from personal experience how mean and unpredictable people can be. I shouldn't be shocked, and yet I am.

My own father, the man who was supposed to love and protect me, he was the one who set me on this path. The path of mistrust and fear and loathing. And my God, I loathed him. I loathed him as much as I feared him.

Jason nods, then shakes his head. 'Yes. No. I don't know!' His feet shuffle about. His eyes cloud over, a darkness there that alarms me. 'He was bleeding a lot from his chest when we left the place. We couldn't hang around to find out.'

'You left the old man to die on his own?'

*So did you.*

A pain shoots across my head. I press my palms into my eyes to blot out all thoughts of the car accident. I didn't shoot anybody. It was a small bump on the bonnet of my car as he hit it. He will have been bruised, nothing more. Tears threaten to spill. I swallow and fight them back. I want to roar to the heavens above at the injustice of this situation.

'I wasn't the one who shot him, okay?' His voice breaks. 'I didn't even know Sonny had a gun with him. If I'd known...'

'Oh please!' I can no longer contain my anger at his levels of hypocrisy. 'Save your breath trying to explain to me how saintly you are. You're apparently shocked and upset at your friend shooting a defenceless old man, and yet here you are, brandishing a gun at a baby!'

Silence, greater and far louder than any shouting could ever be. It crashes in my head, thundering in my ears.

'So where is this friend of yours, then?' Anger and curiosity fight for space in my mind, pushing any fear I feel, out of the way.

'I left him at the services on the border. We stopped for a break and while he was using the toilet, I drove off.'

I go through the scenario in my head, working out all possible endings to his sad little tale. 'He knew where you were headed?'

Jason nods. 'Yeah. We were on our way here to hide out for a bit.'

'So when he realises you've left him behind and taken his gun, he's going to try and find you?'

'With what? He's got no vehicle, has he?' He shrugs and gives me a half smile. 'He hasn't got any money either. I've got it.'

'But he has a phone? And as you've also got the cash, he has an even greater reason to find you.'

'Possibly. Mine's turned off. Without any money or a car, he's fucked. All he can do is hitch a ride and who's going to bring him here? Not as if this is on the main route to anywhere, is it? We're not exactly overflowing with passing traffic.'

My throat is dry. Another man who has no misgivings about shooting frail, helpless old people is possibly on his way here to wreak revenge at being unceremoniously dumped by his partner in crime. If I demand again to leave this place, I'll be stopped. I need to get out of here but I'm going to have to find another way.

I'm not going to wait around for a revenge-fuelled showdown with two individuals who have no scruples whatsoever, but do have a gun.

I nod, hoping he doesn't see through my lies as I put on a show of agreement, all the while working out how I can escape this frightening situation. I pray I can pull it off without any further problems. Maybe this time, I can make it without suffering any life-changing consequences. Unlike that day all those years ago when my mother, my baby brother and I tried to make a bid for freedom and things went awry. This time, I'll get it right. I'll make sure of it. If there is one thing I have learned in this cruel and callous world, it's that we are given very few second chances and if they do come our way, we need to grasp onto them firmly and see them through to the bitter end.

# 23

## 1970

'So, what's going on with you then, Nancy? What exactly is rattling around that empty little head of yours?'

Her hands were clasped tightly on her lap, her skin white and waxy with the effort of keeping her fingers pressed together. She fought to hold herself upright, to shake off the waves of dizziness that roiled through her head, making it feel as if the walls were leaning inwards, the floor coming up to meet her. Every bone in her body vibrated; every sinew stretched to snapping point. A few hours. That was all she needed to focus on: a few hours in which to keep up this act; this exhausting, hideous act of appearing contented. Thoughts of putting a handful of pills in his drink floated around her brain. She dismissed that notion. It would take more than a few painkillers to fell Roger. Besides, if by chance he did fall ill afterwards, or died even, she would be held accountable. Then what would happen to her children as she was led away in handcuffs? No, the safest way was to be her usual self: to remain composed and not allow his mind games to perforate and poison her thoughts. She couldn't ruin things when she had come this far. She was so close now. So very, very close.

'I'm not sure what you mean? There isn't anything going on, Roger.' Her brow was creased in faux confusion. She shook her head and shrugged. 'I honestly don't know what to say?'

Her body was tensed and ready. Ready for the potential blows that were coming her way. She watched his face for signs of anger. His eyes were cold and calculating, evaluating her every move. He was doing his best to see inside her head, and failing. That would rile him, push his mood even further into a dark abyss. In the past, he had often been able to gauge what she was thinking, but not this time. This time, she had kept her secret buttoned down tight.

The sound of his fingers drumming on the walnut coffee table echoed through the room. Nancy stole a glance at his perfectly manicured nails, his slim fingers, and the precision with which he continually tapped out a rhythm that prickled her skin. It was designed to unnerve her. And it was working. This sinister, carefully premeditated performance of his was making her nerves jangle. He didn't know anything of her plans. It was impossible, and yet at some point, she had clearly let down her guard, said something out of turn or acted out of character, and like the suspicious individual that he was, her husband had spotted it, and now he was cornering her, waiting for an opportune moment to strike.

The pulse in her neck thumped. She swallowed, wondering what came next. Her mind was too tangled up to guess how he would react, fear obscuring all rational thought. Whatever he had planned, it wouldn't be pleasant. A smiling assassin, that's what her husband was. A cold, calculating man who thrived on doling out misery and pain to those closest to him. It was his favourite pastime, the enjoyment he derived from these moments reinforcing his belief that he was the victim in all of this and his subsequent actions would be wholly justified.

'Well,' he said, his tone and body language too difficult to gauge, 'I gave you a chance, Nancy. I've tried to be kind and help you along, but you've left me with no choice.'

Her body turned to stone. She sat rigid, waiting. He stood up, his body towering over her, his hands pushed deep down in his pockets. She glanced up at his face. His expression was unreadable. She watched as he turned and left the room. Only when she heard his study door slam shut did she dare to move, her hands covering her face to stem the flow of tears that ran down her cheeks. He didn't know. He couldn't. So what exactly was going on here? Had she slipped somehow – her attitude and conduct not up to her usual impeccable standards? Although a poor liar, she was proficient at smiling when he was in the room and being sombre and invisible if the situation demanded. She didn't believe she had given Roger any reason to think that anything was amiss. What had he picked up on? How did he know that something was going on? Dear God, she just wanted the day to be over with, for the hours to race by without any more drama so she could pack up and leave.

She wiped at her face and stood, determined to not be debilitated any longer by his facetious remarks and incessant probing. For so many years – in fact, most of her adult life – his ego and power trips had been a dominant force in her life, leaving her weak and helpless. But not any more. She could do it now, while he was occupied. She could take Melissa and George and her wad of money and just walk out of that door. It all sounded so easy in her head, so natural and seamless. And yet her limbs refused to co-operate, her brain aching with the idea of such a manoeuvre. What would be the worst that could happen? If she managed to get out of the door with her children, would Roger really be so bold and callous as to assault her in the street where people were mowing their lawns and washing their cars? The answer would be no; he most certainly would not want to lose face in front of the neighbours. Dragging her back inside while she yelled and kicked and screamed would embarrass Roger terribly and the one thing he did not approve of was being publicly humiliated. His ego wouldn't allow it. But he *would* follow her if she left. He would get in his car and track her movements, watching every step she took and keeping tabs on her whereabouts; he would wait, and bide his time until she was alone, and then he would make his move. All it would take was one isolated street, one shady pathway and she would be back in his clutches. Even booking a taxi was an impossible task. Roger was omnipresent, always lurking and listening out. Especially now he suspected something was going on. He was on red alert, pretending to be busy whilst closely monitoring every single move she made.

Above her, Melissa played silently in her room. Would it really be so difficult to sneak her and George out without Roger noticing? She suspected that the answer to that would be yes, but the longer she remained in this house, the slimmer her chances became of ever leaving. Her husband's suspicions were slowly tightening around her like a vice, crushing the very life out of her. Every passing second put her and her children in greater danger. Roger was currently sitting in his study, planning and scheming, his temper slowly building. His fists and feet at the ready, his mind angled towards violence. He would be planning retribution. And it would be ugly and vicious and horribly painful.

She couldn't breathe. Nancy's hand fluttered to her chest, clutching at her neck. The room swam around her. The floor was spongy beneath her feet. She sat down again, her fingers clinging to the arm of the chair. A few seconds. She just needed a few seconds to compose herself, to work out what to do next. How best to deal with this situation, this awful, hazardous situation in which she found herself. She was losing. Once again, he had come out on top and left her feeling anxious and deflated.

*No.*

She took a few deep breaths and stood up, the clouds in her head clearing, a spot of sunlight in the distance sharpening her thoughts. This was beyond ridiculous. She was a grown woman and it was about time she took charge of her life. She had rights. One of those rights was to not be beaten in her own home on a regular basis. And yet, the one time she did dare to be brave and call into the local police station, she was shooed away like an errant child.

'This is a domestic matter between you and your husband, madam. The police do not make a habit of intervening in people's marital affairs.'

A large, brutal-looking officer eyed her suspiciously from behind his desk before turning his attentions back to the documents laid out on the table top. And that was that. She knew then that she was truly alone. Any plans she made to leave would be undertaken on her own using what few resources and little ingenuity she had.

Still, she refused to give up on her idea. She was doing this for the children, for their safety. Roger's violence and mood swings were escalating on a weekly if not daily basis, his anger unspooling. Something had to be done. And quickly.

Nancy moved away from the chair towards the door. It was now or never. And never, in a house that was this cruel and pitiless, was a sentence she and her children could no longer endure.

## 24

## MELISSA

The light outside begins to fade. I can't stay here another day. Gabriel is still ill but marginally better than he was. I thank the Lord for small mercies. None of the incessant screaming or whining that makes Jason edgy. It's one less thing to worry about. Leaving the cottage under the cover of darkness would probably prove to be an easier task than leaving in broad daylight, my movements difficult to detect, concealed by a heavy opaque sky.

We have been here all afternoon, each of us suspicious of the other. I was allowed to feed Gabriel, and nibbled my way through my own measly sandwich with a gun pointed at my back. We can't go on like this. Something has got to give.

'I need your key.' He is standing over me as I lie back on the sofa and nestle Gabriel into my chest to calm him before taking him into the bedroom and settling him down for the night.

'My key? Why on earth do you need my key? I was here at the cottage before you. Why don't you give me your key instead?' I am beyond being polite. I no longer fear him. His accomplice was the one who fired the gun. He's nervous with it. Agitated and using it to keep me in my place. But at the end of the day, it's still a lethal weapon. I don't trust him or his temper. A nervous man with a weapon is likely to make mistakes, to misfire it, and I can't let that happen.

'Because I'm the one with the gun and I don't want you escaping in the middle of the fucking night, that's why!'

I sigh and dig into my pocket, handing it over and watching where he puts it, my eyes half closed as if I'm tired and disinterested. Part of me wants to resist, to see how far he would go if I refused. Does he have it in him to pull that trigger, or is he bluffing? But like the good girl that I am, I relent and now sit, trying to work out how to retrieve my key back from his shirt pocket while he sleeps.

'Put the baby to bed and then you go with him.'

He stares at the bedroom door. I can see him studying the mechanics of it. It opens inwards into the bedroom, not out into the living area. He can't imprison me in there by pushing something heavy up against it. There is no lock and the workings of it give me the advantage. His eyes flicker. He's trying to fathom how to keep me holed up in there during the night. I'm trying to work out how to sneak out while he sleeps. Because at some point, he will have to nod off. He looks exhausted. A man on the edge.

'I need to use the bathroom.' I cock my head to one side, unsure whether I look arrogant or obliging. Truth be told, I no longer care. I just want to be out of this place, to get as far away as I can from him and his friend who is out there somewhere. For all I know, he could arrive any minute with vengeance in mind.

'Okay, but don't be too long. And take the kid with you.'

'You really think I'm about to leave him with you?' I spit out the words, my lip curled into a snarl. I hope he can see how much I loathe him, how his arrival has ruined everything.

He doesn't reply. I head into the bathroom with Gabriel nestled safely in my arms. So intent was Jason on getting my cottage key from me, he has forgotten to confiscate my car keys which are tucked deep in my pocket. It slotted into place in my head as he spoke – my escape route. I place Gabriel on the floor and sit on the toilet. The bedroom window. It's big enough for me to climb out. I can flee during the night while he sleeps. I have the keys for my vehicle and that is all I need. My money is in the bedroom. I'll take that too and head away from this place, leaving this hideous man and his anger and that gun behind. I hope his friend arrives at some point and they end up killing each other.

I stand up and scoop up a sleepy-looking grandson, pressing my face against his. I kiss the top of his head and open the bathroom door, trying to squash down the surge of exhilaration that is coursing through me, making sure to keep it concealed behind a façade of fear.

'Am I allowed to take a glass of water to bed with me? And a few of Gabriel's bottles of milk in case he wakes?'

He thinks about it then nods. Already, I can see what little energy he has left, leaching out of him. I head into the kitchen, collect as many bottles as I can and wedge them under my arm, and then just to show him that I'm not bluffing, I fill up a glass of water and balance it in my hand.

I pass by where he is standing and see him monitoring my little collection of items, his eyes sweeping over me appraisingly. The bedroom door closes behind me and I let out a juddering sigh of relief. A sigh mingled with mild euphoria. It's almost at an end, our time at this cottage. No more being held hostage here by a gun-wielding man who is on the brink of losing it.

I change Gabriel and get a bag of our clothes together along with a change of nappies. I settle down on the mattress and feed him. He finishes in record time and then I remember about needing baby rice.

*Shit!*

I can't risk any screams of hunger from Gabriel. Not when things have calmed down. He doesn't make a sound when I lay him down on the mattress, more intent on playing with his feet than watching me. There is still a deep rumble in his chest but for now, he appears to be improving.

'You wait there, little man, while I go and get some more food for you.'

The door lets out a small creak when I push it ajar. I peek my head around. Nobody close by. No gun-toting, shadowy figures lurking around the corner. As quietly as I can, I shuffle through to the kitchen and collect the rice and cutlery.

I'm on my way back into the bedroom when the bang of a door opening and hitting plaster reverberates through the cottage. It's followed by a deep bellow of anger. I shut my eyes and swallow, my heart a heavy metronome in my chest, my pulse a gallop. He's found us. Sonny is here. Despite the many miles and lack of transport, he has found us. The solid thud of footsteps through the hallway sends me skittering back into the bedroom, dizzy with terror. I stand next to Gabriel and watch him, my ears attuned to every word, every creak of a floorboard and every rustle of clothing. I stand motionless, praying this man doesn't realise we're here, yet knowing he will have seen my car.

'You fucking bastard!'

I hear the muffled clatter of bodies as they hit the floor and then another string of expletives that explode into the air. The almighty boom of the gun being fired ricochets in my ears. And then silence.

It takes me a few seconds to gather my thoughts. I spring into action, grabbing a bag and throwing bottles, baby food, clothes and money into it before lifting up Gabriel and trying to prise open the window. It's jammed closed. I lay him down on the mattress and try again, every movement echoing in my head. I have no idea who fired that gun and am not waiting around to find out.

My breathing is low and irregular as I try once more to open the window. It gives a little, years of paint gradually flaking away to allow a gap between the window and the wooden frame. I gouge at it with my nail, running my fingers along the edges to try and free it up, but it's useless. *My keys*. Flummoxed, and hot and bothered, I find a sharp edge and scrape away the thick layers of paint, then give the window another heave, pressing my shoulder into the glass. It opens with a thunk, the noise loud enough to draw attention to us.

I suck in my breath. Outside the bedroom, I can hear somebody moving about. I grab the bag stuffed with our meagre belongings and pick up Gabriel. He doesn't cry, staring at me instead with wide, bewildered eyes. On impulse, I kick the mattress over to the door hoping to hinder anybody who tries to get in. It won't stop them but it might slow them down. If Jason is out there, then I don't think he will shoot us, but if it's the other guy who has arrived full of hell, then I refuse to consider what he is capable of. He has murdered one, maybe even two people. Killing doesn't faze him. He will do it again.

It's a struggle to hoist myself, Gabriel and the bag out of the long window but I manage it without falling over. My feet twist beneath me as I stagger towards my vehicle.

Behind me, I hear a growl of anger, somebody hollering at me to stop. I ignore it. Nothing and nobody is going to make me turn around and face whoever is inside that cottage. We're out and we are never going back in.

My hands are cold, my face hot. I press the button to open the car and strap Gabriel into his seat, my dexterity surprisingly steady. It's amazing how controlled I can be when danger is close by. When our lives depend on it.

I throw the bag into the back and am about to climb in the driver's seat when he comes running at me, his face contorted with rage. It isn't Jason.

*Shit.*

I take a deep breath and open the door, pushing the keys into the ignition in a clumsy effort to start the car. After a nerve-wracking splutter, it kicks into life. I think of Jason or whoever he really is, laid out on the floor, blood pooling around him, and then I see this man, this Sonny creature. with his long, unkempt hair and straggly beard, his stained, ragged clothes and wild eyes, and I push my foot down hard on the accelerator, but already he is pulling at the door handle. It swings open and he runs along beside me, the gun held tightly in his right hand. I rev the engine and increase my speed, but somehow he manages to clamber onto the footplate and is travelling along with me, one hand clinging onto the roof-rack, one hand still holding the gun. I need to do something. I have to throw him off but I can't risk crashing the car, not with my grandson in the back. My heart thrums. Sweat coats my neck. Our lives are hanging in the balance. Why can't this man just let us go? We mean nothing to him.

'I killed the old man who owned that cottage and I don't mind fucking well killing you!'

He roars at me, fighting to be heard above the howling wind and throb of the engine. A bomb goes off in my head at hearing his words. The old guy in Edinburgh. He's dead. They robbed his house and killed him. I think about what could have happened if I'd visited him later than I did. I would have stumbled across a crime scene. The police would have been present. My plans to take Gabriel would have been thwarted.

*And we wouldn't be here now.*

A pain lodges behind my eyes. Now I understand how and why Jason came to the cottage. They saw the details of the cottage in the old man's house and took a set of keys, intending to use it as a bolthole, somewhere to lie low until the heat died down. But then an argument broke out between the two of them. The old guy wasn't supposed to die. A robbery became a murder. I fight back tears. The police will be on their way here right now. An even greater reason to leave.

I flex my arm and try to elbow him away but he remains in the same position. I turn the steering wheel from side to side in a bid to throw him off but still he clings on. In desperation, I swing the car sharply to the right and brake. It works. He is thrown off the footplate and onto the ground. I press my foot to the floor, leaving a crumpled silhouette behind me. He isn't hurt. In the rear-view mirror, I watch him clamber up and stand motionless, watching as I speed away. Then, arms pumping furiously, he runs after me. I drop a gear and rev the engine as hard as I can to leave him far behind, but still he chases.

And then I realise why. The glint catches my eye. It's on the floor in the well of the passenger side of the car. The gun. It fell out of his grip when I made a sharp turn and ground to a halt. He is in the distance and I have his gun.

A thousand possibilities fly through my head but the one that stubbornly refuses to move is the fact that if Jason is dead, this man can take his car and follow me. And if that happens, then both Gabriel and I are sitting ducks.

I push my foot flat to the floor and head out into the night.

# 25

## 1970

She crept upstairs, passing Roger's study door with as much stealth as she could muster. One rogue creak of a floorboard – that's all it would take to alert him to her presence. Being as quiet as the grave was key. Once she reached the top, she would gather her money and a few belongings for her and the children and she would hide them under her side of the bed. Then in the middle of the night while Roger slept, she would sweep up the children and she would leave this godforsaken house. He knew. Her husband knew. She didn't know how but he had an inkling of what she was about to do and the longer she left it, the more difficult it would be to make her escape. Procrastination was her enemy, as big and formidable a presence as Roger himself.

She stopped outside Melissa's room, trying to work out what to do next. The house was silent, her laboured breathing the only sound to be heard. Blood pounded in her ears. She felt sure Roger could hear her, was able to feel the vibrations of her thrashing heart through the floorboards. The tension in the house caught in her throat, the sensation of it spiking her blood pressure, pushing her body to its limits. She clung onto the doorframe for balance. She couldn't go on living like this, everything on a knife-edge. Her body couldn't take much more of this stress. She was leaving this dangerous, uncompassionate man. She should have left him years ago.

Relief replaced fear as she opened her drawer and checked on her wad of money. Still there. Unseen and untouched. At the back of her wardrobe was a bag. No large suitcases. Too cumbersome to take on a train with young ones. She mentally began to go through the things she would pack and was disturbed by a low shuffle behind her. She turned with a half-smile, expecting to see her daughter standing there and felt her features slacken and her body go limp when it was Roger, his glare steely, his limbs and spine rigid. Dread swirled in her bowel when he closed the bedroom door and walked towards her. She backed away, her hands grappling behind her for something solid to hold onto. She had to stay upright, to not look guilty or apprehensive. That was his intention – to catch her unawares and then go for her exposed underbelly. Roger thrived on her vulnerabilities. Lived for them. She was sure he gained more satisfaction from instilling fear in her than he did from helping patients to heal. That was because he was a monster. An unspeakable entity.

'Sit down, Nancy.' His voice was icy. Sharp and ominous.

She didn't move. Not because she wouldn't, but because she couldn't. Her body was made of stone, solid and unbending, her brain and reflexes frozen.

'I said sit down.' He didn't shout. His voice was now a near whisper. Laced with menace. It was worse than any level of shouting. Much worse, his sibilant tone freezing her flesh and speeding up her blood. Nancy swallowed and tried to stem the panic that crept up her throat. Hours. Just a few until all of this was behind her. If she could get through this next episode, if she could just persuade him that nothing was wrong, then she would be able to flee this prison and never have to endure another of these interrogations. The beatings were bad. Horrific. The lead up to them, his fricative tone, his dead-eyed stare, the rigidity of his body, all those bodily gestures, they were just as bad. They caused the internal damage to her body and mind. The damage that nobody could see.

She sat, her body shrieking at her to run, to bundle up her children and sprint like a gazelle from the man before her. The man she married and once loved. The man who tried to control every aspect of her life and regularly used her as his own personal punchbag.

'See?' he said as she lowered herself into the chair next to the dressing table. 'That wasn't so difficult, was it?'

He sat on the bed, his weight barely making a single crease on the bedsheets. Like an invisible presence. A demon.

'What is it, Roger? I was just about to—'

'Enough.' He held up his hand, his smooth, pale palm facing outwards towards her. 'Enough with these fucking stupid games. I know about you making a call. I know about you using the phone box. Why would you do that, Nancy? What call is so important and so fucking *secret* that you have to walk to the next road to make it? We have a telephone here in the house. Who were you calling? And before you deny it, David from number thirty-six saw you. He chatted to me while you were out, presuming our house phone was broken after seeing you. He offered to let us use his. I hoped you would tell me last night. I gave you every chance to speak to me about what has been going on and you didn't. You have chosen instead to be duplicitous and creep around the house as if I'm some kind of bloody idiot.'

Two pink spots rose in his cheeks. His eye twitched. Nancy wanted to laugh. So he *was* human. Not so infallible after all, but susceptible to emotions just as she was. And then she realised what this was about. She swallowed down the guffaw that was bubbling in her throat. The idea of it was comical. It amused and repulsed her in equal measure. He thought she was having an affair. Her purportedly intelligent husband was irritated, his ego dented and his insecurities exposed because he was convinced she had gone to a phone box at the end of the next street to make a call to another man and on top of that, *worse* than making the call, a neighbour had seen her. Roger had had to suffer the indignity of being confronted by a friend about his wife doing something he knew nothing about. Something furtive that involved another man. That must have stung. She could imagine his reaction, the anger he must have felt at having to cover up the fact that he didn't have an answer at the ready. It will have prickled beneath his skin like sharpened claws.

Hysteria built in her gut. She smiled, trying hard to keep her tone light and free of mockery and ridicule even though she wanted to point a finger in his face and laugh until she cried, telling him how stupid and irrational and pathetic he was. How wide of the mark he was. Not so intelligent after all.

And then she spoke, her voice a whisper, her timbre soft and accommodating as she replied to his question. 'The phone was ringing as I passed it, so I stopped to answer the call.'

She watched the two rouge marks fade from his cheeks, his usual pallor restored. 'Why? Why on earth would you do that?'

'I'm not sure really. It seemed like the right thing to do. I think maybe it was just instinct.'

'And who was it?' Once again, simply because it was part of who he was, suspicion was there in his voice and in his eyes, that dark stare of his that drilled deep into her soul.

Nancy gave a light laugh and sighed as if recalling a happy memory, retrieving it from a store of them in her head; a store that didn't exist. 'It was an old lady. She had got the wrong number and was a bit confused, so I spoke to her for a while to try and help her work out who it was she was actually trying to call.'

And all the while as she told the lie that she hoped he would believe, Nancy's heart thrummed and galloped around her chest. She leaned forwards to disguise her discomfort, hoping David from number thirty-six hadn't seen her dial her sister's number. Hoping he hadn't been there when she stepped into a silent phone box and picked up the receiver. Because Roger would check. At some point, he would find an excuse to visit David to investigate the veracity of her story.

He sat silently, saying nothing while Nancy prayed, hoping this was enough to throw him off her scent. Hoping he wouldn't take it upon himself to visit David on the pretence of borrowing a rake or some other gardening implement. Even Roger knew how contrived that would look. It would paint him as a sad and desperate man. Which is exactly what he was. Sad. Desperate. Insecure. Vicious.

'A bit of a strange occurrence. Why didn't you say anything about it when you arrived back home?'

She swallowed and had to stop herself from rolling her eyes at him. This was beyond the pale. Was there *anything* in her life she could call her own?

*Because I don't have to tell you everything, you wicked, controlling, old bastard. I wish you would drop down dead.*

'I'm not sure really. You were a bit busy and I didn't want to disturb you. I also got caught up with feeding George and chatting to Melissa. I guess it just slipped my mind. Sorry, my darling.'

She widened her eyes in fake innocence and managed a watery smile. Nothing too obvious. Just a low-key expression, a look she had mastered over the years. Nancy wondered how many more beatings she would have had to endure had she not managed to capture the essence of purity and guiltlessness with her facial expressions and body language.

He said nothing in return, watching her closely for a couple of seconds, his features pale and composed. And then he spoke, his words sending a wave of pain pinballing up and down her spine. 'So if I go and check with our daughter, she will obviously tell me the same story?'

Nancy's heart was at bursting point. Melissa. Their helpless, young daughter was going to be cornered by this man. He would show her no mercy, scaring and tricking her with his carefully crafted questions. The poor child wouldn't have any inkling of what was going on, what she was supposed to say, her need to protect her mother an overriding force. With no prompting she would speak honestly and then Nancy's dreams of escape would be over. How did a man like Roger ever father such beautiful, gentle children? He didn't deserve them. He deserved to be alone and lonely, a man whose family deserted him, leaving him to rattle around this house on his own day after day after day.

'Of course she will. Why wouldn't she?' She had to stop him going into Melissa's room. She had to say something to stall him. 'Roger, if you don't mind me asking, why are you so perturbed by this? It was just a mistake that an old lady made. I happened to be passing at the time. There really isn't anything sinister going on.'

'Well, you don't have anything to worry about then, do you? Melissa will surely confirm what you've just told me and then we can all get on with the rest of our day.'

Nancy struggled to breathe. Her windpipe had shrunk, her chest was compressed. This was it. This was the moment when her plan and the rest of her life would unravel in spectacular fashion. She had to get in Melissa's bedroom and speak with her before Roger did. A hundred scenarios filled her mind, ways of stopping him, none of them plausible. It would take more than a fall or a sudden illness to break Roger's current stride. So instead, she sat, her body folding in on itself, her limbs feeble with fear, and waited for the inevitable consequences of her weak and obvious lies to come crashing down around her.

# 26

## MELISSA

There are few quiet country lanes I can take to attempt to cover my tracks. At least the roads are dry now after the storm and I'm not leaving any muddy tyre marks behind. Gabriel is asleep and undisturbed by our earlier encounter.

Once we have covered enough miles and are out of sight of passing traffic, the car shielded by trees, I pull over and pick up the gun, turning it over in my hands, impressed and also frightened by its heft and solidity. I wouldn't have the first idea how to fire it. and yet if that man ever catches up with me, I will have no qualms about using it to protect both me and Gabriel. Daunted by its presence, I put it in the glovebox, the barrel facing towards the front of the car. Part of me considers throwing it away, opening the car door and hurling it into the distant moorland where nobody will ever find it. Another part of me is screaming to keep it. This gun could stand between me and him. I could use it to threaten him. I may not know how to operate it but firearms are a way of keeping enemies at bay. Besides, how hard can it be? A simple pull of the trigger should be enough.

A few seconds pass, the solace and silence giving me enough time to come to a decision. Keeping it is safer than discarding it. I set off again, hoping I see some road signs, something to give me an idea of where I'm headed. All I can think about is getting far away from that cottage. From him and his anger. Distance is safety. Even without his weapon, that man could kill us both using his bare hands and he would do it without breaking a sweat.

I continue travelling on the empty main road. The light begins to fade – something else to be grateful for. Darkness allows for anonymity. The darker the route, the greater our chances of escaping his clutches – that is, if he has even bothered to give chase. He has the money and the car but knows that this gun can link him to the crime. He will give chase, I'm certain of it.

My mind shuts out that unpalatable thought and rakes over what has happened so far, my thoughts centred on going back to England. I have to get out of Scotland. Soon the police will arrive at the cottage. They will find my belongings, my DNA and fingerprints in every room. I have no idea where I'm going from here but I do know that I can't stay in this area.

Home tugs at me, the north east pulling me towards it like a magnetic force. It's all I've ever known. I have nowhere else to go. Going back to my apartment is out of the question, as is going back to the actual town. The road where I live will be surrounded by police vehicles and the whole neighbourhood will be on the lookout for me, but I could perhaps find a rundown guesthouse somewhere on the North Yorkshire moors. Even the wilds of Scotland are no longer safe. A murder hunt is underway.

The more I think about going to North Yorkshire, the greater the appeal. It will mean driving through the night to get there but I can easily manage that. Gabriel is currently asleep. Better I get in as many miles as I can while he is quiet and peaceful than have him screaming in the back of the car because he needs feeding or is cold or needs changing. The rumble from his chest is still there but his temperature appears to be normal. That gives me hope.

I think about heading to Whitby. It's as good a start as any. Once I'm there, I'll be able to find my way to the coast road and find somewhere to stay along the route. No big hotels, just somewhere warm and dry with a proprietor who won't ask any questions and will take my cash, turning a blind eye to our arrival. It's a long drive – I'm guessing six or seven hours with some comfort breaks along the way. No mean feat with a baby strapped in the back and a gun safely tucked away in the glove compartment. I need to stay focused, perhaps even stop for a nap in a layby to make sure I don't fall asleep at the wheel. I also need to drink plenty to stay hydrated. It all sounds so easy in my head. The practicalities of it may prove to be unworkable but what other options do I have?

Gabriel continues to nap while I drive. I keep up a steady pace, my mind still going over past events instead of focusing on the present. I think about that poor old man in Edinburgh, and the man I hit with my car, and whether the police have already reached the cottage. Whether they have even discovered the dead body in Edinburgh. He may be still there, his bloodied carcass slumped on the floor. That's how I miss the lights behind me. They seem to come out of nowhere, the white glare scorching my eyes, the driver of the car narrowing the gap until the vehicle is so close, I can barely see its bumper bar in my rear-view mirror. My heart thumps. I think of Gabriel, and how he would be hit first should we make contact. I should have put his seat in the front next to me where I could keep an eye on him. I think of a hundred things I should and shouldn't have done to avoid this but it's too late now. I can't avoid this and I can't stop. This car in my rear could be nothing at all and completely unrelated to the cottage and those men, but it could also be everything. After what we've been through, I'm not about to take any chances.

I press my foot down hard on the accelerator and we are propelled forwards, the large engine in my car kicking into action. If this vehicle behind us is just another driver, then they will have no reason to try and catch us. Except they do. Within a few seconds, their headlights appear once more in my rear-view mirror, blinding me as they are turned on to full beam. A steady pulse beats away in my neck. I need to remain calm, stay focused. For Gabriel's sake, I need to keep a clear head and not let fear muddy my thinking even though my nerves are shrieking and my insides have turned to liquid. We're travelling at over 70 mph. It's too dark to see if it resembles Jason's vehicle, the one that was parked next to mine at the cottage. One mistake could prove fatal. I want to stop and howl at this person that I have a small baby in my car, *a tiny fucking baby!* but know that we are beyond that point. He is a murderer and no amount of reasoning will stop him doing what he has come here to do. I need to be faster than he is, be sharper and more mindful of my movements. I also need to think as he does and be prepared to put up a fight. I can do that. What I also have in my possession is a gun. That is a sobering thought.

*A gun.*

My mouth is dry, my tongue furred. I stare ahead and increase my speed, my fingers locked around the steering wheel. Everything has turned to dust. My plan for taking Gabriel and spending time with him, being relaxed and happy and showing him how to live in a calm and loving household, has all but disintegrated. We are on a downward trajectory now. Unless something miraculous happens, then I cannot see a way out of this mess. I tried to do the right thing, I really did, but like everything else in my life, it has gone horribly wrong. My plans for love and happiness and a secure family life coming apart at the seams.

I push my foot further to the floor again, the car behind managing to keep pace with us. We're now doing just over 80 mph. If anything happened to us at this speed, we would both be killed outright. If I slow down, the car behind will catch us. He wants his weapon back. And I am under no illusions about his other motives. He wants to make sure I don't identify him to the police, tell them about his admission of murder. He wants to retrieve his gun and turn it on Gabriel and me. I won't let that happen. I may have made mistakes. I may have been rash in coming here at all, not thinking it through forensically, but I'm not an idiot and I don't give in without a fight. This man is a killer, a hideous bully, turning his gun on a frail elderly man.

*You ran an old guy down.*

I clamp my jaw together and keep my eyes on the road. I have to focus on keeping my grandson safe. My father was a narcissist, an arrogant bully, and I refuse to once again to be on the receiving end of somebody like that. A person who feels they have the right to control and manipulate me. I will fight to the bitter end. And as long as there is breath in my body, I will *not* let anything happen to Gabriel.

Up ahead is a right turn. It's dim and shady and extremely narrow but if I can fool him into thinking I'm going straight ahead, swinging the car round at the last minute, I may be able to lose him. It's risky but not half as risky as our current position. At this rate, he will catch us and nudge my car off the road.

The engine growls when I press my foot down even harder. I keep my posture rigid, occasionally glancing to Gabriel, who remains asleep, and then when I am almost upon the right-hand turn, I brake as we take the sharp bend. We're at a dangerous angle, the car feeling as if it's going to topple over. I grip the steering wheel and turn it back around, driving away at speed. Up ahead is another right-hand turn which I also take and before I know it, we are on a tiny lane engulfed by darkness, shrubbery and trees hemming us in on both sides. I slow down and turn on my full beam to give me a better view. I can hear another engine behind us. I can't be sure whether it's my overactive imagination or whether it's real but I'm not about to slow down and take any risks. I glance in the rear-view mirror but it's too dark to see anything. Ahead of me, the road appears to grow darker and smaller, the trees blocking out any remaining light.

My veins shrink as I hear it again. I wasn't imagining it. Another vehicle is approaching behind us. He's turned off his headlights and is somewhere to our rear. I can't see any escape routes, no junctions or narrow lanes I can slip through to try and shake him off. If it is him, that is. My chest rattles as I heave a sigh. Of course it's him. This area is deserted. We're on a tiny road in the Highlands of Scotland. There's nobody else around for miles.

I need to do something to stop him from following me. I should have done it at the beginning. Gabriel's safety is paramount. If he comes to any harm, I will never, ever forgive myself and this guy, this awful *maniac* is now too close for comfort.

Without making any painful, lurching movements, I begin to hit the brakes in a rhythmic motion, touching the pedal every couple of seconds, switching between the brake and the accelerator to knock him off balance. I'd like to say it works but a sudden bump to the back of my car tells me otherwise. I let out a gasp. He's trying to run me off the road. Without headlights, I can only hope he veers off the side and topples over. It's unlikely as my car is illuminating his route.

'Shit!'

My voice is a high-pitched shriek, my throat dry. I feel so sick and tired. I can't go on like this. Something has got to give. I need to dig deep, do something to get rid of him. If he catches us, this man will kill us both. So I brake, the car coming to a halt, my wheels screeching on the road. Then I lean forward, remove the gun from the glove compartment and open the car door.

## 27

### 1970

She would like to say that everything turned out just fine, that Roger spoke to Melissa, who verified Nancy's story. She would like to be able to say that, but of course that didn't happen. Because that's not how life works. The poor child, unable to compete against the labyrinthine workings of Roger's warped brain, capitulated and admitted that no, she hadn't heard the phone ring and that no, it wasn't an elderly lady that Nancy spoke to on the telephone and she wasn't sure who it was. Perhaps it was Aunt Hayley.

Nancy sat on the edge of the bed in the room next door, listening to it all, sickened by Roger's contrived, saccharine tone that rapidly turned sour once he got the gist of what had taken place, barking at their daughter to go downstairs and wait in the living room and that no, she wasn't allowed to take her book with her. Nancy waited, her body one huge pulse of fear. She felt as if her entire body was slowly being ground to dust, every aspiration she had of leaving this place smudged away. She waited for Roger's furious entrance into the bedroom and envisioned herself fighting back, telling him that it was over, that she no longer wanted to be married to a monster. She thought about it, wishing hard for it to happen but the reality, she knew, would be nothing like that. She was a frightened, insipid creature who didn't have the strength to do anything except cower. This was what he had reduced her to. He had sucked all the life out of her. What little strength she had, she used on her children, on cleaning this house, on being the best she could be so her husband didn't feel the need to take his fists to her, pounding and kicking until she could hardly breathe.

The soft pad of his footsteps across the landing after he watched their terrified daughter escape downstairs made the hairs on the back of her neck stand on end. She could hear George's murmurs that would soon escalate into a cry. She needed to go and get him, to feed him and hold her baby boy close to her breast. She craved his closeness as much as he craved hers. She thought of his milky breath and soft skin and fought back tears.

The opening of the door puckered her flesh. She imagined herself picking up a heavy object and smashing it over her husband's head. She could almost feel the weight of his body as it slumped at her feet, the feel of his skin as she drew back her foot and drove it into his face.

Nancy looked up. Roger was standing in the doorway, his face set like stone. He stepped forward and slammed the door closed behind him. Nancy couldn't breathe. Her face burned and her innards roiled. Should she tell the truth? Hope he would understand? She swallowed and ran her fingers through her hair. He wouldn't; she knew that. Trying to explain anything to him was a waste of energy and time. His opinions and perspective on the situation were rigid. It was his way or no way. Always had been and he wasn't about to change. If anything, he was getting worse, the switching of his moods so rapid, the sharpness of his temper so bruising, it was breathtaking.

'Why did you lie to me?' His voice was controlled, each word enunciated with excruciating precision.

Nancy lowered her head, tears threatening to fall. She was tired of this. So very, very tired. A tidal wave of emotions engulfed her; years and years of hatred and fear that had been pushed aside, ignored and squashed out of sight. She looked up at him, a glint in her eyes she hoped would let him know she was at her tipping point.

And then she spoke.

'Why do you think I lied to you, Roger? Ask yourself why I tiptoe around you, too fearful to tell you *anything*?'

A slap or a kick was coming. It was unavoidable but before that happened, for once, she would have her say. She would make him listen, let him walk in her shoes, show him how debilitating and draining it is to be frightened and full of uncertainty. To not know what was coming next. Her words might not penetrate his iron veneer, but it would make her feel better, knowing she had at least tried. Knowing she had attempted to do the best for her children and tried to get them safely to shore whilst swimming against a seemingly unstoppable and ferociously strong tide.

His fists were clenched at his sides, his pallor ghostly. This was new to him, being spoken to in such a brusque manner. Nancy wanted to laugh. She wanted to run at him and push him to the floor then stand over him and watch him squirm.

'I beg your pardon?'

She smiled. His reaction was laughably predictable, his pride already dented by her mild-mannered disposition and polite question. By the fact she dared speak at all.

'Roger, everything I do is wrong. You find fault in every

move I make. Last week, I was slapped because your cup of tea wasn't hot enough. Do you really think it's acceptable to hit and kick and punch another person, especially when that person is your wife?' She should have stopped at that point, she knew it, but something in her brain was pushing her on, making her say the unsayable. 'I am in pain nearly all of the time because of your actions. I am bruised and tired and distressed, and more than that, I am so deeply, deeply unhappy and if you can't see that, Roger, then you must be blind.' Tears ran in thin streaks down her face. She sat, unmoving. Hardly daring to breathe. Waiting.

He was already striding towards her, his eyes tapered, his breathing a low rasp. In the next room, George began to cry. Her breasts tingled, milk soaking through her clothing.

'And if you hit me now, if you beat me senseless, who is going to feed your child?'

He stopped. A twitch pulsed in his jaw. Nancy let out a trembling sigh, her eyes never leaving his. She wasn't able to predict his next move. Inside her husband's head wasn't a place she cared to visit. It was an unwelcoming, dark place that pulsed with terror and violence.

'Go and sort him out, then come back here and we'll continue with this talk.'

Nancy stood, aghast at her readiness to follow his commands. After all these years, it was a hard habit to break. She filed past him and entered George's room, cradling him in her arms as she gently lifted him out of his crib, his small body giving her a modicum of reassurance that not everything in this house was contaminated by Roger's toxic, abrasive ways. There were still pockets of innocence in this house, pleasure to be had when her children were laid in her arms. They were her future. They were all she had.

George fed from her, alleviating the pressure in her breasts, giving her some time to consider her options.

She carried him into their bedroom and sat down on the mattress. George laid contentedly in her arms, his eyes locked onto her face.

'He needs to go back in his crib.' Roger's voice was cold.

'He's been in his crib for too long already. I can't just leave him in there. He isn't tired and he needs to be held and stimulated.' She stared at Roger, eager to see his response as she spoke. 'Would you like to hold him for a while?'

His shock was palpable. She almost laughed. For once, she was ahead of him, playing him at his own game. Being strong and daring to question his authority.

'I'm sure he's more than happy with you.' A flush crept up his neck. Spots of crimson peppered his face.

'You wanted to continue talking, Roger?' She smiled and tipped her head to one side, waiting for his reply.

His brows knitted together, a line of creases bunched above his eyes, ageing him by a decade or more.

'Melissa said you were talking to your sister. That you were going to visit her and you were taking the children with you. Is that right?'

She took a trembling breath and held her nerve as best she could. 'Yes, that's right. I thought you would enjoy the peace and quiet for a few days while we were gone.'

He laughed and shook his head then stood and strode around the room, hands slung deep in his pockets. 'I know what you're doing. Don't think I don't understand what all this is about. If it was your sister on the phone then why lie to me and why not call her from the house phone? You've done so in the past.'

She didn't reply, the hammering in her chest making it difficult for her to speak. Seconds passed, the interminable silence a painful thing to observe. Then Roger's voice cut in, breaking the moment, rupturing their last few seconds together before everything fell apart.

'I'll tell you why; it's because you didn't call your sister at all. And it wasn't a sweet, confused old lady who got the wrong number. I know exactly who you were ringing.'

She waited, the clanging in her head a discordant screech that made her want to scream until she was hoarse, tearing at his face with her nails until his skin was a bloody unrecognisable mess.

Her voice was reedy when she finally found the courage and the strength to speak. 'Who was I ringing, Roger? Because I know for certain that it was my sister I spoke to. I'm not sure who *you* think it was?'

His sneer and the darkness in his eyes scared her. 'Do I have to spell it out to you, Nancy? Are you really that dumb? Or is it that you think I'm too stupid to see through your lies? Hmm?'

He moved closer to her. She pressed George into her chest, her arm protecting his head from any possible blows.

'What's his name and where did you meet him?'

She shook her head and sighed. She wanted to shriek with laughter. Not this again. This preposterous idea he had that she was seeing another man. Could Roger not see that she barely had enough energy to wash and dress herself, let alone conduct an illicit affair? Could he not see that living with him had put her off ever loving or trusting any other man? It was laughable. Except it wasn't. He was deadly serious. And his anger was mounting, his energy reserved for violence, unspent within him. His face reddened as he edged ever closer to her, his eyes locked on hers. She wanted to reach up and gouge out his eyes. Make him suffer and cry out in pain. Make him feel her pain, the pain he had spent years inflicting on her. She could do it. Resentment fuelled her hatred of him, gave her a layer of strength she didn't know she possessed. It made her want to slap his face and hit him hard with something heavy and solid. She could place George on the bed and put up a fight. For once in her life, she could stand up and retaliate.

Except she didn't. She sat immobile, hoping to reason with him, hoping she could make him see sense, inject some compassion into his stone-cold, emotionless body. She didn't react or strike back or scratch or claw and lash out for one simple reason and one reason only: because she wasn't a monster. Unlike him, she wasn't a fighter, driven by white-hot fury that burned her insides. She was a gentle soul, solicitous and reserved. Thoughts of beating him senseless remained in her head; the levels of consideration she had for others, even Roger, overriding all other emotions. Overriding her need to defend herself. She was also half his size. Roger wasn't huge but he was taller and broader than she was. A mountain of a man compared to her comparatively diminutive frame.

'Roger, it isn't that at all. You've got it all wrong. I was going to—'

The slap knocked her to the floor. George fell from her arms. Their screams merged, her baby's cries twisting at her guts as she curled up into a ball and wept.

## 28

## MELISSA

The gun is a deadweight in my hand, the cool of the metal in stark contrast to my burning flesh. Despite the tremble in my fingers and the sudden weakness that has taken hold in my arm, I keep it steady and walk towards his vehicle, the barrel pointing at his windscreen. It must be loaded. His slack features and wide eyes tell me he is scared. His gaze follows the possible trajectory of an escaped bullet while his fingers remain curled around the steering wheel. I stand, counting my amplified breaths and wheezes to ensure he is focused on what I do next, then lift the gun high into the air and throw it as far and as hard as I can, into the nearby woods.

His mouth contorts in anger. Before he makes a move to get out of his vehicle, I slide back into my own car and screech away. I didn't know what else to do. I couldn't keep that gun. The thought of him catching up and wrestling it from me, using it against me and Gabriel, knotted my insides. Disposing of it was, as far as I could see, the only sensible course of action. I'm not a sharp-thinking shooter or military expert. I'm a middle-aged woman with zero knowledge of firearms. At some point, he would have caught up with me. I could only out-manoeuvre him for so long.

We're alone on the road now. Locating that gun is more important to him than tracking me. It's his link to the robbery, to that murder. I think again of the old guy: his decrepit house and the possible stash of money that he kept lying around. I wonder if word had spread, people gossiping about the wealthy old man with minimal security, making him a target for the likes of Jason and Sonny.

In the back, Gabriel stirs. I continue driving, keeping a close watch on him as well as keeping an eye out for service stations. I need fuel and I need to feed and change him but for now, I have to make sure I put plenty of distance between us and that psychopath.

We manage another hour before he wakes properly, his falsetto yowl telling me he's hungry. In the distance, I spot the unmistakable green and yellow glare of a petrol station. I can stop there, sort out Gabriel, fill up my car before making tracks. Half an hour and we'll be back on the road and heading to England. We can't be too far from the border, but in truth, I don't know where we are. I used a map to get to the cottage after dumping my phone, but left it behind when we made our escape. I'm driving blind using only my intuition and road signs.

An irregular bumping sensation as we approach the distant lights frosts my flesh. An uneven camber of the car while I try to hold it steady pushes any notions I have of an early exit from this pit-stop out of my mind. A flat tyre. My stomach plummets. A tyre I can change but feeding, changing and soothing a fractious baby at the same time will prove problematic.

We limp along on an empty stretch of tarmac, Gabriel's crying rattling at my nerve endings. I try to stem the panic that I feel rising in my throat. It expands, restricting my breathing, sitting in my chest like a sleeping serpent. I rub at my eyes and sigh. So far, I have encountered gun-wielding criminals and dealt with them effectively and swiftly. I have nursed Gabriel through febrile convulsions when I was convinced he was going to die. This current dilemma pales into insignificance besides those events. I'm tired, hungry, low on energy as well as petrol. Everything feels chaotic, time and circumstances working against me.

We reach the service station as my patience runs low and Gabriel's cries reach a crescendo. By the time I pull up, my temples are throbbing, my eyes gritty and heavy. The forecourt is bereft of other vehicles and a bored-looking young woman is inside, her face illuminated by the clinical LED lights overhead. I fill up my car, unstrap Gabriel and head inside to pay.

I hand over the cash and the assistant looks at me as if I've just given her a severed limb. I raise my eyebrows and she shrugs, her bottom lip jutting out like a petulant child about to throw a tantrum.

'Hardly ever see anybody use real money these days. All cards, ain't it? Especially since Covid.'

'I like to keep an eye on what I spend. Too easy to forget when you just flash a bit of plastic around.'

I swivel my head, glancing at the shelves behind us. 'Odd request, but I don't suppose you sell baby food?'

Another hard stare and a frown. 'Not that odd since you've got a baby with you, is it?' She nods to an area in the far corner and then gives me a smile. 'Over there. Not got much but there is some baby formula and stuff.'

Relieved, I pick up a few jars of rice and some pre-prepared cartons of formula milk as well as a bag of nappies, and put them all in a handbasket. I grab a pack of sandwiches and a bottle of juice and put them in as well, then hand over my cash.

A deep voice stops me at the exit before I reach my car, its projection and intonation hard to ignore.

'Looks like you got a flat.'

I suppress an eye roll and grit my teeth. Interventions and simple obvious remarks I can do without. If I can just clamber into the back seat, get Gabriel fed and changed and strapped back in, then I can change the damn tyre myself. I'm more than capable, but right now, I'd just like to have to deal with one crisis at a time.

'Yes, I know. Just going to get this little one changed, then I'll sort it.'

I nod at the tall stranger who is standing, watching me. I turn my back to him and strap a crying Gabriel into the car, throwing my purchases into the footwell. All I need is some time and space: the time and space to drive a few seconds over to the other side of the forecourt, to feed and change a screaming baby and grab a snack for myself, and then I can set about changing the fucking tyre.

'I can give you a hand. You look like you've already got enough to do.' His voice is gentle, his face soft and expressive, but the less I have to do with other people, the better. I operate more efficiently on my own. People cannot be trusted.

'Thank you but I'll be fine.'

Gabriel lets out another scream and the man's face creases with concern.

'It's really no bother. If you want to sort out the baby inside, I can have your tyre changed and you can be on your way in half the time.'

I want to refuse, every part of me screaming to shut him down, drive away, ignore his offers of help, but find myself nodding and thanking him. Gabriel is reaching fever pitch with his crying. I'm tired, I'm cold and I am hungry. My meticulously thought-out plan is disintegrating before it has barely had time to take shape. It is the dusty remnants of a slapdash attempt to salvage what is left of my life.

'Thank you. I need to move it away from the pumps.'

'I'll do that for you.' He holds out a large, upturned palm for my keys.

Suspicion balloons in my chest. I glance over his shoulder. His own vehicle is parked nearby: a Range Rover, worth at least three to four times the value of my old Ford. Probably more. Why would he take my old jalopy and leave his own car behind?

I hand them over, a feeling of surliness at being thought of as helpless twisting in my gut.

'Why don't you go inside and feed the little one? It's warmer in there and there's a tiny seating area at the back.'

I nod and am walking in the direction of the brightly lit service area when he calls after me. 'Do I know you from somewhere? Your face looks familiar.'

It was only a matter of time. My flesh puckers. My scalp prickles. Every part of me feels hot and bothered. I unglue my tongue from the roof of my mouth and reply, trying to sound jovial. Nonchalant and unmoved by his question. 'I don't think so. I'm not from this area.'

He laughs. 'Me neither. I'm from the north east of England and on my way back from a business meeting in Scotland.'

*The north east.*

Gabriel is suddenly twice as heavy in my arms. I'm weak and dizzy, muted by his words. Is this a set-up, some kind of covert police operation to lure me in, or just a bizarre coincidence? My legs almost buckle as I walk inside, my need to be away from him so strong, it's a physical thing pushing me on. I should have taken notice of my instincts and refused. I should have fed Gabriel, strapped him in his seat and changed the tyre myself but instead, in a moment of weakness, I succumbed to his offer of help and now here I am, being monitored by a stranger who thinks he knows me. My buzzing head, my stiff set shoulders and squirming innards all tell me it's wrong being here. I want to disappear, for the ground to open and swallow us both up.

Instead, I sit at the back of the shop on a chair next to the coffee machine and give Gabriel one of the pre-prepared formula drinks in his bottle, then spoon out a couple of measures of baby food. It's not easy and I'm all fingers and thumbs but at least he quietens down, allowing me to think clearly. As soon as that guy is finished changing my tyre, we'll head straight off. I can eat my sandwich while I'm driving and stop further on to change Gabriel's nappy. I'm even prepared to pee in the bushes as long as I can make my escape from this place as soon as possible.

Outside, the sky is dense, a veil of darkness peppered with the occasional cluster of tiny, diamond-like stars. I shiver and bounce Gabriel on my knee, eager to keep him quiet. While he is content, I decide to use the toilet.

It's cold inside the baby changing room. Gabriel neither notices nor cares, gurgling and smiling at me as if everything is fine in our world. The world that is slowly collapsing around us.

I finish up and gather our things together. The tyre-changing stranger is standing, waiting for me when I open the door, my key fob dangling from his index finger.

'All done.'

My skin flushes hot and cold simultaneously. 'Thank you. You are really very kind.'

'It's no problem. You probably have a slow puncture but I've pumped it up so it should get you to where you're going.'

I think about my erratic swerving and nod, wondering if I caused it. 'Thank you again. I think I'd better get going. Need to get this one strapped in and be on our way.'

His eyes bore into my face. Heat pulses in my neck, climbing up into my hairline, an arc of warmth making me uncomfortable. Eager to leave. I dab at my face with semi-dexterous fingers.

'Are you sure we've never met before? You do look really familiar.'

Air expands in my lungs. I try to speak but the words refuse to come so instead, I shake my head and walk towards the exit. I manage a quiet, dutiful, 'Thanks again,' over my shoulder before heading out into the chill of the night.

A strong sense of liberation blossoms in my core when I put Gabriel in his seat and strap myself in, ready to leave. It's short lived. The tall stranger is watching me. I see the realisation dawning as he opens his mouth to speak and raises his arm, a long finger pointed in my direction.

*He knows.*

Trepidation slithers beneath my skin, curling and looping itself around my vital organs. I watch him pluck out his phone from his pocket and punch in a number.

Blood pounds in my head. Everything is closing in on me. I press my foot down hard, the wheels spinning on loose bits of gravel. We screech out onto the main route, the drama and urgency of my exit adding to my anxiety. I feel nothing but relief at leaving him and the bright lights of the service station behind and let out a protracted gasp as we head into the anonymity of the darkness.

The unexpected sound cuts through my fear, the shrill pitch of a ringing phone piercing the air. *My* phone. It vibrates in my pocket. A coincidence, nothing more. With my free hand, I fish it out and stare at the screen, then take a left turn off the main carriageway and pull up into a layby. I dim the headlights, press the button, and wait for somebody to speak.

'Hello? Are you there? It's Lorna from the supermarket. Look,

I know you probably don't want to hear from me and I'm sure you've got your reasons for doing what you did, but I've just been watching the news and I think that perhaps—'

I end the call. A grenade explodes in my head, the shrapnel blinding me. I rub at my eyes and glance in the mirror, my reflection always a shock to what I expect to see. I'm old, tired looking, my skin grey, a nervous, dark expression evident in my eyes. And worse than that, I look like me. No disguise. All the items I acquired to mask my appearance are back at the cottage. No wig, no thick applications of make-up. No glasses after dumping them and reverting back to my contacts. Nothing at all. And people are now onto me. Possibly even tracking that call. The police could be on their way as I sit here, wondering what to do next. On instinct, I climb out of the car and look around for some kind of inspiration or guidance, and find none. I'm truly alone. Companionless and set apart from the rest of society. I took this journey alone and I'll end it alone.

I glance at the roughly laid tarmac, then drop the phone to the ground and stand on it, crushing and grinding it with my heel until it lies in tiny fragments. I reach down and pick up the broken pieces, then throw them as far as I can in different directions into the nearby shrubbery and woodland before getting back into my car and heading back out onto the main road and into obscurity.

# 29

## 1970

Waves of pain ricocheted through her body. Nancy's face, the sharp angles of her limbs where she landed after the fall, throbbed and pulsated. She lay rigid and unmoving. He was somewhere in the room. She could feel his presence, his anger still a profound force. And something else. Or someone else. There was somebody else here.

*Melissa.*

Oh dear God. Please don't let her daughter have witnessed any of this. Nancy blinked, her eyes clogged up with tears and blood. She had to get up. She desperately wanted to move, to stand and scoop up her children, and to flee this wretched house, but feared that this time, something was broken, a vital part of her shattered beyond repair. So she lay, concentrating on her breathing. Trying to gather her strength. Focusing on staying alive.

And then a sound. Somebody crying. Not her husband. Definitely not Roger. He wasn't built for tears or remorse or any shows of sentimentality. It was her daughter.

*George!*

The memory flooded back into her brain. George had been in her arms when the attack happened. Her baby boy. She needed to find him, to hold him close to her and make sure he wasn't injured. She couldn't bear it if anything had happened to him. He was a baby. Just a helpless, defenceless baby. Roger had had no qualms about striking her and knocking him out of her arms. At that point, it wasn't possible to hate anybody more than she hated her husband. She felt nothing but malice at the thought of him and knew that even with the passing of time, those feelings would never abate or waver. He had done the unthinkable, and in doing the unthinkable, he had lost the right to dictate to her whether she was able to leave this house. She was going, that much was certain. She just needed her body to work properly, for her limbs to move and flex and help lever her torso up off the floor, and for the bleeding to stop. She was tired, so very weary, but a fire burned deep in her belly. Flames of rage and determination that would help her escape this hideous house and marriage. Help her to escape from this awful, joyless existence.

'I've got baby George, Mummy.'

More tears misted Nancy's vision. She lifted and turned her head, a blurred image of Melissa coming into focus. She was sitting on the floor, a small, white bundle laid in her arms.

'His eyes are closed but at least he's not crying any more.'

A weight pressed down on Nancy, pinning her to the floor. She had to move, to get up and see to her baby boy and her daughter. They needed her. She needed them. Roger was somewhere close by, his ominous presence as big as the room itself.

A small sob from Melissa and then an anguished cry. 'I'm frightened, Mummy. I'm really, really scared. It's George. He's not moving. He's not moving and I've tried whispering into his ear and stroking his face and cuddling him but he isn't looking at me or making any noises. You need to help me make him better, Mummy. You need to get up and help.'

Nancy rose, an inner strength driving her on. She knew that she had it in her; she just knew that somewhere deep within herself, she possessed enough force, resilience and bravery to bring an end to all of this.

Through clogged-up lashes, snot and blood and saliva marring her sight, she could see Roger standing in the doorway. Melissa, their young, frightened daughter had picked up their child, not Roger. His own son, and her husband had left him there on the wooden floor to cry, oblivious to his injuries, to his distress and pain. A baby.

She ran at him, arms outstretched, nails at the ready. A roar exploded out of her throat, a volcanic eruption, hot, relentless and unavoidable.

Behind her, she could hear Melissa cry, then the wails of George merging with her own screams. He was alive. Her baby boy was still alive.

Like the coward she knew him to be, Roger ran, his feet thundering down the stairs. She followed, throwing herself at him as he tried to open the front door, their bodies colliding, her weight pinning him up against the frame. Then something else. Small footsteps. Melissa behind her with George still swaddled in her arms.

'The kitchen! Go to the kitchen, Melissa!'

The fight had left him, Roger's body putting up little resistance to her clawing and slapping, his arms covering his face, protecting himself from her blows. He had gone too far, hurting their baby boy, and was now trying to redeem himself, standing inert. No counter-attack, no fists or feet directed at her. He just stood there. Pretending he was weak and mild-mannered. They both knew what an irascible, difficult man he was, his propensity for violence a putrid thing so deeply embedded in him that it would never leave. It was indelibly scored in the very centre of him.

A scrape of metal from behind, the faint patter of footsteps accompanying it. And then unable to contain his anger any longer, Roger sprang into action, his fury combusting. Nancy fell back onto the floor. Pain shot through her, delaying her reactions, slowing her down. He was upon her, his hands clasped around her throat, his eyes bulging. Spittle hung from his mouth, hanging in long strands over her face. Her vision attenuated as he applied more pressure, darkness creeping in at the edges.

A baby crying somewhere nearby. A quick movement. Then a low howl as Roger slumped to one side before scrambling away down the hallway, blood trailing in his wake. The slam of the kitchen door as he made his exit. Then silence.

Melissa stood above her mother, the knife smeared with crimson, small beads of Roger's blood dripping onto the wooden floor. Nancy let out a moan, the pressure on her windpipe easing. Her eyes caught sight of George, laid on the bottom stair, his pale face angled her way. His eyes watching her. He was alive. Thank God. Her baby was still breathing. Gasping for air, she watched as her daughter marched into the kitchen, knife in hand, turned on the tap and rinsed the blade under a stream of water until it gleamed.

* * *

The ambulance arrived in less than five minutes, Nancy gasping her instructions into the mouthpiece while her daughter watched, George bundled in her arms. She told them nothing of Roger's injuries when they got there, saying he had left her for dead after throwing their son to the floor and hitting her repeatedly in a fit of pique before attempting to strangle her, telling them that it hadn't been the first time but it would definitely be the last. No, she replied when they asked of his whereabouts, she didn't know where he had gone and neither did she care.

* * *

Nancy and George were discharged from hospital the same day, her current injuries and historic scars testament to a life of abuse at the hands of her monster of a husband. George, surprisingly, suffered little, and was treated for a slight cut to his shoulder where he landed after falling from her arms.

Roger's car was discovered at the top of the cliffs twenty-four hours after he disappeared. His body was found on the beach below a few days later. He didn't drown; he had been mangled by the rocks before he hit the water, their sharp, unforgiving edges tearing and shredding his skin as he tumbled to his death. Even the sea didn't keep him, spitting out the poisonous and the unwanted, thought Nancy bitterly. The knife wound wasn't too deep and didn't warrant a mention, the injuries inflicted by the rocks far greater and more perilous than any swipe of a bread knife inflicted by the small hands and clumsy, unskilled fingers of a child. But that swipe stopped Roger from strangling her. It saved Nancy's life.

Word spread of his abuse. Nancy spoke freely, tired of keeping secrets. Tired of protecting Roger's image and status. His friends and colleagues held a memorial service for him, unwilling or unable to believe what he had done, their allegiance to him too strong and lasting to sever. Nancy pictured them as they sat next to each other in the church, listening to the priest extol his virtues, telling the world what a brilliant doctor he was: a great family man, albeit a little misunderstood and under tremendous pressure. But at the end of the day, he was just an ordinary, hardworking individual who made one terrible mistake.

They were all there, his friends and colleagues and their respective spouses. Except for Jeanette Whitcome, who spent the day of the service sitting by Nancy's side in the living room, their fingers interlaced in a show of strength and solidarity. Many of his friends stuck by his memory, blind to his destructive ways. Some knew the truth, the real story behind the carefully constructed fabrications of Roger's life. And many simply turned a blind eye, too wrapped up in their own lives and day-to-day existences to care.

'I just wish I had spoken up sooner. I am so very sorry for what you went through.' Tears welled in Jeanette's eyes. She spoke softly and Nancy was grateful for her warmth and soothing tones.

Every day upon walking, Nancy's head ached, dreams of the future and visions of the past clashing and jockeying for position in her brain, each becoming entangled in the other until she could no longer distinguish one from the other.

Sympathy cards flooded in, cluttering up her house. She disposed of them; their words of comfort were neither needed nor wanted. Roger was dead. Life was going to be glorious. Besides, her emotions were still a work in progress. It was difficult for her to process anything resembling sympathy or compassion, having endured nothing but violence and harm for as long as she could remember, but it was a skill she was working on. Something she longed to embrace. In time, it would show itself but for now, she was content to just be. So reading cards dripping with solace and fake empathy did nothing to console her, to advance her life or make her any happier. Every day, she rose from her bed knowing she could do and say whatever she pleased. And that, for the time being, was enough.

The house was quiet with Melissa still learning to live with what she had witnessed. What she had done. They never spoke of that day, how her daughter had helped to save her mother's life by using brute force against her own father. But it was there, that dark memory. Nancy worked on extinguishing it by showering her child with love. Using shafts of shimmering light to banish the darkness. And Melissa reciprocated by helping Nancy to take care of George, her protection of him as fierce as any lioness looking after her cubs. Hayley visited, carrying out household chores, making sure meals were cooked and eaten, the house clean and habitable. They had a routine of sorts. And they had each other.

A month after the funeral, Nancy received the coroner's report for Roger's death. His passing was recorded as misadventure. Nancy wanted to scream at the heavens, the truth of his death masking the reality of his life. She filed it away in a box on the bottom shelf of a cupboard, vowing that as long as there was breath in her body and strength in her limbs, she would never glance at it again. It was an insult. Even in death, Roger still had the upper hand, so many of his friends and colleagues continuing to believe that the incident with her and George was a terrible accident. A one-off. Continuing to believe that a man of his standing would never act in such a brutish way. They didn't know him. Never had.

And so Nancy did what she had always done day after day: caring for her children and being the best that she could be. It was just the three of them now and despite the injustice of it all, despite everyone continuing to think that Roger had made just one hideous mistake, she was content and settled, the dawning of each day breathing warmth and luminosity into her life.

## 30

## MELISSA

My mind is a snarl of thoughts and memories as I drive into the gloom of the night. I'm tightly compressed, my skin flashing hot and cold, my brain firing in all directions. Without warning, parts of my childhood I would rather lay dormant, elbow their way into my mind. That day: the day it happened – me standing at the doorway of my parents' bedroom, watching as my father hit my mother. Watching in stupefied silence as my baby brother fell from her arms onto the floor. The sudden cry. Then the silence while I cradled him, praying he would wake, every bone in my body, every nerve ending straining for him to open his eyes and make a sound, and the shrill pitch of my own fear that crackled in my head during that wait. And then of course, the knife. The heft of it in my hand as I pushed it at my own father, trying my damnedest to pierce his skin. A surprisingly difficult thing to do. I had no idea human flesh was so tough, so thick and impenetrable. Perhaps it was my tender years. Maybe if I had been a few years older, a little bigger and stronger, I would have killed him. Not that it mattered. I shocked him by fighting back. Drew blood. Watched him scurry away like a frightened rabbit. I didn't manage to kill him. But I wanted to, oh how I wanted to. He died anyway. At his own hands, but either way he was out of our lives and we were happier for it. But those few moments, seeing George lying there, the pallor of his skin, thinking he was dead – it has haunted me ever since. I dedicated my childhood to protecting him, making sure he wasn't ever put in the path of danger again.

George upped and left us recently, taking him and his family off to warmer climes, their life in Australia something to be envied and embraced. We spoke little of our father as adults, my memories of him charred, George's memory of him and that time of our lives, non-existent.

I wipe away tears. My hands are trembling, my fingers bone cold. I don't miss my father, more the idea of having one. A caring, functioning father, somebody we could have looked up to and admired. He was a cold, calculating man, as distant in death as he was when he was alive. Besides, what could be gained from raking over such a traumatic time? We survived and that's the most important thing.

The dreams still haunt me though, those terrible, nightmarish visions of bruised and bloodied babies, their screams echoing in my head, even after waking. All the specialists and child psychologists tell us that children are resilient creatures, that they can cope with trauma far more easily than we give them credit for, but I don't believe that is the case at all. I believe that trauma buries itself and reappears when we least expect it, creeping in bit by bit until eventually, it becomes anchored so deep in our bones that ridding ourselves of it becomes an almost impossible task.

Gabriel sits quietly in his seat, his face shrouded by shadows. Even with all the earlier stress and anxiety, it's still a huge comfort knowing he is close by. He may be small and helpless but right now, he is all I've got. Since Stuart left, things have been difficult. More than difficult. I gained my independence while my loneliness grew. It hasn't been easy, but I survived. And now, it feels as if everything I have achieved has all been for nothing. All my assistance, my attempts to rescue Gabriel and save him from a life of neglect are nearing an end. The police will soon be swarming the area. I need to get back to England before they start setting up roadblocks on all the major routes out of Scotland. After checking road signs, I estimate it's going to take me another two hours or so to reach the border. I need to move quickly, to concentrate only on driving, not getting dragged back to the past. A past I cannot change.

I turn on the radio for background noise, the sound of another voice enough to ease me and quell my nerves while I manoeuvre my car through the endless, lonely roads in the darkness.

I look back to Gabriel, who has begun to doze off. I'm lucky. His fever seems to have gone and whatever infection he had has hopefully abated. After all that has happened in the last few days – and it has been frightening and overwhelming – we are still here and we're still together, despite every odd being stacked against us. I smile. Life may feel as if we're stumbling down a rocky path, but when I think about it, we have broken the back of our problems. Whatever lies ahead can't be half as bad as what we've experienced in the past few days. I tell myself that because it's easier than facing up to the truth, and the truth is that I have nowhere to go and soon, Gabriel will be taken from me.

The music on the radio stops and the newsreader begins to speak. I switch it off and tap my fingers on the steering wheel, trying to remain upbeat. Trying to break the near silence and act normal even though this scenario is completely abnormal. I have no real plan, no place I can go where I know we will both be safe.

Once we get holed up in a room in North Yorkshire, then I'll have time to sit down and think things through, but for now, I need to stay calm and be methodical. No more upset or unnecessary complications.

I pass a slip road off the main route and see blue flashing lights in the distance. My heart thumps in my chest. I take a few deep breaths and grip the steering wheel even tighter.

I can't continue like this, my nerves fraying every time I see or hear something out of the ordinary. I'm not a bad person. I'm a good person doing what should have been done many months ago.

I focus on the road ahead, trying to banish old memories and negative thoughts but they continue to find a way in. I think of Stuart and how inseparable we were in our younger years, how much in love we were before it all went awry, our marriage crumbling, our lives taking us in separate directions. Then I think of my mother in the nursing home, how her memory became fractured towards the end of her life. Perhaps that was for the best. She forgot about her past, although every now and again, her eyes would glaze over and she would speak of those times, reliving the terror. There were tears on occasion but mainly happiness and relief at my father's absence. He wasn't missed. George remembered nothing of him and we thrived without having our father in our lives.

The fact I haven't visited my mother's grave recently looms large in my mind. I would like to do that when I get back to England, although I suspect the police will be waiting near all my familiar haunts in case I turn up – my home, the graveyard, perhaps even the house where I grew up, although that is questionable. It all happened such a long time ago. Decades. My life is pretty insular these days, the places I visit, limited. They won't have to cast a wide net to catch me. That's why I plan on finding a small room somewhere in North Yorkshire. Just me and Gabriel, waiting it out together until they grow tired of searching for us.

I ignore the voices in my head, the ones that are telling me that none of this this is going to go away, that they won't ever stop searching for us and that hiding is futile and will become more and more difficult until in the end, I won't have any safe spaces left, and will either be caught or more humiliatingly, be forced to hand myself in. Ignoring that voice in my head is easier than addressing it because that would mean admitting defeat. And I won't do that. Gabriel would be returned to his feckless parents and then what would happen to him? The neglect would start all over again. After all the effort I've put in, all the love I've shown him, for that to happen is unthinkable. So I will go on with this campaign for as long as I can. I may have broken the law in taking him but as the wonderful Mr Charles Dickens once wrote, the law is an ass. We have to employ our instincts to override some ancient rules put in place many centuries ago that are outdated and no longer meaningful. That's what I have done and I have no regrets about it. I would do it again in a heartbeat, regardless of the consequences.

Cars pass us. Headlights behind, rear lights up ahead. An HGV rushes past, its engine a deafening roar, my vehicle swaying as we become caught up in its slipstream. Then the traffic thins out until we are the only people on the road. That reassures me. Nobody tailing us. No police sirens or flashing blue lights in my rear-view mirror. Once we're back in England, I will get us both to a place where we will be warm and dry and completely anonymous. Just me and Gabriel and nobody else.

I drive in silence for an hour before turning the radio back on. My body is tense as I listen. I expected the taking of Gabriel to make it onto the news, but it still takes me by surprise, knocking all the air out of my lungs when I hear my name being spoken out loud, our disappearance the headline story. Vibrations fill my head as I sit there listening, absorbing every little detail, bemused by what I hear. They've got it wrong; some of the specifics are incorrect. Important specifics. I'm mystified by this glaring error but don't spend too long dwelling on it. Lazy journalism, that's what it is. Besides, the greater the mistakes, the less chance they have of finding us. I hope their stories and descriptions are riddled with clumsy blunders and erroneous details.

*Cleveland Police also want to question Melissa Crawford about a hit and run incident that took place on Wilson Road. The victim, an eighty-four-year-old man, suffered serious injuries and is currently in hospital receiving treatment.*

I swallow saliva that has gathered in my throat. A clenched fist sits at the base of my gut. I switch to a different station, trying to dismiss their words, driving even faster, my foot pressed down hard on the pedal. I blink and rub at my eye to banish the tic that has taken hold there, humming softly to myself as I listen to an old, classic pop song, shaking all thoughts of what I've just heard, right out of my head.

# 31

## 1970

Only after the third phone call from the funeral home to request she pick him up did Nancy finally decide to collect Roger's ashes. It wasn't out of any sense of guilt for leaving it so long. Far from it. She had plans for his remains. He would not, even in death, dictate to her. Roger would baulk if he knew what lay ahead for his ashes. All the more reason to go ahead with it.

Melissa sat in the back of the car as they travelled to the funeral home, her face expressionless, George cooing contentedly in his seat. Nancy prayed that what took place, what her daughter witnessed and what she actually *did*, taking a blade to her own father, wouldn't leave any lasting damage because Nancy now knew that contusions and broken skin healed faster and more efficiently than bruised and dented feelings, and dark memories. Those things were embedded deep in the brain, and sometimes, they didn't mend at all. They stayed put, festering and multiplying, appearing uninvited at most inopportune of moments.

They pulled up outside the funeral home, Melissa slipping silently out of her seat. Nancy unfastened George, gently lifting him out, and took her daughter's hand, surprised at how cool and thin it was.

They stepped inside, Nancy hoping the person behind the desk wouldn't attempt to offer any hollow platitudes for her loss, and was relieved when Roger's ashes were handed over without any drama. She put them in the footwell of the car and they set off towards her planned destination. Roger's final resting place. The only place he deserved.

# 32

## MELISSA

Gabriel's cries force me to pull over into a service station. I had planned on driving through the night but after an hour or so, he stirs, the noise impossible to ignore. It irks me, having to stop, but something is clearly wrong, his shrieks evidence of something more than just hunger.

I pull up in a dark corner of the parking area and climb into the back with him, the heat emanating from him a sure sign that he isn't over his illness as I had hoped. My stomach drops. This I can do without. I don't have any medicine. Most of our things I left behind at the cottage, taking with me only the essentials. I thought Gabriel's fever was a thing of the past. This isn't the case at all. I feel as if dark forces are conspiring against me.

The service station looks well stocked. I'm certain they'll have what I need but after my previous experience, I'm reticent to go in there, fear of being recognised again, making me jittery.

I slide into the back of the car, lift Gabriel out of his seat and pluck a bottle of milk out of the few things I managed to salvage from our belongings. He turns his head away, refusing to latch on, and lets out a howl that makes my blood run cold. Even in the near darkness, I can see his ruddy complexion, his mottled cheeks and obvious distress. I want to weep. I want to weep and rage and scream that none of this is fair, but it's a waste of energy as it won't change a damn thing. It won't stop his crying and it won't rid him of this fever that just goes on and on and on. I fight back the tears and rub at my face, hoping ideas will present themselves. Ideas that will help ease his suffering and give me enough time to find somewhere for us both to stay. Somewhere warm and dry where nobody notices me. Somewhere with a decent supply of antibiotics to rid him of this infection. I know he needs medical attention; I *know* that. I'm not an idiot and I'm not cruel, keeping him from doctors and professionals who can ease his suffering, but what I am considered to be at this point is a criminal, my name and purported crime making national headline news.

I take a sharp breath, lift Gabriel out of the car and march into the service station. I'll take my chances. If the off-the-shelf medicine doesn't work, then I will take him to the nearest hospital. I'll face my fears and hope they don't have me on some kind of list. I could give them a false name. They're not going to deny treatment for an ill baby just because they can't find him on their computer system. A small voice nags at me that they can however, call the police or social services but I ignore that voice. I will just have to wait and see whether the painkillers help and if they do, then none of those worries will matter.

I squint against the sudden stark glare of the lighting, Gabriel nestled to my chest while I scan the shelves for that magical bottle of liquid that will make him better. Even if it only alleviates the fever for the next few hours I'll take it. A few hours is better than nothing. It's up on the top shelf next to a line of skin creams and unguents. I grab a bottle and keep my head dipped, avoiding cameras, attempting to be as unobtrusive as possible, then scoop a few items of food and a bottle of juice off the shelf into the basket and head to the counter where a sharp-featured young lad in his twenties is standing, watching me. My palms are clammy. He scans the items and with my free hand, I count out the required amount.

'No fuel?'

'No,' I snap, eager to get away.

His eyes appraise me before handing me my change and sitting back on his stool. I watch him in my peripheral vision as I leave, relieved to see no recognition in his expression, just a dull acceptance at having to do a thankless job in a lonely, soulless environment.

In the car, I give Gabriel the medicine and he takes a small amount of the milk. This gives me hope that this recurrence is just a blip, that everything is going to be okay. His temperature is still raging but he has quietened down. I sit with him for a few minutes, stroking his face, my fingers cradling his head and the back of his neck until he calms. Everything will change once we reach a place of relative safety: this transient way of life, continually shifting from town to town. I say relative because nowhere is completely safe. Not in the current climate. We are a couple of fugitives. Living this sort of life is nothing short of torture. It is not as portrayed in the movies. Plenty of worry and drama and angst without any of the added adrenaline and excitement. I long for a peaceful life, sedate surroundings where we can be ourselves, just me and my grandson. A place where we can wander freely without fear of being seen and recognised. I realise how implausible that sounds but if I don't have that thought in my head, something to aspire to and dream about, then why am I even doing this? There must be an end point to my endeavours, something to aim for, otherwise I may as well just give up, and at this moment in time, that is not something I am prepared to do.

We all have to fight for what is right in this world, for what we truly believe is the morally correct thing to do. This is my fight and Gabriel's welfare and happiness is the prize. It's not completely out of my reach. I just need to work a little harder to get it, that's all.

The small, still voice in my head continues to shout at me that I need to give up, that I will never win this one. I ignore it. It tells me that it's all over and they are closing in on us. I ignore those words too because life is brutal and if I allow him to be taken from me then my existence will be empty and the thought of that emptiness is terrifying. It stretches out ahead of me, a long, dark road without end. So, no, I will keep on with this, just me and Gabriel together until the bitter end.

# 33

## 1970

The car park was full, busier than she would have liked, but then what did she expect? It was the middle of the day, everyone working, people visiting patients. Nancy thought of all those doctors and nurses inside the large redbrick building: Roger's colleagues and friends, beavering away in the hospital. Listening to people's health issues. Attempting to cure them. She tried to imagine Roger sitting in his office, how he used to be; his soft voice lulling his patients into a comfortable sense of security as he assured them that they were in safe hands. The same hands that he regularly used to beat his wife senseless. If only they knew. She thought of them all now, mourning his absence, telling everyone what a wonderful, thoughtful physician he was. None of them knew the real Roger Fitzgerald, the monster that lurked beneath the surface. Nancy was the only one able to describe him in fine detail, stripping away the outer, shiny veneer that fooled almost everyone, to reveal the hateful, horrific man underneath. Nobody's death pleased her, but then Roger was no ordinary man, and she wasn't ashamed to admit that she was glad that he was dead.

Melissa sat in the back of the car, reading her comic book. George slept peacefully. The sight of their faces continually warmed her heart.

'I'll only be a few minutes, honey. You wait here. I'll lock the doors. You can see Mummy from where you are. I'm just going over to the main entrance.' Nancy pointed her long, slim finger towards the double doors. Melissa raised her eyes, scanned the area, and nodded approvingly.

The box of ashes was still heavy despite the fact she had scraped out a handful for use later at home. Nancy held it tightly, carefully. Not out of any sense of loyalty but because she didn't want it to fall. Not before he had been scattered in the correct place. The only place he deserved. Nancy didn't want him and neither was he worthy of being put anywhere green or peaceful. The people in this place were the ones who supported him, the same people who put their belief in a man long after it was proven he held no love or respect for his own family. A man who saw fit to hurt and maim his wife and ignore his own children. They were welcome to him.

Nancy climbed out of the car and closed the door behind her, locking it and giving her daughter a little wave. She glanced around, saw nobody was watching, then spat on the ashes before striding over to the main doors and scattering them on the bare concrete. For added effect and just because she could, she gave them a little kick, smearing them with her foot, grinding the particles with her heel. Then she headed inside, placed the empty box on the reception desk and left without uttering a single word. A printed label on the top of the box displayed Roger's details. She hoped one of his fawning colleagues would realise what she had done. It felt like a small victory but a worthy one. She had waited years for this comeback. It was her moment of glory. Would these people who worked alongside her beast of a husband realise why she had done what she had done? Probably not. Their allegiance was unswerving, each of them too terrified that their neat and carefully crafted house of cards would collapse around them should they ever be brave enough to face the truth that people like Roger – professional, middle-class individuals – were capable of such atrocities. That they could live two separate lives. It would terrify his colleagues if they were forced to delve deep inside their own hearts, minds and souls and realise that not only had they been lied to, but that they, intelligent, well-educated people had all been too dim and too adulatory in his presence to see beyond his ghastly charade. They should have dug deeper. They should have helped her. She hoped it was a lesson they would learn in order to better themselves, not just as physicians but as human beings.

* * *

The journey home passed without any mishaps. She felt lighter, the band of anxiety around her skull, loosening. She had just one thing left to do, a churlish thing for sure, but she wouldn't feel completely free until her dead husband was disposed of in a way that suited his lifestyle, a way that befitted how he had treated her and their children while he was alive.

Melissa played in the living room with her toys. George kicked about on the floor, his sister keeping a careful eye on him. Since Roger's death, Nancy had allowed her daughter to play wherever she wanted, encouraging her to dance and shout and clap and be as loud as she could be, to inject some laughter and fun and levity into their home. No more creeping around. No more moving through the place ghost-like. She was a child. The days of tiptoeing around, of salting themselves away, terrified of possible imagined slights and transgressions, were behind them. Only light and warmth ahead.

Nancy took the rest of Roger's ashes into the bathroom, tipped them into the toilet, then removed her trousers and underwear, sat down and urinated on them. She stood up and flushed, watching as the last of her husband's remains disappeared. A fitting end for a supposedly upstanding man who behind closed doors, committed the most heinous of crimes. He was where he belonged – in the sewers with the rest of the human waste.

# 34
## MELISSA

By the time we arrive in Whitby, the darkness is absolute. It's late and despair has set in as we pass row after row of *no vacancies* signs, each proudly displayed like a badge of honour, a proclamation of their busyness. In the back, Gabriel cries, his howls so raw I pull over at the side of the road to attend to him. Heat pulsates from his small body, hitting me in waves when I slide onto the back seat. Alarm bells go off in my head. I rummage around and give him yet more medicine and milk, then hold him close, rocking and whispering to him until he quietens down. I'm not sure I have the strength to do this any more. Everything appears to be stacked against me. All the odds of keeping Gabriel by my side, keeping him happy and healthy, are diminishing with every passing second. I have broad shoulders, but this is becoming awfully onerous and I'm buckling under the weight. With nowhere to stay for the night, I feel a pressure begin to build behind my eyes.

'I'm sorry, my love,' I say as I strap Gabriel in again and clamber back into the driver's seat, my body as heavy as stone. Fighting the burden of fatigue that sits in the dead centre of me is becoming harder and harder. I glance at my reflection in the rear-view mirror, wincing at my pale lined flesh and the dark rings that sit under my eyes. I no longer need a disguise. This journey, this whole fucking awful undertaking has stripped me of my usual identity. I look like a corpse, my hair dry and matted, my skin hanging like melted candle wax. 'Just another short drive and we'll settle down for the evening, I promise.'

I pull into a layby on the outskirts of Whitby. It's pitch black and so very cold but our chances of resting our heads on a soft pillow in a room somewhere close by are zero. We have fuel in the car, enough to allow me to leave the engine running so we can keep warm until first light. Then I will head elsewhere, find us somewhere safe and dry to stay.

The car seats fold down, leaving us a flat area in which to sleep. I place the baby chair in the well of the passenger seat and we use the blankets I had stored in the boot for covering the area where we'll sleep. I use my padded jacket as a mattress for Gabriel and cover him over, tucking him in after changing his nappy and giving him another dose of medicine and a tiny amount of milk. He is still hot and feverish and appears tired but aside from that, he is okay. Not great but at least we don't have a gun-wielding psychopath chasing us. A decent night's sleep and hopefully he will wake, alert and happy, having shaken this thing off once and for all.

My throat is dry and I'm hungry. I take a swig of juice and watch as Gabriel closes his eyes, his raspy breath an indicator that his breathing is regular. Once he is properly asleep, I climb out and squat in the bushes to pee. Not my finest or most dignified moment but my choices are limited. Come sunrise, we'll set off before anybody sees us and I'll let my head lead me to a place where we can find a room. Something will turn up. It always does.

* * *

My eyes are glued together, my thoughts muddled. Outside, the sun sits sluggishly on the horizon, its watery hue illuminating the pale sky. I blink, press the heel of my hands into my sockets and glance at my surroundings. It only takes a few seconds for my thoughts to come sharply into focus. Gabriel is lying beside me, his breathing a series of growls and crackles.

Sleep was fitful. My back and neck creak and groan, my joints are a collection of aches and pains when I sit up and stretch. Another brief glance in the rear-view mirror tells me that I look as haggard as I feel. Even worse than yesterday. I drag my fingers through my hair, knots snagging at my nails, and take another swig of lukewarm juice to clear the taste of stale morning breath that coats my gums and the roof of my mouth.

Outside, the road is deserted. Once again, I step out of the door and squat to relieve myself. Gabriel continues to sleep. It's almost 7 a.m. If he doesn't wake in the next half hour, then I'll have to pick him up and hope he stirs from his slumber. We need to get back on the road before any passers-by notice us.

I move about, gathering up blankets, making plenty of noise, hoping it rouses him. I listen to his laboured breathing, my ears attuned to every gasp and rattle in his chest, the intensity and harshness of it scaring me. It isn't normal, that level of rumbling, the rapidity of it. He needs help. He needs more attention than I am able to give him. That thought disturbs and frightens me.

Once again, Stuart punctures my thoughts. I can hear his voice, coaxing me, trying to reassure me, telling me that I need to do something. No more inactivity. No more sitting around, waiting for things to miraculously improve. No more burying my head in the sand, pretending the bad things are going to disappear. They never leave. Ever.

Images of injured, elderly men fill my mind. Guns, car crashes. And blood. So much blood. Thick, glutinous smears, streaking across cold, hard surfaces, faces of the injured and the dead contorted in terror. Then their bodies turning cold, their flesh mottled and grey as death takes hold and does its thing.

The distant roar of an engine cuts into those unwanted visions. The tight ribbon of anxiety around my head loosens a fraction. I turn away as an HGV thunders past. It will be the first of many. We need to get moving, although where to is anybody's guess.

Beside me, Gabriel begins to stir, his eyes flickering. His skin is pallid, his lips dry and cracked. His breathing is deteriorating. The earlier rumble is now a wheezing gasp, his chest pulsing as he tries to get more oxygen into his lungs. Fear stabs at me, pinpricks of terror needling their way deep into my scalp.

I pick him up, holding him close to my shoulder. His clothes are damp with sweat, his head and skin hot to the touch. I grapple round for more medicine, knowing it's futile. A tiny drop of over-the-counter medication isn't going to help against this raging infection. I'm swimming against the tide. A tsunami that is going to swallow us both whole.

With my free hand, I raise the back seats, throwing blankets and bags out of the way.

'You wait here, little one, while I rearrange your seat. We're going to make you well again.'

Against my better judgement, against everything I had planned for us – our new life, our solitary existence – I decide that I'm going to have to take him to the nearest hospital, hoping I haven't left it too late. If anything happens to Gabriel, I will only have myself to blame. I've been selfish because of my fear of being recognised. He needs help. Sickness swills in my gut. No wig, no make-up. Just the face I was born with. The same face that is barely recognisable as me. Worry, fatigue and living like a vagrant have done enough damage to hopefully ward off anybody noticing or recognising me.

Without any resistance, his weakened body too frail to cry out, he watches me helplessly as I strap him in once more. I slide into the front seat and drive towards the hospital in Whitby, my heart being squeezed by an iron fist.

Less than four minutes. That's how long it takes us to arrive, my eyes misted with tears as I swing the car into a parking space. I unstrap Gabriel and carry him inside, his body heavy with exhaustion. I march to the reception desk and bark out a command.

'He's ill. My grandson is ill. He's hot and he can't breathe properly. We need to see somebody straightaway.'

The man behind the desk scrutinises me, suspicion carved into every crease and groove of his face. Perspiration has stained my jacket and I probably smell dreadful.

'Okay, if I can just take some details.'

'He needs to see a doctor right now!' His flippant manner and lack of urgency sets off a fire inside me. Fingers of ice creep up and down my spine as I glance at Gabriel, his pained expression and glassy eyes tearing at my soul.

'We just need to take a few details and a doctor will be with you as soon as possible.'

As if suddenly alerted to the situation, Gabriel lets out a hacking cough and vomits, regurgitating a fountain of viscous yellow fluid that lands on the desk between us. He follows it with a prolonged, high-pitched shriek that turns heads in our direction.

They appear out of nowhere, the team of bodies that descend, and before I can protest, we are bustled away to a side room. Gabriel is lifted from my arms as a medical professional examines his chest, listening with a stethoscope, her face giving nothing away.

I stand and watch, my limbs watery with dread. I shouldn't have come here. Now the questions will begin. The police will be called, a team of social workers will descend and they will snatch my grandson from me. Fear unfurls itself in my abdomen, stretching and reaching out, its dark tentacles slipping inside my veins. They're going to take him from me, I can see it in her expression. I can't let that happen. Gabriel is mine. He's all I have.

I step forward and shout at the doctor. 'We have an appointment in town. Can we have some antibiotics and then we can get going. I don't want to be late.'

She turns and glares at me, her lips puckered in annoyance. 'How long has he had these symptoms for?'

The walls close in. I can't breathe properly. They're going to do it; they're actually going to try and keep him. Visions of George pierce my brain: the feel of him after I gently picked him up off the floor. My mother's battered and broken body, unconscious at my feet. And then my father, that look on his face, the terror I felt as I watched him stride towards me, his eyes flicking between me and my baby brother. Then that final expression when he realised what he had done, that he had hurt George, knocked him out of my mother's arms. That there was no going back. He could have killed him. For the first time in my life, I stared at him, holding his gaze until he turned away, an expression in his eyes that I couldn't fathom. Perhaps it was fear. Or perhaps it was shock because I had dared to challenge his authority by meeting his dark-eyed stare and refusing to break contact. And then I remember what I did before he left the house for the final time. I can still feel the bulk of the knife, the gleam of the blade. The satisfying swish as it slid across his flesh. I wanted to drive it in, to end it there and then, but didn't possess the physical strength to do it. He was going to kill my mother and I couldn't stand by and do nothing, but in the end I did what I could and it was enough. And all the while, George lay on the stair, blissfully unaware that our mother was only seconds away from death. I spent the rest of my life protecting my brother, right up until he stepped on that plane with his wife and children. I'll do the same for my grandson. It's who I am. A carer. A protector. A grandmother.

'He just needs some antibiotics, that's all.' My voice sounds ethereal. It doesn't belong to me. I'm operating on autopilot, my reflexes taking over.

My usual reserved demeanour is absent as I rush past her and grab Gabriel, his hot, little body pressed against mine when I snatch him out of her arms. She's going to keep him. I can sense it. Any sound he makes as I grab him back is drowned out by the voices of the doctor and nurses shouting at me to put him down, that he is very ill and needs to be admitted to hospital.

I run out of the main doors and into the parking area. A sob erupts out of my chest. I can hear them calling after me as they spill out of the exit in an attempt to catch me.

I don't strap Gabriel into his chair. There isn't time. I lay him on the front seat and push my jacket up against him to stop him falling, then manoeuvre my vehicle out of the car park and out onto the main road, pressing my foot down hard on the accelerator, desperate to leave all the unwanted attention and the accompanying melee behind.

# 35

## MELISSA

He doesn't scream or cry and, I don't know which is worse – his usual croaky, ear-shattering howling or this dreadful, haunting silence. I'm not comfortable with what I did. Leaving the hospital, denying him the care that he clearly needs. But I panicked, allowing my emotions to overrule all logic, and now my grandson is seriously ill and I have no proper medicine for him. No antibiotics. Not a damn thing. And I don't know what to do next.

I find a quiet, secluded spot and pull over, lifting Gabriel carefully back into his seat. I lean forwards and kiss his cheek. He gives me a half smile and I pray that his fever is breaking. At some point, he has to get better. Children pick up all types of bugs and viruses. They all recover eventually. Don't they?

Convincing myself that everything is going to be okay, because the alternative is too dreadful to consider, I set off again, driving slowly, scouring the nearby area for anything resembling a café or a B&B. We pass through a quiet village and I spot a sign next to a small, white building. It's a community centre set back from the main road, and a board set out on the pavement states that they're holding a coffee morning. We could lose ourselves in there, use the local amenities and buy some refreshments without anybody bothering us. It doesn't look overly busy. In fact, a quick glance at the car park tells me it's almost empty. We're early. I could use the baby changing area to clean and change Gabriel and then I can feed him and buy myself a coffee. These sorts of places are usually run by volunteers who will be too busy making and serving food and drinks to notice or care about us. We'll be anonymous in their midst, drifting in and then leaving soon afterwards, refreshed and restocked with supplies.

With few or no guesthouses around, our choices are limited. This may be the closest thing we will come to having some home comforts for the next few hours. It's a risk, but one I'm willing to take simply because I don't know what else to do or where to go.

I lift Gabriel out of the car. He is still hot and tired. My heart aches for him. All I ever wanted, all I *still* want, is for him to be happy and healthy. I've failed in so many ways. Fighting back tears, I carry him inside and look around at a large hall that is devoid of people. Tables adorned with white tablecloths are set up at the back, but the place is empty.

'Ah, I'm sorry, we don't open for another forty-five minutes.'

I spin around at the sound of the voice behind me and am transported back in time when I see him standing there.

'Moussa?'

His eyes cloud over in confusion before crinkling at the corners as he smiles at me. 'Mrs Crawford?' He sneaks a glance at Gabriel, then stares at me, an anxious look on his face. 'Everything okay? What you doin' here?'

I shrug my shoulders and slump into the nearest chair, Gabriel's cheek close to mine. The wooden seat groans under my weight.

'I could ask the same of you. What brings you to this part of North Yorkshire?'

He smiles and shoves his hands in his pockets. 'My aunt helps run this centre. I still live in Stockton but I can drive now and am insured for my mum's car, so here I am.'

My heart swells for him. An ex-pupil who came so close to throwing away his future by hanging out with the wrong people, being lured into troublesome situations, and having skirmishes with the police. And now here he is, helping at a community centre, serving coffee and cake with his aunt. A lump is wedged in my throat. I needed this moment to show me that life sometimes does reward those who are prepared to work hard to achieve their goals. Not all dreams are destined to end in pieces.

'That is so wonderful to hear. So how are you getting on now, Moussa? And how is your brother?'

He smiles at me, such joy stemming from him. It's like he doesn't have a care in the world, like his life hasn't been a path that has been littered with complications and difficulties. I recall his mother falling ill and he and his brother being taken into care. And now his aunt is here, living with them in this country and he has matured into a caring young man. I swallow down tears.

'Oh, I'm really good, Mrs Crawford. I help out here a few days a week and I'm doing a course at college as well. Learning how to be a plumber an' all that.'

'That's brilliant, Moussa. So good to hear. And what about Seydou? Is he okay?'

He rolls his eyes and sighs. 'Ah, y'know what he's like. Our mum, she said if he don't pull his socks up and get a job, she gonna send him to live with our uncle in Dabou.'

'He'll pull himself round,' I say quietly, still marvelling at how much this young man has matured, how big and strong and polite he is. The same young man who refused to pick up a pencil almost every day for the two years that I taught him. The same young man who swore at staff and ripped down wall displays if he was asked to open a textbook. All he needed was love and security and a chance to flourish. And now here he is, sitting opposite me, holding a conversation, looking at the world through adult eyes and comprehending it all with a mellowed, measured brain. Only a few years ago, all of this seemed out of his reach.

He places his hands together, pressing them onto his knees. His feet tap out a nervous rhythm on the tiled floor, the sound echoing around us. He turns and gives me a worried, sideways glance. I can feel the heat from his body. Even now, he still holds me in some sort of high regard, as if I am always going to be his favourite teacher, the person he went to when the world seemed to be set against him. The person who listened and cared. And I did. Still do.

'I saw you on the television, Mrs Crawford.' The tapping on the floor grows louder. His voice when he speaks is husky and close to breaking. 'Your photo was on the news.' He glimpses at Gabriel then back at me. 'That baby – it ain't yours, is it?'

I wait a couple of seconds before replying, a thousand horses galloping through my body, stampeding across my chest, making it almost impossible for me to speak. My voice is reedy when I do finally find the strength to reply.

'Sometimes, Moussa, doing the wrong thing can feel like the right thing at the time. Do you know what I mean?'

I watch him closely. He isn't smiling any more but he nods and I can see that he understands what it is I am implying. His rigid posture has softened and his loud, rhythmic tapping dulls, the sound less abrasive, melodic even.

'But even so,' he says, his head lowered as if he is suddenly too embarrassed to look at me, 'it's somebody else's baby, Mrs Crawford. You need to give it back. His mum will be worried an' all that. It ain't right. And I know you're a big believer of doin' the right thing. That was what you taught me. You remember?'

I do remember. I also recall telling him that sometimes, principles trump everything; that on occasion, we must stand alone when we do something we believe to be correct, because not everyone has walked in our shoes or seen the world through our eyes. Experience shapes our desires and values and beliefs. It shaped me.

He reaches into his pocket and places his phone on the bench next to where I'm seated.

'You do know that Gabriel is my grandson, don't you, Moussa? I didn't just steal a random baby off the street.'

He looks at me, confusion creasing his brow, and with every passing second, I can see that already, our once strong bond is slackening, the fine threads of it fraying and unravelling.

'His mum and da are really worried. They didn't give you permission to take him, Mrs Crawford. I think maybe we need to call somebody, let them know where you are and that the baby is safe an' all that.'

I nod. He is trying to do the right thing. I should be proud of this young man. He is now trying to get me to do the right thing as well, repeating everything I taught him verbatim.

'You're right.' I sigh and give him a sorrowful smile. 'I'll need to use your phone, if that's okay, Moussa? I'll give them a call, tell them where I am and that they can come and collect him.'

He swings his whole body around to look at me. His eyes are wide and he is nodding, his grin lighting up his handsome, young face.

'That's all I wanted to hear. I think that would definitely be the right thing to do. You just need to swipe it to the right. There ain't no code.'

I give him a long, hard stare and raise my eyebrows.

'I know, I know. Stupid to be so lax, ain't I. I'll put one in once you're done with it, I promise.'

I pick up the phone and stare at it. Something inside me stirs, a jerking sensation deep down in my stomach. 'If you wouldn't mind, Moussa, I'd rather make this call alone. I'm going to ring my husband, tell him where I am. You're absolutely right; doing the correct thing is always the best course of action.'

His voice lifts, relief apparent in his eyes, the way they lighten and sparkle as he watches me closely. 'Well, you should know, Mrs Crawford. You was the one who taught me that rule.' He stands up and looks as if he has grown a couple more inches in the last few minutes. 'Tell you what, I'll go and make us a drink in the kitchen while you make the call. Will a weak coffee do you? We ain't got too many cakes to spare as they're all going to be sold later on when we open up, but I do know we got plenty of coffee and milk.'

'Ah, that would be perfect. White, no sugar,' I say, trying to emulate his happiness and relief. Trying to end our conversation on a high.

'Right. Well, I'll leave you to it.' He begins to walk away then turns to face me, his rubber-soled shoes squeaking on the tiled floor. 'I'm glad we had this chat today, Mrs Crawford. It's been really good seeing you again. And I suppose maybe he does look a bit like you. The baby, that is. I didn't know he was your grandson and I'm not that good with little ones or nothing like that – I mean, I like 'em and everything but I can see he's got the same colour eyes as you.'

'Thank you, Moussa,' I whisper, guilt for what I am about to do filtering into my bloodstream and clogging up my veins. 'Thank you for being here and for being so calm and understanding.'

*And not calling the police.*

He flashes me another smile, nods, and then carried along by a wave of relief, he all but dances into the kitchen and closes the door.

Gabriel is still cuddled into my chest, his wheezing dulling the euphoria I feel at what I am about to do. I push Moussa's phone away from me, stand and walk over to collect the long broom from the far corner of the room, then as quietly as I can, I slide the wooden shaft of it between the handles of the double doors of the kitchen where Moussa is currently making my coffee. I whisper an apology to the boy who came close to leading a lawless existence and to the man he is now: the young man who made all the right choices in life, then I head out of the building into the soft, morning breeze.

# 36

## MELISSA

I need to leave Whitby and the surrounding areas. I need to leave North Yorkshire. Once Moussa manages to get out of the kitchen, he'll call the police and they will close in on me. I hope he understands why I did what I did. Keeping Gabriel by my side is my main aim in life. He may not be as healthy as he should be, but this time in our lives will surely pass. Once he is better, we can make a fresh start, be the people I always dreamed we would be.

I can't go back to Stockton-on-Tees. Far too risky. The place will be on red alert, everyone on the lookout for us. And I can't stay here. Even if Moussa doesn't call the police, then the hospital will have surely alerted them. I can't go back to Scotland either. The death of the owner of the cottage will be headline news, his link to the cottage under investigation which will in turn lead them to me. I refuse to wonder what happened to the gunman. I refuse to expend what little energy I have focusing on his whereabouts, whether he ever found that weapon and whether Jason lived or died. My focus remains firmly on me and Gabriel, finding somewhere we can hide out. I'm being hemmed in on all sides, events pushing me into a corner. My safe place is no longer safe and going back to my home is out of the question.

My fingers are cold as I drive, Gabriel's rasps filling me with dread while I stare at the road ahead. I peer at the sky, begging God for help. Just a chance for my grandson to get better, for this fever to lift. That's all I want. If he grants me this one thing, I will never ask for anything ever again. I'm an independent, self-sufficient woman. I've had a life full of ups and downs. A life beset by trauma. More than my fair share. But I'm not going to wallow in self-pity. Life is short. We need to take opportunities wherever and whenever we can. I took mine, travelling down a road strewn with bumps, potholes and dead-ends. And I haven't given up. Not yet. I'm still here, putting in the effort and the miles, doing what I can to make a success of it.

The next half hour is a blur. I hear sirens everywhere and nowhere, and see lights flashing in the distance, a spread of blue across the horizon as they grow closer, giving chase and trying to catch me. I blink and then they're gone. I take a deep, rattling breath, blink again, and they're back. By the time I reach Guisborough, I am doubting my own senses and questioning my state of mind.

I take the bypass road, avoiding the probing eyes of high-street shoppers, all the while aware I'm getting closer and closer to places I should be actively avoiding. This wasn't and still isn't, my intention but with nowhere else to go, I find myself being drawn towards old, familiar haunts. I'm like a homing pigeon, always returning to the place where I spent most of my life. The place I should be circumventing. I hope that the police are still out in the wilds of Scotland or lining up along the coast near Whitby and not here searching for me.

My foot is almost flat to the floor. I'm going too fast but can't seem to control anything any more. Even above the sound of the engine, I can hear Gabriel. His breathing is a rasp, his chest rattling and rumbling. He's struggling to breathe.

I suppress a sob. I'm beyond weeping, my emotions in tatters. There has to be an end to this situation, I just can't envisage what it looks like. I'm bouncing from one catastrophe to another without any breathing space in between.

We reach the roundabout and I brake too late, the wheels screeching on the tarmac. I'm acutely aware of my low mood and reckless driving. I'm aware that I need to curb my behaviour, if not for me then for Gabriel's sake. I'm allowing anger and exasperation to guide my thinking. I take a few deep breaths and drum my fingers on the steering wheel while I wait for the traffic to start moving again. I cast my mind back to the past, my brain firmly secured in that period of my life. My father's face has taken root in my mind as I slip the car into gear and drive.

* * *

I have no recollection of getting here, but find myself parked up in front of my childhood home on Daisy Lane. Thoughts bulldoze their way through my brain as I sit, staring at the house, dark images becoming snarled together. A pain takes hold in my breastbone. I place my hand there and stare at the house, all those old fears and that sense of dread returning. Even after my father left, I couldn't summon up feelings of happiness. Constant fears of George being hurt in some way stayed with me. My father's presence hid around every corner, springing out on me every time I stepped into a room. He never left. Not really. Even in death, he was overbearing, taking up space in my head, visiting me in my dreams. His friends and colleagues remained faithful to his memory, leaving me, my brother and my mother very much alone.

I take a long, stuttering breath and stare at it. The house on Daisy Lane. Such a misleading name. When I first met Stuart and told him where I had lived as a youngster, he said it made him think of a contented area, a road filled with flowers and happiness. A house filled with love. How wrong he was. It was the place where I was born, the place my father left after I took a knife to him. A place of terror and violence.

A line of white noise sizzles in my ears as I scrutinise the outside of the house with its freshly painted shutters and carefully manicured front lawn. New windows and doors have changed the appearance of the exterior but sitting here looking at it still gives me a chill. It's immaculate. My father also kept the outside pristine. A beautiful, well-kept house does not make a beautiful, happy home. Those things don't go hand in hand. 12 Daisy Lane held toxins within. It had a rotten heart with poison at its core and as I sit here studying it, I only hope that the current owners have managed to shake off any residual memories that may have clung to the walls, corroding the bricks and plaster and eating away at their lives. I pray that misery and terror can be cast out with love and tenderness. My mother, George and I lived here for a few years after my father died and we tried to make it work, but shadows lurked, memories pricking at us. The house was sold and we moved a couple of miles away to a neighbouring town to a house that became a home. Our home. A place free of darkness. A place filled with love and laughter, and the endless chatter of contented children; the same sounds we were too fearful to make at Daisy Lane.

After marrying Stuart, I began to realise that he would never be able to comprehend what me and my mother had been through. That was partly our undoing, the point at which our marriage began to crumble – his lack of concern and the fact he was bereft of care and compassion. After my mother died in a care home, her mind paralysed by dementia, I also lost a part of me. George was already making plans to emigrate and I felt as if I had been cut adrift. The one woman who knew what it was like to live with a monster, the only woman who understood me, had gone. My mother's death rendered me a middle-aged orphan and that was when I realised that I had missed having a father. Not my father. A decent, loving father capable of affection. One that hugged me, sat me on his knee and read bedtime stories to me. A father who loved me and actually wanted me in his life.

I think of Stuart and our son, Robin; how Stuart used to bathe him, give him supper, then tuck him in bed at night, the two of them whispering and giggling as Stuart turned the pages of Robin's favourite book. I swallow and rub at my face. And then the tears come.

The sound of sirens drags me back to the present. I slink further down into my seat, glancing behind me, relieved to see that Gabriel is asleep. His breathing is still a deep, gravelly rasp. The worst isn't over just yet. It never is.

For the final time, I cast my eyes over the house in Daisy Lane. The telephone box where my mother made that call is no longer there. I still see that phone box in my dreams, the image of it so real that I wake, convinced I am there, standing outside, peering into George's pram while my mother made the call. The call that set off a chain of unforgettable events.

People come and go in the street, filing in and out of their houses, getting into their vehicles, unloading bags of shopping, chatting with neighbours. I don't recognise any of them. Everyone from that era has moved on, sold up and left the area, or died. Except for one. David Griffiths from number thirty-six, the man who spied on my mother. The man who told my father about her using the public payphone. Now an old man in his late nineties, he still resides at the same house. I know because I have kept a close eye on him for all these years. What he did that day was despicable. Was it really idle chatter on his part, or was it something more sinister that drove him to speak to my father and tell him that my mother was doing something out of the ordinary and calling somebody from a phone box? I recall that he and my father spoke often, my father the perfectly mannered, genteel man as he mowed lawns and dug weeds, the pair of them tending to their gardens like normal people when all the while, demons danced in my father's head. Did they have common ground, he and my dad, David Griffiths also doing unspeakable things to his own family once the doors were closed and the curtains drawn?

I sigh and wipe away tears with my sleeve, and then stop, a pocket of air compressed in my chest. A young woman is leaving David's house. A carer or a nurse, her blue clinical outfit incongruous against the white picket fences and freshly mown lawns. She climbs into a vehicle, sits for a few seconds, head dipped as she writes some notes, then pulls on a seatbelt and leaves. Anticipation and anger bubble in my gut. This could be my chance to tell David Griffiths what I really think of him. We were leaving anyway, my mother's plans for our escape already in motion. All David did was speed them up and bring about another beating for my mother that resulted in George being knocked out of her arms. He could have died that day. It was sheer luck that he wasn't seriously injured, or worse still, killed. Had it not been for me grabbing that knife, my mother would also have died.

The road is empty once again. I get out of the car, unstrap Gabriel and march up to David's door, rapping against it as hard as I can, the effort sending small ripples of pain through my hand.

Seconds pass with no movement inside. I count them,

wondering about his current condition, wondering if he is too frail to answer, perhaps even bedridden. I am about to give up hope of ever seeing him again, to turn tail and get back into my vehicle, when the door is opened and there he stands: an elderly and barely recognisable David Griffiths. Trails of silver, wispy hair lie atop a shiny, bald pate. His skin is almost translucent and speckled with liver spots. Grey, rheumy eyes sweep over my face. He doesn't recognise me. That's no surprise. I was a child when we moved from this road. A child when I attacked my father with a knife to try and stop him from strangling my mother. She would have died that day had I not intervened. All because this man let his tongue run loose, telling tales and poking his nose into other people's business.

'Hello, David. Can I come in and speak with you, please?'

Without waiting for a reply, I push past him, closing the door and marching through the hallway into the kitchen. His house is a mirror image of the one in which I grew up. His face shows surprise but no fear. He uses a walking frame, following me, his feet shuffling along the long, carpeted entrance hall, stopping at the door to speak.

'I don't keep any money in the house and I don't want to buy anything.'

'That's good,' I say over my shoulder, 'because I'm not selling anything.' I attempt a smile but feel such hatred for this man that it rapidly fades, morphing into a grimace.

I sit down at his old pine table, Gabriel huddled close to me, and look around at the dated kitchen units and small, old-fashioned tiles.

'Then what do you want and why are you here? Did the nursing agency send you because I've spoken to them about that last one who—'

'I'm not a nurse. I haven't come here to take your blood pressure or wash you or dress your sores.'

*Thank God.*

I glance down at Gabriel and look up again at him, raising my eyebrows as I speak. 'I'm not here for any of those things.'

'Then what do you want?' he asks, his voice a near whisper. 'Who are you and why are you in my house?'

# 37

## MELISSA

The expression on his face shows no signs of sorrow or remorse, but I can see that there is a flicker of fear in his eyes. He doesn't trust me. He is right not to have any faith in me. I'm angry. Resentful. He is elderly and in poor health. Anything could happen. Anything at all.

'I don't remember much about that time.' His voice is feeble, no longer the strong, powerful man he once was. The voice and body of a very sick and fragile person. He looks away and leans back in his chair, the padded cushions behind him almost swallowing his stick-thin body.

'Really? I do and I was much younger than you. How odd. Maybe you're choosing to not remember?'

His face reddens, colour spreading over his pale cheeks. He attempts to stand up but flops back into the chair, unable to put up a fight, exhausted by the sudden exertion.

'I barely remember speaking to your father that day. It was a passing comment. Nothing more, nothing less. I knew you had a house phone and thought that perhaps it was broken.'

'That passing comment almost killed my mother. My baby

brother was injured. Have you any idea how damaging your *passing comment* was? Your interference could have wrecked our lives.' I spit the words out, my heart hammering in my chest. 'But in the end, you did us a favour. Your friend, the man who beat my mother senseless day after day, killed himself and we were all better off without him.' I'm snarling now, my mouth twisted with malice, each word designed to maim.

He heaves a sigh, each breath he takes a huge effort, his chest convulsing beneath his clothing. I should feel sorry for him and yet I don't. As old and weak as he is, I feel nothing but contempt and loathing for this man. What would have become of me had I not grabbed that knife? My mother would have died and George and I would have had to spend the rest of our childhood with a man who would have turned his violence on us. A cold, unfeeling man who didn't even like his own children.

'Why speak to my father about it anyway? Why not ask my mother? She was the one using the damn phone!' I can hardly breathe. I should leave, let it all go now I've had my say but something is driving me on, making me unpick his argument until the hole in his story is so big, it can bend light.

He doesn't reply, his chest suddenly deflating, his eyes cast downwards. He looks so small. So insignificant, as if a strong gust of wind would blow him away. Just as tiny pinpricks of pity start to puncture my skin, he looks up and our eyes lock in combat. His voice is a hiss when he speaks, his tongue running over his wet lips in a repulsive, snake-like movement, a predatory reptile about to strike.

'Nobody believed your mother's story. Nobody! Your father was a decent man. A good doctor and well-liked round these parts. What happened to him was a tragedy. Now you need to leave my house before I call the police. Go on, get out. Get out!'

He pulls himself upright and I feel all the blood drain from my face as I digest what he has just said. Him as well. All my father's colleagues and friends, all of them sticking together, ignoring my mother's bruises, her battered body and broken mind. I picture myself placing Gabriel on the sofa before marching towards this man and pushing him back down onto his chair while I hold a cushion over his face. He is too sick and infirm to put up a fight or try and stop me. I could do it with minimal effort. I can almost feel the tremble in my arms as I press hard and hold it in place until his lungs are devoid of oxygen. But I don't do such a thing because unlike my father, I am not a monster. Instead, I stand and carry a sleeping Gabriel towards the kitchen door, then turn and face him.

'You are a disgrace, David Griffiths. A despicable man. You're as bad as my father, condoning what he did and blaming an innocent woman. Shame on you, you lying, deceitful bastard. Shame on you.'

Fifty years of hatred spills out of me as I lift my hand and sweep it across the shelf next to where I stand, ornaments and a collection of glass bottles falling to the floor and smashing. The fragments scatter across the kitchen and hallway and even though I know he is too ill to clean them up, I feel no guilt. I want to kick the table over and wreck his house. I want to push him to the floor and watch him struggle and suffer. It's clear he knew my father for what he was, and even if he didn't, all these years later with the facts of that day now fully available, he still doesn't care.

Without waiting for a reply or even glancing at his face to see his expression, I leave the house, get into my car, and drive away, leaving his house and this hideous road behind me, never to return.

# 38

## MELISSA

I think perhaps that deep down, I always knew where I was going to end up. I'm laying old ghosts to rest, trying to come to terms with my fractured past by piecing together a new future. I could have gone anywhere after leaving Scotland but I didn't. I came back here, pulled by an invisible force that is dragging me closer and closer to a painful period of my life.

The graveyard was empty when I landed, the police unaware of the strength of the invisible cord that will always keep me by my mother's side. I knelt by her grave and told her how I had tried to speak to David Griffiths, to let him know how wrong he was. And to tell her that he was blind to what he had done. I also said my goodbyes because it may be some time before I am able to visit again. It's coming to an end; I know it for sure. Gabriel is ill and I have gravitated back to the north east. None of what I had planned has worked. My attempts to save Gabriel have failed. I am not about to hand myself in to the local police station. Not just yet. I'll cling onto hope for as long as I can. And when all hope is gone, then I'll know that it's time to stop. I have no idea what lies in store for me after I take that step but whatever it is, it cannot be as bad as what I've already been through. I've lived a hundred lifetimes, endured the best and worst of times, and survived. Another day, week or month of misery won't make any difference.

I stop at the top of Saltburn Bank to take in the view of the raging sea and distant horizon, before heading down and taking a right onto Saltburn Road and winding my way back up to the top of the cliffs, taking a left turn towards the old coastguard cottages. This is where my father parked his car all those years ago. This is the exact route he took after realising that he had taken things too far, that his own daughter hated him as much as he hated her. He was weak. A coward. My father did what he did to avoid losing his reputation. He didn't do it because he was sorry or wracked with guilt. He did it because he was too cowardly to face up to the consequences of his actions that day, the fact he injured his own baby and almost killed his wife. He did it because he was too frightened and embarrassed to go to prison. I hate him for that. I hate him for escaping without being brought to justice, his atrocious actions pored over by a jury, the details of his violence printed in every newspaper. At least by doing what he did, my mother and I didn't have to spend years dreading his release from jail. No appeals, or desperate pleas for parole. No worrying ourselves sick as the years passed that he would one day be free and able to come looking for us, ensuring our lives of torture could start all over again. The end of his life was the beginning of ours. We were finally free. Just me, my mother and George. Aunt Hayley visited often as she could, as did Jeanette Whitcome. She stayed by my mother's side for many years and after Mother's passing, attended her funeral, where she read out the most beautiful eulogy, moving most to tears with her carefully crafted words of wisdom that outlined my mother's dignified life. A life that for many years, was filled with terror but thankfully ended with love.

The road comes to a halt as I reach the row of cottages, the tarmac narrowing to an uneven path. We will have to take it on foot from here. I lift Gabriel out and grab a bag full of his things. He needs feeding and soon he will need changing again. It's a never-ending process, looking after a baby. Harder than I imagined, our time together charged with problems and difficulties.

We set off along the track that forms part of the Cleveland Way, a 100-mile route that stretches from Helmsley to Filey. It has been well trodden over the years by ramblers and members of the public. It was well trodden that day by my father. I wonder what was going through his mind as he made his way to the cliff edge? We weren't that well acquainted when he was alive, his dislike of me obvious. Trying to delve inside his head now he is dead isn't an easy or pleasant task. I have no idea what drove him to do any of the things he did. He was a damaged man. A heinous individual. The hatred I had for him used to burn bright in me but has dulled over the years, now reduced to no more than a flickering flame. He isn't worth it. Keeping raging hatred and malice alive within oneself is exhausting. It's a soul-destroying pastime, allowing it to rule one's life. It damaged my marriage, my inability to let it all go, to put it behind me and try to focus on the future. The time has come to extinguish that flickering flame once and for all.

Behind me, I hear a voice. I stop, my skin prickling as I tense my body. The voice grows louder, the icy wind carrying it towards me.

'Hello?'

A female voice. Loud. Powerful. Designed to make me stop. My instinct tells me to ignore it. I don't. Why draw more unwanted attention to myself? So I turn, Gabriel tucked tight against my body, and see her standing there, arms wrapped around her midriff for protection against the strong gusts that buffet us. I guess she is mid-thirties. She is tall and dressed in black leggings and a beige sweater that comes down to her knees. Long dark strands of hair blow around her face.

I remain silent. Nothing to say. I didn't come here to make conversation with a stranger. I came to be alone.

'Excuse me, I saw you pass by my house and wanted to catch you before you go any further along the path.'

I widen my eyes and shrug my shoulders, willing her to leave me be. That's all I ask, to be left alone.

'It's just that the path is really uneven and I was thinking that carrying a baby might prove to be a bit difficult.'

I say nothing, my silence prompting further explanations.

'I live in one of the old coastguard cottages. I know the track pretty well. I'm not sure if you're aware, but part of the cliff crumbled away recently. It can be really unstable and this wind is meant to strengthen even more in the next few hours.'

She glances at Gabriel, her eyes fixed on him with a steely glare as if to emphasise her point, before shifting her gaze back to me.

'We're fine,' I say lightly, standing up straight, trying to project an air of bravery. 'I also know this track really well. Trust me, we'll both be fine.'

She stands, arms still tucked around her body. The way she is watching me, the way her eyes are tapered, her mouth set in a thin line, there is something. I count the seconds, waiting for something. Anything. And then it comes, the rush of her words knocking me off balance.

'You're her, aren't you? You're that lady off the television.'

My heartbeat pounds in my ears. I can feel it in my throat, a low pulse that climbs up into my gullet, choking me.

I take a long, irregular breath, shake my head, and turn away, my pace steady and brisk. I look behind me, relieved she isn't following. She is just a figure in the distance, the wind pushing against her slim frame, her hair fanning out in the strong breeze like seaweed fronds.

Gabriel feels solid and weighty in my arms. I stop, hoisting him further up on my hip, then set off once more. The wind picks up speed, growing more powerful the closer we get to the cliff edge. Huge waves roll in below us, crashing against the rocks with astonishing ferocity. She was right about one thing – I will need to be careful up here. The path is taking us close to the edge. I say path. It's more of a muddy track. A well-worn route fit only for experienced walkers. It's true what she said about it not being a suitable place for babies or people like me who are not equipped with the correct walking boots or footwear. And yet here I am, tracing my father's footsteps, wondering where he finally came to a standstill. Wondering how long it took for him to step forwards and peer down. Did he apologise for being such a bastard and make his peace with the world before he leapt to his death? Or did he simply think nothing, his mind empty of sorrow and regret and the other emotions that make us human, the fear of a possible prison sentence driving him on and directing his movements? I am inclined to think the latter. I may not have known him as other children knew their fathers but I knew of what he did. How cruel he was to his family. How distant and judgemental he could be. Men like Roger Fitzgerald aren't capable of feeling grief or shame, and are especially impotent when it comes to feeling guilt for their crimes.

I shiver and snuggle Gabriel closer in to me. Cool, damp air nudges its way beneath my collar. Sea spray splatters my skin and settles on the earth around us, wet and oily, making it even more difficult to keep a firm footing. Gabriel babbles and wheezes in my arms and then lets out a mournful cry. I look behind, relieved to see the woman is leaving, heading back towards the row of cottages. I walk a little further then slump down onto the edge of the muddy track and reach in for a pre-prepared bottle of milk. It's lukewarm but it's all I have.

Gabriel lies back in my arms and drinks, stopping every few seconds to catch his breath. Even the act of sucking is tiring him out. I swallow down the lump that is bobbing about in my throat. I should now savour every moment we spend together. Our time is limited. I'm not an idiot. I know defeat when I see it. And I know what comes next.

He takes less than a third of the bottle. I stand up again and begin to walk, unsure of where I'm going. The track is narrower and closer to the edge than I anticipated. A death trap. This is the part that has crumbled. The weight of Gabriel nags at the base of my spine and nips at my upper body. I wait a few seconds to catch my breath, lifting him higher up onto my hip once more. He responds by clamping his little legs around my midriff and pushing his head into my chest. I take a shaky breath, the reassuring bulk of him, and the warmth of his body setting free more tears. Despite the howling wind and the roar of the sea below us, I feel at peace up here. I want to remember this moment, to drink in Gabriel's scent and study his face, to try to cast to memory every single little thing about him – every flutter of his eyes, every smile, every breath. I want to savour them all.

I continue walking, imbued with an iron will and a small sense of triumph. I'm on top of the world up here. My time may be limited but I'm determined to make the most of what little I have left. I wipe away more tears and raise a small toast to myself in my head, amazed I've made it thus far without anybody catching up with me. My being here at all is proof enough that I am a fit and stable person and able to take care of my grandson.

They won't see it that way, the people who will eventually track us down, but deep in my heart, I know that I am a decent woman. I've been one step ahead of them all the way. I have fed and clothed him, kept him warm and safe while his parents neglected him and the authorities raced around in circles searching for me. They will take him soon enough though. I know that and I'm prepared for it. The lady from the cottage will have already called the police and will be at home waiting for them to arrive. I can almost see her, standing on the path, her long hair a flowing halo around her head as she points them in the right direction, a self-congratulatory smile on her face. The concerned citizen. The hero of the hour.

The footpath narrows, following the curve of the cliffs. We are perilously close to the edge now. The wind grows stronger, pushing at my back and biting at my flesh. I pull my jacket over Gabriel and fasten it up, pressing him closer to me, doing what I can to protect him from the elements. I glance down at the top of his head and small crop of light-brown hair. The sight of him never fails to make me happy, his perfectly formed features and long, dark lashes taking the breath right out of me. He is small enough to stay curled up beneath my clothes but big enough to fill my heart. This little person, this beautiful boy would have helped fill the void that sits deep inside me; given more time, his presence in my life could have made me whole again. But I guess some things are simply not meant to be.

My feet slip, twisting about on the damp ground. I gasp and straighten my spine. My fingers cradle the back of Gabriel's neck. Small pieces of gravel are strewn around the track, making walking that bit more difficult. I kick them aside and continue, my senses attuned to every noise, every movement around me. No sirens yet. It won't be long. Soon they will arrive in a blaze of glory, the blue hue of their lights telling me that it's at an end.

The rumble and crashing beneath us is both captivating and terrifying in equal measure: the way the sea lashes at the side of the cliffs, a brutal, unrelenting force of nature. I stop to listen, watching how the waves bounce around. It's mesmerising. I have always loved the changing of the seasons; the way the final vestiges of summer can suddenly turn on a sixpence, cold air sweeping in and whipping the sea into a frenzy, or how the sea welcomes spring after a long, cold winter, its swells and surges calming in readiness.

It scares many, being up here: the sheer height, the erosion, being exposed to the elements. But it doesn't scare me. I've faced worse, lived through more daunting situations and been exposed to greater dangers that are far more hazardous than a raging sea and strong winds.

Beads of perspiration coat my face and scalp despite the cold weather. A flood of fresh tears bites at the back of my eyes. I carry on walking, Gabriel's small mewls growing louder. He's probably still hungry. I perch on a patch of dry grass and fish out the bottle. Once again, he takes tiny amounts, his breathing loud and laboured, his chest wheezing and rattling as he tries to suck from the teat. By the time he finishes, I can feel him beginning to wilt, even the effort of feeding too much for him. His eyes flicker and he is asleep in seconds.

Above us, birds circle; seagulls screech, dipping and diving, searching for their next meal. Life goes on. Ill babies and dead fathers mean nothing up here. Wildlife and the flora and fauna show no mercy. There will be no pity or sympathy and no easy way back should the weather take a turn for the worse. The wind grows even colder, picking up speed. I shiver but am immune to it. Gabriel's body is melded into mine, a shared heat warming us both.

I think of my poor, browbeaten mother, her inability to fight back, to stand up for herself and her children and do the right thing. She should have taken me and my younger brother a long time before it happened, escaped from that place wearing only the clothes we had on our backs. In the end, I did it for her, showing my father that we weren't prepared to put up with any more of his violence.

I quash those negative thoughts. My mother did what she could under the worst of circumstances. I focus instead on my father and his many failings, thinking about how badly he treated her, how scared she must have been. None of it was her fault. She was crippled by fear, her mind fogged up by pain and the regularity of the blows. She lived her life in a constant state of terror. We both did. I remember those long days when he was in the house with us – the uncertainty of his behaviour, the oppressive atmosphere that descended whenever he walked into a room. The changeability of his moods. There weren't ever any triggers, nothing we could do or say – or more importantly, not do or say – to avoid the conflict. It was always there, simmering below the surface: his fury and resentment. A ticking timebomb.

My eyes are heavy, my mind once again, clogged up with memories of the past. I yawn and with Gabriel nestled into my chest, I lean back on the long tufts of grass and let myself be carried away by a wave of exhaustion. The solidity of him is a crushing bulk against my ribcage. As carefully as I can, like lifting a delicate flower, I remove him from the inside of my jacket and lay him down on the ground. He'll be perfectly safe here with me. I'll make sure of it. I know this area well. Nothing bad will ever happen to him while he's by my side.

Fighting off the fatigue, I move us both closer to the edge of the cliff, away from the swarm of insects that buzz around us. On impulse, I lean forward and peer over the edge. It's a long way down, the route a terrifying journey filled with crags and crevices, the sea below us an unforgiving, ill-tempered force. Such a hideous way to spend one's last few seconds. I can't even begin to gauge the height. 200 feet? Or maybe 300? Perhaps even higher. I can imagine the peacefulness that would follow such a departure. No questions. No interrogations. Nobody telling me I had stepped onto the wrong side of the law by taking Gabriel. Because they will. Already, I can hear their voices, their accusatory tones as they call my name, attempting to hold me to account for a crime I didn't commit. I visualise their dark expressions, the collective lowering and shaking of heads as if I were a lowlife criminal. A damaged individual. I did the right thing, removing this child from the poisonous clutches of his feckless parents, and nobody will ever convince me otherwise. And if anything untoward were to happen to us before they get here – anything final – well, it would mean that it would be just me and Gabriel, together forever, which would be no bad thing, would it? I am, after all, the one who has loved him unconditionally and kept him alive these past few days. The only one who appears to care.

The tiredness swamps me. It's been an exhausting couple of days. I lie down next to his small body, the wind that sweeps in from the sea a welcome distraction from the murky thoughts that continually swill around my brain. I'm becoming mired in them. It's being here, so close to where my father ended his life that is causing it. Or maybe it's simply because my life as I know it, the life I tried to forge with my grandson to keep him safe, is about to come to an end.

A sharp gust of wind catches us, cooling my flesh and dragging all the air out of my lungs. I gasp and close my eyes, wishing there had been a better way to finish this, wishing fortune had been kinder to our plight. If I had had an unwavering faith, maybe God would have given an insightful response, but He didn't and now we are here on the edge of the world, exposed to the changing weather, alone and waiting.

I sigh, thinking of all that has gone before, and everything that is yet to come. My limbs and my mind succumb to a sudden wave of dog-tiredness, its jaws clamped firmly around my body as it drags me beyond a heavy, dark veil and into nothingness.

# 39

## MELISSA

The overhead screech of seagulls wakes me, rousing me from a sleep where I dreamt of prison cells, crying babies, and drowning in icy waters; huge waves dragging me out to sea while Gabriel lay on the cliff edge, alone.

I lie still. I'm tired, so very tired. When I open my eyes, he is gone. Jagged blades score and scratch at my flesh. Terror renders me immobile. I want to shriek and howl, to weep for an age until I have no tears left. My mouth is a gaping void as I try to shout his name, my throat constricting until I can no longer breathe. I'm still asleep. This is a dream. A hideous nightmare. I sit up and sweep my hand across the still-warm grass where Gabriel should be. He has slipped. Somehow while I slept, he rolled and now he is gone. Tears slide down my face. The shriek finally escapes from my throat and goes on and on and on, a ghastly echo in my head.

I crawl to the edge of the cliff, dreading my fate and yet at the same time, resigned to it. Resigned to the fact that Gabriel has fallen over there, that he has woken and somehow managed to turn, slipping over the rocks and falling into the sea. I need to be with him, to feel the force of gravity as I hurl myself over, my body plummeting downwards, but instead, feel fingers touch me when I inch closer to the drop. I don't have to look, to turn my head and glance behind me because I already know who it is. They have found me. In a moment of weakness, I slept and now they're here. I've reached the end of the road. It's all over.

Except it isn't. Not yet.

I shake myself free of the fingers that are curled around my shoulder and stand, suddenly released from their clutches. I run as fast as I can. Who would care if I stumbled, or if the earth beneath my feet breaks away and cascades into the sea, taking me with it? I've nothing left to live for. And yet something in me refuses to give in without putting up one last good fight. I will run until my legs buckle and my lungs are fit to burst because giving in is a sign of weakness and I am not my mother. I will keep going until the bitter end.

Behind me, the air is filled with noise: a blend of voices calling for me to stop, telling me that there isn't anywhere left for me to go and that the path is dangerous. I know this. I know how dangerous it is. The man who almost ruined mine and my mother's life ended his own up here. The man I wanted to kill. The police failed us all those years ago, ignoring my mother's pleas for help, and they are still failing me now. All I ever wanted was to do the right thing – taking a knife to my father. Taking Gabriel. They were both acts of love, a way of protecting the vulnerable. And yet I'm the criminal.

I continue running, my chest tight, my breath misting in front of my face. The path becomes a thin rut, no more than a line of sludge that impedes my progress. I lower my eyes, focusing on every step I take. Heat combusts beneath my clothes. I pull at my sweater, loosening it and yanking at the collar. The sound of heavy footsteps closes in behind me. More shouting for me to stop. I ignore them, putting even greater effort into sprinting away. One foot in front of the other. Just keep going until all my energy is gone. To my left, the ground rises, a hillock that obscures my view of the sea. Anxiety scratches at me. Gabriel. He's over there, the waves crashing around him. I need to be able to see the water, to feel close to him. We shouldn't be apart. My thighs and calves throb and burn as I leave the path and scramble up the small bank, spiky tufts of grass coming away in my hands when I grab at the ground for purchase.

More calls for me to stop, screams and hollering that I'm only making things worse and that there are people who want to help me. I don't want their help. All I want is Gabriel.

I keep climbing until I reach the brow of the bank, the view of the foaming sea and the sheer drop to it a sobering sight. My legs are suddenly heavy, my chest tight. I slump to the ground, a tremble taking hold in my upper body and limbs. I'm weary. My body is aching.

'Melissa, please stay where you are. Don't move any closer to the edge. We want to help. We can see that you're upset.'

I almost laugh at their attempts to talk me round but don't have the energy to do anything except sit and stare at the horizon. I wonder what would happen if I sat here for the next hour, refusing to capitulate to their demands and their sloppy appeals for me to move away. Would they lose patience? Send more people to try and coax me away from this place? Or would they become angry, insisting I do as they say, using force to restrain me, putting me and themselves at risk?

'We know about your family and why you're here. Please come and speak with us; we can sort all of this out together. We have people who can help you.'

Tired of their tactless requests for me to reconsider my current position, I stand up, my feet apart, the wind a constant force at my back. It's difficult to remain upright and not get pushed forwards into the rocks. A strong gust catches me unawares and I slip, my legs scissoring down the other side of the bank, my breath concertinaed in my chest. I gasp when I topple forwards and fall, my body splayed on the cold, wet grass. I'm lying on my stomach, my head hanging over the precipice. I'm close now, so very close to taking that final leap. Do I feel frightened? It's hard to tell. I'm not sure how or what I feel any more, my senses dulled, my emotions a dry collection of thoughts and memories that no longer feel like my own.

I lie still for a few seconds, trying to piece everything together, trying to imagine my own passing. Would I die before I hit the bottom? From this distance and trajectory, I can see that I would hit rock before the water got to me, the curve of the cliffs and the large indent halfway down too deep for me to escape. Millions of years of erosion from the sea and powerful winds have scooped away the central parts of the cliff and the bottom now juts out like a huge, monstrous claw, ready to catch whoever lands there.

I count my breaths and listen to my heartbeat. It throbs in my throat and ears. I can hear it above the sound of the sea and the wind, and wonder if I'm already dying. Perhaps my body is already in shutdown, the anxiety of this situation and the grief of losing Gabriel raising my blood pressure, pushing my heart to its limits. I would rather be dead. It's a more comforting thought than the void I have to face every day. No Stuart, no mother, George thousands of miles away, and now no Gabriel.

Gravel and rough grass scrape against my bare stomach as I shuffle forwards. It's time. No more delays or excuses. I take one last, trembling breath, my eyes closed tight. Even at this point, as close as I am, cowardice still streaks through my veins. This is who I am – a failure. I wasn't brave enough to drive that knife deep into my father's belly or to keep my marriage afloat, and I haven't been brave enough to save Gabriel. I continue shuffling, fear making me tremble, anger at my own ineptitude filling me with shame.

I sigh, sadness at who I am and all I've done, blooming inside me. I slither closer to the place where all my problems will disappear, every part of me damaged and cast out to sea.

The wind stings my face. I'm nearly there. Just a few more inches and it will all be over. I stop, sensing somebody close by. I can feel their body heat and the warmth of their breath on my neck. A heavy hand is placed on my shoulder, strong fingers clutched around my upper arm. I'm pulled up onto my feet and dragged away from the edge and back onto the footpath. I am spent, my body too fatigued to fight them off any longer.

A cacophony of noises: voices calling, shouting. The crunch of approaching footsteps.

'Gabriel. I have to see Gabriel. Please just leave me be...' My voice is hoarse, my breathing heavy and irregular.

'Come on, let's get you down from here, shall we?'

The gentlest of touches soon turns into me being forcibly led away, my arms held fast behind my back. I scream out my grandson's name over and over and over until my voice breaks and my throat is tight and sore. A blanket is placed around my shoulders to stave off the chill. I don't feel cold. I don't feel anything at all.

Somebody spins me around and we walk back over the track and towards the main road. Something catches in my throat, a jarring sight causing me to cough and splutter. He's there. I can see him, in the distance. Gabriel, my beautiful, baby boy, lying in the arms of a stranger. A police officer. I try to scream out to him but hear nothing and wonder if I actually said it out loud or whether it was only in my head.

The woman holding Gabriel leans in to him, snuggling her face close to his, whispering to him, stroking his soft cheeks while I stand, useless and inert, my strength sapped, my will to live leaching out of my pores and disappearing into the ether. The drop behind me still holds great appeal. I should have done it before they reached me. I should have emulated my father's last moments and taken that death leap. I try to imagine what it would have been like, stepping over and hitting that craggy cliff-face, my bones snapping and cracking, my flesh ripping and tearing, until there was nothing left of me. Just a lump of damaged flesh and broken bones. A better ending than what lies in wait for me. Bars on windows. Waking up each day in a room that is barely bigger than a broom cupboard. That is my future. Dread eats at my insides, burning my skin, making me light-headed and woozy. None of these people will ever understand why I did what I did. They think I'm unhinged, viewing me through the lens of the law. A law that works against families, allowing parents to neglect and hurt children and vulnerable babies. A law that protects the aggressors and leaves the victims scrambling about in the dirt.

I stagger on unsteady feet as I'm led across the path to the waiting police car. I keep my head low, unwilling to look anybody in the eye. I won't give them that pleasure. The pleasure of seeing how distressed I am. How desperate and full of anger. I've lost the battle. After all the effort I have put in to keep my baby boy safe, they now have him while I have nothing. I am empty. A person-sized shell. Nothing left to live for.

## 40

## MELISSA

They're being kind to me, that much is true. Treating me with kid gloves. No shouting, no bitter recriminations. I have no complaints. I spoke to the police again today and have also been questioned by a team of mental health specialists and now here I am, talking once more to a gentle-voiced doctor who, it would appear, is interested in what I have to say. For the first time ever, somebody is listening. Somebody who appears to care.

Stuart has been here too, his eyes full of sadness. His face creased with concern. I wish I could recall when it was he visited but time has run away with me, one day merging into the next, time losing all meaning.

'I'm sorry.' Those were his first words when he came and sat next to me. 'Just tell them everything, Mel. Start from the beginning and tell them everything that has happened. They just want to help you. We all do.'

He placed his hand over mine, gave it a squeeze, wiped away my tears, and left. I felt such deep sorrow as I watched him go. Sorrow for all those wasted years. Sorrow for our married life that is no more. But most of all, sorrow for a future we may now never have. And we could have had so much, Stuart and I; we could have *been* so much, and now we have nothing. We *are* nothing. I'm hollow. A hopeless, lost soul.

I manage a small smile, thinking back to my other visitor, his friendly face, eyes brimming with love and compassion. George.

'You're back?' I said to him as he sat opposite me. I reached out and took his hand, our fingers touching, the warmth and feel of him sparking deadened parts of me back to life.

'I am. Just for a short while.' He didn't put a timestamp on it, probably afraid of my response. Afraid of my tears if he told me he was returning to Perth the following day.

So we pretended that his visit was for forever, speaking of our shared childhood, our teenaged antics and the time we spent together as a family. We sat, pretending the geographical distance between us didn't exist. I asked after his wife, Brenda and his twin daughters, Zara and Hannah and he told me they were fine. Thriving and happy in their new environment. Relief tinged with sadness was like an arrow in my heart. Thriving. They would never return. Australia was their home now. And this was mine.

The doctor's voice snaps me back to the present. 'My name is Rhys. If you would like to talk freely then you can, or I can ask questions and you can answer when you feel ready?'

I shrug and sigh, not yet ready to open up completely and reveal all of me. That's because I don't know all of me. I have a lot of missing parts. I guess that's why we're here. Why I am here and not currently holed up in a cold, dark prison cell somewhere. At least they know I'm not doing it on purpose – being obtuse and forgetful, that is. I am the way I am because the things they are telling me appear to have slipped out of my brain like water through a sieve. Maybe I chose to forget them. Easier that way, I guess. Less painful.

'I don't quite know what to say. Where to start.' I place my hands in my lap and clamp my teeth together, a polite smile feeling like a step too far. For now, speaking clearly and keeping myself upright is all I can manage. True and complete happiness is out of my reach. I'm not sure I can even remember what it feels like. The time I spent with Gabriel was brief, a hiatus from my usual, drab existence.

'How about we talk about your son, Robin, and his son, Gabriel? Your grandchild.' He lowers his voice to a whisper. He picks up a pen and then places it back down on the small table. 'Are you comfortable with that?'

Things begin to take shape in my mind. My head buzzes, the noise filling every crevice of my brain. My throat is dry. I swallow and rub at my eyes. It feels hot in this room. Hot and airless. I touch my face, surprised at how cool I actually am. Am I comfortable with that subject? I no longer know what comforts or distresses me. I'm a stranger in my own mind, my thoughts scrambled and disparate. My memories full of sharp corners.

'Robin and Gabriel?' I say, my tongue too big for my mouth, my lips and gums as dry as sandpaper.

'Yes, if that's okay? We just want you to tell us what you can remember about the death of your son, Robin and his son, Gabriel. Your child and grandchild.'

The sudden drop in temperature makes me shiver, the cold a heavy shroud that presses against my flesh. Gabriel. My grandchild. Robin, my only child. My beautiful boys. Both of them gone. A drum pounds in my skull. I press the heel of my hands onto my forehead to alleviate the pain that is building there. I swallow and lower my head to stop the vomit from rising.

'A car accident.' The words are out before I have time to think. 'They were in the car – my car.' My brain is on autopilot, a stream of words spilling out unchecked. 'Robin's car had broken down so I went to collect them. He was up on the embankment of the A19 with Gabriel in his arms. It was dark, the rain was torrential.' I swallow and pick up the paper cup from the table, then take a sip of water, the violent shaking of my fingers making it difficult for me to hold it steady. Pain flares behind my eyes.

'Take your time. Just tell me whatever you can remember.'

I don't know that I do remember back to that time in my life and yet I must if I am here speaking about it. The words are flowing freely but the memory seems to be stuck somewhere in the recesses of my brain, a disconnect between the two.

'I pulled up on the hard shoulder. There wasn't anywhere else for me to stop. I got out and scrambled up to them but Robin was already on his way down with Gabriel. They were both soaked through and Gabriel was tired.'

*Thanks for this, Mum. The recovery vehicle was going to take another half hour at least.*

I recall those words and say them out loud to Rhys who is sitting, watching me closely, waiting for me to continue.

'And then my mobile phone rang. It was Adele, Robin's wife. He had tried calling her when he first broke down but hadn't received an answer which is why he rang me. I stayed up on the embankment to speak to her and explain what was going on while Robin put Gabriel in my car.'

'Can you recall what happened next?' Rhys shuffles about in his chair and places his hands on his knees, a careful, methodical pose designed to calm me. It doesn't work. I'm hot and bothered, yet freezing cold at the same time. My mouth saying things I don't want to say. His well-practised pose won't work. I will never feel calm again.

'I couldn't hear Adele because of the noise of the lorry. It came out of nowhere. It was travelling so fast – too fast. The driver didn't see my hazard warning lights. He should have seen them. And she shouldn't have rung me. Adele should have answered the first time when Robin made that call!'

'So you blame your daughter-in-law for what happened?'

Something snaps in my head, a taut band finally breaking free after being tightly wound around my skull for so long. The break jolts me into action. I sit up straight, my voice filling the room.

'Of course I blame her! It was a huge knock-on effect – her missing Robin's calls, then ringing me at that very moment when a huge truck was driving too quickly in the pouring rain. Of course I bloody well blame her! This is all her fault. She should have picked up the first time, then none of this would have happened. My son and grandson would still be alive if only she had answered that fucking call!'

I can't see for tears, my vision blurred, and then out of nowhere, it comes hurtling at me: that evening, those images. They are catapulted back into my brain like shrapnel. Designed to injure and maim. The truck, the spray of water. The speed. The almighty sickening sound as over forty tonnes of metal ploughed into the back of my car. And then my screams. My never-ending hoarse screams as I stood there and watched it happen.

I wipe away tears and cover my face with my hands. I've been screaming ever since that day, a loud, wailing noise that fills my head and won't go away. It just goes on and on and on. An eternity of it.

'I think perhaps we've talked enough for today. You should get some rest. We'll speak again tomorrow.'

And with that, he is gone and I am led away by a nurse who places her hand on my shoulder, her touch as light as air as she guides me back to my room.

# 41

## MELISSA

I stifle a yawn. I wonder if I'm being given sedatives while I'm a patient in this place but am too tired to ask. Yesterday's session left me feeling exhausted and deflated and then last night, I was plagued with vivid dreams and nightmares – crying children who wandered around graveyards unaccompanied, cars driving into the sea. Faceless babies screaming for their parents. I awoke with a film of sweat covering my skin and a deep headache that took hours to shift.

'You were telling me about taking Victor,' Rhys says.

He has nice teeth, this man. Such a ridiculous thing to notice but that's how it is lately. As if I'm just waking up to my surroundings, memories and thoughts finally slotting into place in my head. Hearing that name jars. I sit up straight and shiver.

'Victor?'

I don't like the deep hammering sensation that sits inside my head. I rub at my face and just stop short of clawing at my own flesh to try and stop it.

'The baby. We need to talk about the baby, Melissa. The one you took from outside the house close to where you live. He needed medical attention. After finding him on the edge of the cliffs, he was taken into hospital with pneumonia. He's recovering but he was very ill. Do you have any thoughts on what happened?'

I'm immersed in cold water. I feel numb and detached from this room, from this situation. Nothing seems to fit, my memories becoming knotted again, my thoughts a jumble of names and events that are alien to me.

'No, I don't want to talk about Victor. I don't know him.'

Rhys nods sagely, his eyes never leaving my face. 'Okay, shall we talk about Ted?'

Heat grows in my chest, an expanding force as it climbs higher, burning at my throat, making it difficult for me to breathe or speak. He wants me to ask who Ted is. I won't. I'm not being led down this path. A path scattered with hidden meanings that are designed to catch me out. I say nothing, sitting as rigid as stone.

Rhys fills the gap with his questions and statements. I am under no illusions as to who is in charge here. He may be easy-going and gentle with his constant reassurances but he is the doctor and I am his patient. Our relationship is professional, an asymmetrical alliance.

'Ted Fremantle spoke to you just after you had taken Victor. He saw you with the child and told you about his daughter and how she passed away. Now do you remember? He recognised you as a neighbour. He was the one who told the police that you had taken Victor when he was interviewed in hospital. He thought it was your grandson. Is that what you told him?'

Rhys's tone is soft and encouraging but his words are loaded with menace, phrases and carefully crafted questions aimed at cornering me into a confession.

'Ted is an elderly gentleman in his eighties and he's still in hospital recovering from his injuries. Can you recall how he got those injuries, Melissa? It would be really helpful if you could cast your mind back and try to think about that day. Do you think you can do that?'

I sit silently. Listening, not speaking. His words are a dagger to my chest. I think that perhaps I do know. No, I'm being disingenuous, lying even to myself. That's because the truth is too hard to face up to. I know that I know. The image of him lying in the middle of the road forces acid up my throat. I swallow it down, rubbing at my eyes. I'm not a bad person. I didn't mean to hurt him. I panicked. I had to remove Gabriel from that house and time was against me. Except it wasn't Gabriel, was it? It's a slow dawning in my mind. A realisation that is a gut punch, hitting me in my solar plexus and knocking me off kilter.

Not Gabriel.

We spoke about this yesterday. How could I have forgotten? Gabriel is dead and so is my son, Robin. They are both gone. I took somebody else's child.

A neighbour's baby. I kidnapped him. I thought it was Gabriel. I desperately wanted it to be him. Still do. I would give everything I own for it to have been him.

Oh dear God, what have I done?

A noise fills the room, an unearthly sound that rattles in my skull and ricochets around us, bouncing off the bare walls. I place my hands over my ears to block it out, to stop the terrible howling, screeching sound and it's only then that I realise the noise is coming from me.

* * *

My throat is parched and as gritty as silt. I run my fingers through my hair and rub at my face. My skin feels coarse and yet greasy.

Grimy, that's what I feel. Dirty and thoughtless and grimy. I asked if I could take a bath and was given permission as long as I leave the bathroom door open. Like a child. That's what I am now, an errant youngster who can't be trusted. Even my thoughts are no longer my own. Every day, I sit in that room and empty the contents of my head onto the table for people to sift through and dissect. It's undignified and humiliating. Is it hardly any wonder I leave each session feeling filthy and wrung out.

People pass by while I sink down into the bathwater, my head in a different place to where it was last week. A different place to where it was even yesterday. It's slow progress but I'm getting there. I've been told that the two men from the cottage in Scotland are still alive. Jason, or whatever his real name is, is stable in hospital and the other guy is currently on the run and wanted for the robbery and murder of the old man who leased the cottage to me. A passing rambler heard Jason's moans and rang for an ambulance. Without the walker's assistance, he would be in a morgue. The police didn't tell me their full names and I haven't asked. Not enough energy to rake over every detail. I have just about enough energy to come to terms with my own misdeeds. Every day is a trial: a step closer to discovering the real me. I'm in there somewhere. I just need to give it time. Had it not been for that robbery, I would still be there in that cottage. Or maybe not. Maybe Gabriel's illness would have forced my hand. I check myself. Not Gabriel. I took somebody else's baby. His name is Victor.

*Victor, Victor, Victor.*

I say it over and over in my head, followed by a whispered apology. I didn't mean him any harm. I genuinely thought he was my little boy. Wanted him to be my boy more than anything else in the world.

Grief has me in a stranglehold every morning when I wake. I

relive that day over and over – the day Robin and Gabriel were cruelly snatched away from me. I think of myself as the blighted one. Tragedy follows me around, a part of who I am. But not for much longer. I am getting help. I don't have to trudge down this winding, rutted route on my own. I pushed Stuart away after we lost Robin and Gabriel, becoming wrapped in my own wretchedness and misery. I didn't give him any time or space to grieve, my own needs obscuring his. It's a substantial thing, like a living entity that had burrowed beneath my flesh, this mantle of misery that is bearing down on me; I can feel its talons scratching and gouging at my innards. If I can ignore its incessant clawing, then I know that somewhere out there, there are rays of sunshine beckoning. I just need to learn how to let them in.

# 42

# MELISSA

*Eighteen Months Later*

The breeze caresses my face. It feels good to be out, the air clear, the sky a perfect shade of blue. I shouldn't be here really, near this house. Near them. It breaks the conditions of my probationary period, but I found it too difficult to stay away. A fifteen-minute train journey and here I am, back to where it happened. I'm also aware of Ted living close by and need to be careful. His injuries stripped him of his confidence and now he prefers to stay indoors, sitting by his living-room window, watching the world go by. When I was in hospital, I wrote him a letter, apologising for what I did, and asked if the staff could forward it onto him. I didn't receive a reply and am okay with that. Not all sins should be forgiven. I was unwell and according to the police and doctors who spoke to me, he understands, and that is enough for me. As for the individuals who robbed and killed the elderly man in Edinburgh – Jason recovered enough to stand trial. His partner in crime was caught at Glasgow airport with a false passport and the money they stole from the poor man in Edinburgh stuffed into a false compartment in his luggage. He was arrested for murder and attempted murder and the trial date is set for a few months' time.

I stare over at the house. Just one look, that's all I want. One last look at that child and then I'll leave this place, safe in the knowledge that he is happy and cared for.

It feels strange being here. This neighbourhood is no longer my hometown. I sold my apartment with the help of Stuart. Coming back to live in this area wasn't possible so we both made the decision that I would move in with Stuart. He has been a rock throughout, visiting me while I was in hospital and overseeing the sale. We talked and talked until our mouths ran dry and we were all out of words. We have a long journey ahead of us but we want to travel it together. Softly, softly. That's how it is now. We're taking things slowly and are both hopeful of a positive outcome. Maybe even a long and happy future together. We haven't made any definite plans but it looks promising.

None of what took place was the fault of Adele, my daughter-in-law. It was a terrible, tragic accident. If anything, she saved my life. Had I not taken her call, I would have been in the car with Robin and Gabriel and I wouldn't be here now. My splintered, grieving mind lashed out. I wanted to blame somebody. My life had been ripped apart and I didn't know where to turn. Anger and grief drove me. I am now in a stronger position, able to control my own thoughts and emotions, no longer forced into a dark corner where demons lie.

What I did was wrong, I know that now. Gabriel is gone. Victor is here. Different children. Different parents. But my intentions were true, because the one thing I got right was the neglect. That part is real. Standing here at a distance, I already can see that something is terribly awry. I know for certain that my actions were justified. The front door of their house is open and I can hear their voices inside, raised in anger. Shouting and yelling profanities. I am also able to hear something else – a child's cry. A heart-rending hollering that cuts me in half.

*Gabriel.*

I bite at my lip and fight back tears. No, not Gabriel.

*Victor.*

Then I see him: the toddler who was my baby for a short period of time. Victor. He appears at the door, an unaccompanied infant, dressed only in a vest. No nappy, his face smeared with dirt. I can see behind him, to his parents as they make their way outside. They appear in the doorway, cigarettes dangling from their mouths.

Victor lets out a wail, his arms reaching out to his mother who in turn, aims a playful kick at his backside that knocks him to the floor. His cries tear at my emotions. Desperate for attention, he gets up and walks over to his father, who scoops Victor up, jiggling him up and down, doing little to alleviate the child's distress. And then he does something that almost takes my legs from under me – a cigarette is placed between the child's lips while they throw back their heads and laugh. The cigarette falls, catching Victor's bare arm before dropping onto the floor. He kicks about as if in pain. I'm too far away to see any possible injuries. I put every ounce of strength I have into not marching over there and snatching him out of their arms. Because I can't. If I do, I will be taken back into hospital with no idea of when I will be discharged. If ever. So I do the thing I should have done in the first place. The thing that would have ensured that poor Victor didn't have to be subjected to such cruelty at the hands of his parents: the people who should love and care for him and keep him from harm. I retrieve my phone from my pocket and search for the number of social services. I know from my time spent teaching, that an anonymous call can be a powerful tool, alerting a team of social workers who have no option other than to investigate.

I will find the telephone number and tell them what I have just witnessed. I will be a concerned neighbour, a passer-by, a close friend who wishes to remain anonymous. I will be whoever I need to be to ensure they send somebody out to check on that poor, neglected child. I will alert them to the recent cigarette burn on his arm. I will ask them to check him for bruises. I will do whatever it takes to make sure Victor is kept from harm and if that means him being removed and living with strangers, then so be it. This isn't over. It may never be over.

My chest tightens as I step into an alleyway, the shadows and darkness swallowing me. I was right all along. I was right with my initial beliefs about that house and the people in it, but nobody took any notice, dismissing my concerns as flimsy and unfounded. The psychiatrists, the team of specialists. They told me I had taken a perfectly healthy and well cared for child, that I was unwell and in need of psychiatric assessment. That part may have been true. They questioned me endlessly, sending in teams of psychologists to delve inside my head. But they didn't check on Victor's well-being or his home life. He was hospitalised and given medication for his physical ailments but nobody thought to check up on his parents. Nobody made any attempt to probe inside their heads the way they probed into mine. They were the victims, making TV appearances, calling for his swift return. Telling the world how much they loved and missed their only child. Victor was handed back without question. But soon the police and doctors will realise how wrong they were, how they made a huge error of judgement. When they check his stick-thin limbs, his many scars and bruises, then they will see the evidence of the neglect that they all missed the first time around.

I punch at the buttons on the screen, making sure to withhold my own number, and take a deep breath when somebody answers after the second ring. A woman's voice speaks at the other end: soft, welcoming. Helpful. I take a long, trembling breath and pray that somebody somewhere will care enough to do something to help keep that little boy safe.

'Hello,' I say, my voice gravelly and low. 'I'd like to make an anonymous report about a child being neglected and abused. I've seen them harm him, his parents. I've seen them kick him and give him a cigarette. He is currently distressed and needs urgent care and attention. Somebody needs to come out as soon as possible. Do I know his name? Yes, his name is Victor.'

# ACKNOWLEDGEMENTS

This was a tricky one to write! It needed lots of adjustments and I would like to thank my editor, Emily Ruston, for her advice and guidance without which, this book would have very possibly ended up being discarded and thrown into the sea from a great height. I would also like to thank Emily Reader who gave sound advice for my copy edits, making sure the story was as finely tuned as it could possibly be. A big thank you also, to Rachel Sargeant, my proof reader for finding those pesky errors that despite various edits and re-reads, still slipped through the net!

A huge thank you to Valerie Keogh and Anita Waller for putting up with my endless moaning! You two are amazing. My writing days would be long and drab without having you at hand.

I would hate to miss anybody out when writing acknowledgements so am not going to name people personally but I would like to give a massive thanks to my ARC group who are just the best, and also to all the bloggers and reviewers who read and help promote my books, spreading the word and saying the most wonderful things about my stories.

A final thank you to Nescafé and Cadburys who make writing difficult novels just that little bit easier. I'd be less wired and two stone lighter without you but would never have managed to pen eighteen books in the last seven years.

I am available to chat on social media. Feel free to contact me at:

www.facebook.com/thewriterjude
www.instagram.com/jabakerauthor
www.x.com/thewriterjude

Best Wishes

J.A. Baker

# ABOUT THE AUTHOR

**J. A. Baker** is a successful writer of numerous psychological thrillers. Born and brought up in Middlesbrough, she still lives in the North East, which inspires the settings for her books.

Sign up to J. A. Baker's mailing list here for news, competitions and updates on future books.

Follow J. A. Baker on social media:

facebook.com/thewriterjude
x.com/thewriterjude
instagram.com/jabakerauthor
tiktok.com/@jabaker41
bookbub.com/authors/JABaker

## ALSO BY J. A. BAKER

Local Girl Missing

The Last Wife

The Woman at Number 19

The Other Mother

The Toxic Friend

The Retreat

The Woman in the Woods

The Stranger

The Intruder

The Girl In The Water

The Quiet One

The Passenger

Little Boy, Gone

When She Sleeps

The Widower's Lie

The Guilty Teacher

Hush Little Baby